DEAD
JEALOUS

SHARON JONE'

ORCHARD

ORCHARD BOOKS
338 Euston Road, London NW1 3BH
Orchard Books Australia
Level 17/207 Kent Street, Sydney, NSW 2000

First published in 2013 by Orchard Books

ISBN 978 1 40832 754 8

Text © Sharon Jones 2013

A CIP catalogue record for this book is available
from the British Library.

1 3 5 7 9 8 6 4 2

Printed in Great Britain by Clays Ltd, St Ives plc

Orchard Books is a division of Hachette Children's Books,
an Hachette UK company.

www.hachette.co.uk

For Christian, whose star fell too soon.

PROLOGUE

It was a good place, a peaceful place. The kind of place where the past could lie, forever.

At the foot of the hill the lake was frozen in a dead calm, a dark mirror reflecting the clouds that rolled in above. Not that those weirdos down at the festival would be turning in any time soon. No, they'd be partying into the early hours, but still, best to do it now, rather than wait.

Do it now and get it over with.

The earth was waterlogged after two days' rain. It would be heavy going, but that was OK.

Good, honest hard work: burying the dead.

Took an hour to dig a hole deep enough and dark enough that not even the full moon could penetrate. But still, her stiff pale hands were visible against the lacy black dress. And her eyes...her eyes were open, shining like silver coins.

Staring.

Watching.

Sods of clay rained down until she was properly hidden, until there was nothing but trampled-down earth to remember that either of them was ever there.

Shit. What if someone noticed she was missing?

No. It would be OK.

People got lost all the time. Especially people like her.

It was a good place for her. A peaceful place.

A place to be forgotten.

CHAPTER ONE

Poppy Sinclair hooked her thumbs into the back pockets of her jeans and snorted.

At the centre of the uneven half-circle of tipis, yurts, rusty caravans and nylon tents was a wicker man. Standing twenty foot tall, its body of tangled branches glowed golden-brown in the sinking sun. Ivy dripped from head and beard, and two tree branches protruded at angles, forming stag-like antlers.

In each spindly hand, the giant effigy held a three-foot wooden scythe. And if that wasn't off-putting enough, this year someone had seen fit to give him a little – no, *massive* – extra.

Mum slammed the boot of their beat-up silver Saab, glanced over her shoulder and grinned.

'Don't tell me that's where you're going to do it?' Poppy asked. 'You can't seriously be thinking of getting hitched under an enormous—'

'—It's traditional.'

'For who? Porn stars? The guy's got a three-foot penis, Mum! What happened to the goddess? Thought this Pagan lark was all about the sacred feminine, but no, it turns out it's about a guy with an enormous willy.'

'And there's something wrong with honouring male

fecundity?' Jonathan asked, draping his arm around Mum's shoulders.

Mum smiled and nuzzled her face against his unshaven chin, like a love-starved Siamese. Their matching brown curls mingled together.

'Ugh! Get a tipi.'

'Hmm?'

'I said, I thought we agreed that if you were going to be my stepfather you would limit your use of the F word.'

Jonathan giggled in that slightly girly way that never failed to make Mum smile.

After all the pills, the Reiki and the thousand and one other therapies Mum had tried when Dad left, it turned out all she needed was Jonathan. Ironic, given she'd sworn off men for life and nearly moved them to a feminist commune.

Jonathan untangled his arms from Mum's shoulders and stretched. 'Want to give me a hand with the tents?'

Poppy shrugged. 'Nahh. I wouldn't wanna get in the way of all the *Boy Power* that's floating around here.'

The secluded field was a brightly coloured mishmash of canvas and cars. Instruments were being tuned, sound systems tested. People who in the real world wore jeans and suits were donning flowing cloaks and painting their faces with stars and flowers.

Poppy turned back to see Mum and Jonathan

sucking face again. She considered reminding them that canvas was in no way soundproof and, for the sake of her mental health, she'd like her tent to be erected far, far away from the matrimonial tipi.

'Think I'll go and have a look round.'

'You will come back for the opening ceremony?' Mum asked, a note of pleading in her voice. 'It would be nice to go as a family.'

'No way!' She planted a kiss on Mum's cheek. 'I said I'd be there for your big...thing. Although that was before I knew it was happening under a *big thing*.'

'Poppy!'

Jonathan smirked. 'This something we need to talk about, Pops? I never had you down as being uncomfortable with the male form.'

'Ha! No thanks, Herr Freud. I'm out of here. You two have fun with your psychobabble tantric whatevers.'

'Hey, hold on!' Jonathan fished his wallet out of his shorts pocket. 'Take this, just in case you need anything.' He held out a tenner.

She hesitated. It still felt weird taking money from the guy, even after a year and a half of him living with Mum. 'It's OK, I don't really need—'

He raised his eyebrows, and gave her his I'm-serious look. The one that was mostly followed by the I'm-analysing-every-move-you-make look. The trials of having a therapist for a stepfather.

'Jonathan,' a voice said.

Poppy turned to see a guy with a smooth tanned head that was shaved apart from a little tuft of green hair at his forehead. He was tall – really tall – and the Doc Martens, combat trousers and army vest he was wearing made him look like an escapee from a post-apocalyptic Hollywood film.

'Oh, hi,' Jonathan said. His voice remained neutral, but the way he squared his shoulders suggested he wasn't exactly thrilled with his visitor. 'I'm sorry, I thought we'd arranged to meet later?'

'I need to see you now.'

'Umm – no. I'm sorry, but I need to set up the tent.'

The guy shifted his weight from one foot to the other like he was struggling to contain some unruly emotion. Anger or despair, Poppy couldn't tell which, but something was tearing him apart. His hands squeezed into fists and he took a deep breath as if in a last-ditch attempt to pull himself together. 'But I really need to talk to you.'

'And we will talk,' Jonathan said. 'Later.'

The guy ran a hand over his face. Then, for the first time, his gaze connected with Poppy's. His jaw fell slack. 'No!' he said, shaking his head. 'This is *not* happening.' And, without another glance at Jonathan, he stormed off.

Poppy watched him go. 'What was *that* about?'

When she turned back to Jonathan he shook his head and held out the tenner. 'Take this. Unless you've changed your mind and really do want to help with the tent?'

'Nahh. I'll – er – leave you to it.' She stuffed the note in her pocket beside her iPod and made a run for it before she got roped into a conversation about the optimal alignment for the tipi, or some other psycho-spiritual crap.

She set off across the field and was immediately enveloped by jangling bells and blacked-up faces. Yellow and black striped Morris dancers swarmed around her like a cloud of angry wasps. She picked up speed and dodged between them only to walk smack into a column of billowing red silk. Fifteen feet up, a face grinned.

'Ahoy down there!' the guy shouted.

What the...? She backed up and realised she'd barged into a stilt walker. 'Sorry,' she called, waving an apologetic hand, and dashing between his legs.

The first time she'd been dragged to one of these gigs she was eight years old and felt like she'd fallen down the rabbit hole into Wonderland. She'd thought all of this stuff pretty damned cool; crystals and auras, tarot cards and totem animals. What kid wouldn't want to live in a world where fairies and elemental spirits were taken seriously? But that was then. Now she saw it for what it was, unlike Mum and Jonathan who seemed unable to live in the real world with normal people.

She pulled out her iPod, stuffed the buds into her ears and hit play. A line of sharp strings blocked out all the Pagan noise. Vintage Verve – the album Michael had made her download at three that morning, his text message assuring her it was going to change her world. She'd heard some of it, but she'd never really listened to the lyrics before. She must have replayed the album at least five times, until the words were buzzing in her veins.

Michael was right – the whole album was a work of crazy genius.

She fought her way to the edge of the festival ground, and found a clear passage between the woods and the backs of the various falafel vans and baked-potato sellers. Spicy smells prompted an ache in her stomach, reminding her that she'd skipped lunch. Jonathan's tenner would come in handy.

But as a guitar picked up the second track, a lump rose in Poppy's throat banishing all thought of food. She flicked onto the next song before *Sonnet* could worm its way into her brain. Michael wouldn't have got the significance, but she had. She'd been kept awake through the early hours by a barrage of angry tears.

Angry about wanting what she couldn't have.

That was it. No more, she told herself. She was finished feeling like that. The whole Michael thing was a phase. She'd known him her whole life; it was inevitable that at some point she would wonder whether their friendship was something...more. But it wasn't. Time to accept it and move on.

Sighing, Poppy gave in to her grumbling stomach and took a tour of the food vans. Organic this, wholefood that – it all looked disgustingly healthy, until she reached the very last one. The chipped white trailer would have looked more at home at a travelling fair or in a layby off the A57.

Poppy caught the unmistakeable whiff of chip fat. Finally!

'Chips please,' she said, yanking the buds out of her ears and having to stand on her tiptoes to see over the counter. She fished in her jeans pocket for the ten pound note Jonathan had given her.

'That'll be two quid, love,' a voice called back.

Still unable to lay her hands on the flaming tenner, she looked up and smiled. 'Sorry, I—'

The guy behind the counter wiped his brow with the back of his hand, brushing a lock of black hair away from his eyes. He looked questioningly over the counter and on seeing Poppy, he grinned. 'Salt and vinegar?'

A wave of heat billowed off the fryers, almost knocking her over. She swallowed against her dry throat. 'Umm – maybe nothing, actually. I seem to have lost my money.'

For a moment he just looked at her, then he folded his arms on the counter and rested his chin on them so that his face was level with hers. 'That's unfortunate.' His dark eyes twinkled and his cheek twitched as if he was trying to stop himself from laughing.

'Yeah.'

He wet his lips and rubbed his cleft chin against his arm. 'Tell you what, why don't you take the chips and pay me later.'

'But you don't know me from Adam. I might run off and never come back, and then what would you do?' Wow, that almost came out like flirting. But she never flirted. She was crap at it.

His grin widened. 'Then I'd have to come looking for you.' It sounded more like a promise than a threat. A delicious promise. Poppy ran her hand over her hair, trying to remember the last time she'd put a brush through it.

He straightened up and began shovelling chips into a white polystyrene tray. 'Can I get you anything else?'

She caught herself smiling. Then, over the tightly muscled and tattooed shoulder that stuck out of his sleeveless black vest, she spotted something. 'Oh my God! You do burgers!'

'Yeeeeeeah?'

'As in dead cow? As in a slice of flesh between two hunks of bread, not a vegetable in sight?'

His eyes narrowed. 'Is that a problem?'

'No! Jesus, it's a flaming miracle! I've never been to one of these gigs where you can buy actual honest-to-goodness dead animal. Normally it's anaemic aubergine burgers all the way. How the hell did you smuggle them in?'

'Friends in high places.' He rested his hands on his hips. 'Is this a roundabout way of saying that you'd like a burger?'

'I think I might love you forever.'

The guy laughed and shook his head. He had the kind of laugh that was comfortable, the kind that made Poppy want to laugh too.

'That seems like a fair deal. What would I get for cheese?'

'That would take us to a whole other level.'

The guy took a deep breath and began building a burger. Three slices of cheese, she noticed. And a cheeky smile as he did it.

Her heart ticked like a clock that had fallen out of time. She felt giddy, slightly dizzy and not at all hungry.

She folded her arms and sneaked another glance at him. Not her usual type. He clearly spent more time lifting weights than reading books, but to each their own, right?

'Hope you don't mind me saying so, but you're not like the other people here,' he said, glancing at her from beneath eyebrows that could do with taming.

'My mum and stepdad are having their handfasting

– err – wedding kind of thing the day after tomorrow.'

'Right. Families, huh?' The guy handed over the burger and chips.

'Yeah, families.'

He smiled and Poppy thought that she could look at that smile forever. It took several moments to realise that she no longer had any excuse to be standing there gawping at him. She cleared her throat. 'I'll bring you the money tomorrow – if – if – that's OK?'

'I'll look forward to it. I'm Tariq, by the way.'

'Poppy.'

'It's been a pleasure.'

She smiled and reluctantly walked away, carrying the warm glow of the van with her. Wow. Just – wow!

She'd only gone a few steps when she heard:

'Hey, Poppy!'

She turned to see Tariq had jumped down from the trailer and was jogging after her, his white apron flapping over his black jeans and vest.

He pushed a can of coke at her. 'In case you get thirsty.'

She took the freezing cold can, unable to stop herself from grinning like a maniac.

Tariq shoved his hands in his pockets and shrugged. 'I have to work tonight. But maybe tomorrow, after your mum's thing, if you're not doing anything, maybe I could buy you another hunk of dead animal?'

* * *

18

The festival occupied a crescent-moon of a field that hugged the pebbled beach of Scariswater, an hourglass-shaped lake that stretched out between an overhanging cliff edge on one side and a cushion of dense fir trees on the other.

Poppy floated away from the bustle of the festival ground. She needed somewhere quiet to sit and contemplate the burger, its maker and a rare moment of successful flirting. Was this it – the breakthrough?

Jonathan was always going on about the breakthroughs his patients made. *Yes! She figured out her dead grandmother was never coming back. Alleluia: finally he saw that what happened wasn't his fault!*

Was this her *Yes!* moment; when she realised that she actually could fancy guys who weren't named Michael Quinn? And here, at this flipping festival, where the fit guys were usually at least ten years too old to notice her. But Tariq could be no more than twenty-one, twenty-two? Definitely within the margin of possibility. And talk about hot! You could fry an egg on his biceps. Maybe griddle a steak on his abs...?

Before her rose the steep embankment that marked the outer edge of the campsite. The festival-goers were supposed to stick to the field, but what would it hurt to take a look at the view?

Behind her, a horn sounded. As if a blanket had been thrown over the whole crowd, a wary silence descended.

A deep sonorous voice called, 'Hail! Spirits of this place. Ancestors, friends!'

'Hail!' the crowd responded.

Somewhere back there, Mum would be searching the faces around the campfire, hoping to see her. But she just couldn't stomach it. Not when she had important, real-life stuff to think about.

Carefully, she scrambled up the side of the gravelly bank. She was so caught up in trying to stay upright that she didn't see the lone figure standing looking out over the lake. Only the glint of the sinking sun in the bottle dangling from the young woman's hand caught her eye.

The figure spun around, her eyes wild, furious. She pressed a hand to the pale skin between the lapels of her studded leather jacket.

'Sorry, I didn't mean to disturb you,' Poppy said. 'Wasn't expecting anyone to be up here.'

The young woman's face relaxed into a smile. She tucked her bobbed black hair behind her ear. 'You didn't. I'm just keeping out of the way of the celebrations. Not really my kind of thing.' Her voice was low, with a lilting Scottish accent. 'Fancy a drink?' she asked, shaking the half-empty bottle of Jack Daniel's.

'If this isn't your thing, what are you doing here?' Poppy asked the girl, who'd introduced herself as Beth.

They sat down on the stubbly grass and Poppy opened the white polystyrene container, releasing a tantalising whiff of steamy vinegar.

'Ah. Now there's a question with a long and complicated answer. Why aren't you down there, dancing naked around the fire?'

'I don't think they allow skyclad,' Poppy replied, shoving a soggy chip into her mouth.

'More's the pity.' Beth cast a glance at Poppy from under thick fake eyelashes. 'You got a boyfriend?'

Poppy shook her head.

'Girlfriend?'

Poppy inhaled the chip she was chewing. 'No!' She coughed and discreetly tried to wipe away the potato sludge that dribbled down her chin.

Beth smiled.

'Sorry. I didn't mean to sound—'

'—Like it's the plague? That's pretty much how my parents feel about it.'

Poppy's cheeks burned. She glanced across the field to where the opening ceremony was in full swing. The crowd had formed a large circle around four bonfires. White-robed figures stood around the wicker man, their hands outstretched to the twilight. It looked like a scene from a seventies horror film.

'How about you? Do you have a...*girlfriend?*' Poppy asked, in an attempt to recover her live-and-let-live credentials.

Beth's blood-red lips stretched into a smile. 'Aye, well, I have a habit of falling in love with people who are never going to love me back.'

A sympathetic 'hmmph' escaped Poppy's throat.

Beth unzipped her leather jacket and leaned back on her elbows. 'A fellow sufferer!'

'No, not really.'

'You're gonna have to try harder than that to convince me. Who is he?'

Poppy picked at a chip but then dropped it and wiped her fingers on her jeans.

Beth laughed. 'Wow! Y'really do have it bad.'

Bad? Yeah. The secret had squatted in her chest for years. Some days it got bigger with every breath she took. She was petrified that one day the secret would burst and she'd say something – or worse, do something – that she'd never be able to take back. And that would be it. Finito. Her and Michael's friendship would be over. Forever. And she wouldn't let that happen. So much for her being finished with thinking about it!

Tariq, she reminded herself. Actual flirting with a cute, single guy. Probably single. Jesus, he'd better be single. Not like...

'Michael,' she murmured.

'And you're in love with him, but he doesn't love you?'

Poppy pressed her lips together, unable to deny it, but not wanting to admit it either. She couldn't deny the ache that sat in her chest. A throbbing, howling boil of self-pity.

Beth turned her face to the sky. The heavens were closing in purple. The only light came from the pinky-orange glow that hovered like a celestial fried egg over the lake, and the newly dawning stars that drew in the night. Beth closed her eyes and smiled, as if she could feel the heat of those distant suns on her skin.

'I should tell you to walk away. Forget him if you can. But love's not like that. Love's a bitch that doesna let you go.' Beth fell silent. Her kohl-lined eyes remained closed. Her shiny black hair fell around her shoulders like shards of onyx.

She wasn't exactly pretty but she had strange angular features that reminded Poppy of a face from the cover of *Vogue*. And for a fleeting moment, she wondered what it would be like to kiss a girl. Was it so very different from kissing a boy? Were girls less hassle than guys? 'Who is she? Your—'

'—Maya. *My Maya.*' Beth sang the name like it was a love song. 'She was my best friend.'

'What happened?'

'Last year she came to this bloody place with her bastard boyfriend and I never heard from her again.'

'Is that why you're here? To find her?'

'That's what I told myself. But I knew—' Beth clawed chipped red nails to her chest, like she would rip out her heart if she could. '—I knew in here that I wouldn't find her.' Her eyes flashed open. They were glassy with tears. 'I fucking knew.' She grabbed the bottle of Jack Daniel's, swigged back several gulps and swiped the back of her hand across her mouth, smudging the edges of her lipstick.

Down below they were singing now. A happy-clappy Pagan number. Lines of bodies danced in concentric circles. Drums beat, keeping time, keeping them in line.

'So this guy, he straight?' Beth asked, eventually.

'Yeah.'

'Girlfriend?'

A billboard image of Julia nuzzling up to Michael filled her head. Her perfect blonde hair, her perfect little upturned nose. Poppy screwed her eyes shut and forced the image away.

'Have you kissed him?'

'No.'

'Have you tried?'

'No! He's my friend. I can't – can't risk losing him.'

'Seems to me that's exactly what you're risking.' Beth sat forward. 'Look, I'm in no position to tell you what to do. But what'll happen if you do nothing? If you say nothing? Watching him with someone else, it'll eat you up, Poppy, until there's nothing left. Love is like fire: unless it's channelled it destroys everything.'

Beth got to her feet and glared at the lake, so flat that it could be a sheet of glass. With a grunt, she launched the bottle into the sky. Droplets of whisky formed an arc, a perverse black rainbow. The bottle hit the water with a splash, sending shockwaves towards the shore.

Beth raked both hands through her hair and sniffed. She turned to Poppy and laughed, but there were tears in her eyes.

'Y'know, when I first saw you, I thought I was seeing her ghost, or sommat. But it was just this place playing games with me.'

'What will you do?' Poppy asked.

Beth didn't seem to hear. She stared down at the festival ground where lines of people were snaking around, to a reel of fiddles and drums. If it wasn't for the flickering bonfires and the smell of burning, it could have been a kids' fancy dress party.

'They'd like this place to be about peace and the earth and all that crap. But something stinks,' Beth muttered.

'Yeah, it's called self-delusion.'

'No. They believe something. I can respect that. Maya was into all this stuff. Was always going on about me being psychic.' Beth snorted and shook her head. 'But this place, don't you feel it? It's a dark place.'

'I'm not sure I—'

'—Stinks of shit. And the thing about shit is that eventually some of it floats.' Beth zipped up her jacket and stuffed her hands into the pockets. The attitude vanished and suddenly she looked small and exposed.

'What would you do?' she whispered. 'If it were you looking for this Michael? Would you keep looking, even if you knew he'd never love you back?'

Michael. With his slightly turned-down mouth that always made him look so damned sullen. Eyes so steady, so knowing, that they sometimes frightened her. Would she ever be able to let him go?

Beth glanced out at the dying rays of the sun and nodded. 'Aye. I reckon I'll keep looking.'

CHAPTER TWO

The air smelled of burning.

Whispers of smoke rose up from the scorched remains of bonfires. At the centre of the crescent-moon field, the hollow body of the wicker man remained tall, untouched by the flames of the night before, and monstrous in the half-light. There'd been a stay of execution. But Saturday they'd be celebrating Lughnasadh and Big Willy would burn.

Poppy shivered. Bloody barbaric. Even if it was just an effigy.

Zipping her hoodie against the chill, she crept past Mum and Jonathan's tipi, towards the lake. It had been a long night. The drums and tin whistles had kept her tossing and turning. Along with thoughts of Michael, and Tariq, and Beth, that seemed to play on an endless loop in her head.

Only a few half-conscious bodies stumbled around the makeshift village, most of them heading for the foul-smelling chemical loos and then straight back to their tents. Understandable – it wasn't even five-thirty and last night had been a late one for most.

Up on the bluff overlooking the lake, at the place where she and Beth had sat, a lone figure was silhouetted against the dusty orange and purple sky. At first she wondered whether it was Beth, but the outline was too solid, too thick to be her. She wondered whether Beth had found her friend.

Friend – ha! That word hid so much.

The campsite seemed uneasy, as if the whole place was holding its breath. A shiver tickled her spine and she thought about slipping back inside her tent and zipping up the flap until more people were around. But there were people all over the place, she reminded herself, just hidden by canvas. And this was the middle of the Lake District, not the middle of a city. What was there to be frightened of? Rampant foxes?

Maybe it was all that stuff Beth had been going on about that had unnerved her. Was there really something bad happening at the festival?

The thing about shit is, eventually some of it floats.

Poppy would be the first to admit that a fair few of the festival-goers were running some kind of scam. *Cross my palm with thirty quid and I'll tell you everything you ever wanted to hear about your past lives!* But she figured that in the long run, it all worked out. They all scammed each other and eventually everyone got their money back. Everyone except people like Bob – her might-as-well-be-granddad – who seemed to have endless funds to give to 'folks who were having a hard time'.

Poppy massaged her tense shoulders and picked her way through the sagging tents, passing a yurt with a door that looked like the entrance to a hobbit house. The dewy grass was slippery beneath her Converse, but was soon replaced by hard pebbles as she reached the water's edge.

Scariswater. The lake stretched out before her like a swathe of shot silk. The ripples reflected all the colours of the morning; inky blacks and burnt oranges. A ghostly full moon graced the sky, even as the sun was stretching its rays from the east. The scene was so beautiful, so otherworldly, that she almost got it – the need to thank someone or something. She let her eyes fall closed and breathed in the fresh damp smells of the lake and hills. But in a flash, gratitude was replaced with terror. She was back there, in that other lake. The freezing water blinding her. Burning in her lungs. Drowning her.

She forced open her eyes and gasped in air.

Air, not water.

Breathe – *breathe!*

The lap of water against the pebbles made a hypnotic swishing sound, the lightest of breezes lifted the hair from the back of her neck, blowing away the memory but not the fear.

She'd grown up in Cumbria. Lakes water pulsed through her veins and she couldn't imagine ever living anywhere else and yet that day, nearly a year ago, a lake just like this one had nearly killed her.

It had been an accident. A freak fricking accident! It

wasn't going to happen again.

She leaned down, quickly undid her laces, pulled off her socks and stuffed them into her Converse. She refused to be afraid of something she loved. She just had to get over it. She'd been unlucky that day, that's all.

The pebbles felt like dry ice cubes beneath her bare feet. She hopped around for a moment until she could stand the cold. Her jeans were skinny, and she had to yank the denim to get it past her calf muscles, but with her jeans as high as she could get them, she braced herself and edged into the lake.

The shock of the water made her gasp and then giggle. The water tickled as it lapped over her toes. Freezing, but not too bad. She'd been in colder.

As she stepped out, the feel of the pebbles beneath her feet transformed. They were no longer rough, but slippery, covered by a layer of slime. Poppy tried to concentrate on what her feet could feel instead of the frightened voice in her head telling her to get out of there. Sharp edges needled between her toes; moss tickled.

The bottom of the lake sloped gently down, and by the time the water was above her ankles, she was wondering where the inevitable shelf was, where the ground would disappear and she would find herself plunged waist deep and in need of a change of clothes.

Ahead, darkness swirled beneath the surface. It

stretched out towards her like a shadow. Maybe this was it – the drop. But no, she could still see shapes beneath the water. She took another couple of steps forward and stumbled. The water hit the back of her knees, like a slap with a wet kipper, and soaked her jeans. A nervous giggle escaped her throat. Or was it a cry?

It's OK, she told herself. She was safe.

The water was so cold, her feet so frozen, that she almost didn't feel it – the gentle caress against her skin.

Fish?

She peered down into the water and saw something pale move, just below the surface.

Definitely fish.

She shifted her foot, hoping to get a better look and something cupped her leg. Something even colder than the lake.

It was then she saw it: a pale hand gliding towards her.

She screamed, but it was too late. Her foot slid from under her. She plummeted backwards. Icy cold water filled her eyes and mouth.

And the sky disappeared.

CHAPTER THREE

Michael Quinn stamped on the clutch and punched the gear stick into fourth. The car kangarooed forward, raising a whimper from his back seat passenger. He glanced in the rear-view mirror. Wide black eyes pleaded with him.

'Sorry, mate. Not used to this thing yet.'

As he turned his gaze back to the narrow country lane, he felt a large rough tongue slurp his ear.

'Eww – no! Eugh!' Michael yelled, nearly swerving into the hedgerow. 'Dawkins, don't do that! Not while I'm driving. Not ever!'

Hot doggy breath made him gag. 'Oh God!' He felt for the window control and held it until all the windows slid open, letting in a blast of clean fresh air.

The promise of the great outdoors drew the giant poodle away from him and soon the dog's nose was stuck out of the window, long white ears flapping in the wind as fields and hedgerows flashed by.

OK. Good. The bloody dog had caused enough trouble as it was without causing him to total his mum's new car.

Or rather, Poppy had.

She could say what she liked, but he knew that the only reason she had gone to the wacky Pagan thing –

and dumped him with her dog – was to get out of going to Julia's eighteenth. She hadn't been to one of those festivals since her mum decided she could stay home alone. Sure, there was the wedding thing, but before she'd known Julia was having a party, Poppy was all for not going. Said she'd been to the registry office, the rest was just sentimental fluff.

Sentimental fluff – she'd actually said that.

He'd purposely not told her about the party, waiting to announce it only after she'd admitted she had nothing on. But then Julia went and sent her an invite. And that was it. Suddenly Poppy had to be with Meg and Jonathan for their handfasting ceremony. What kind of daughter would she be if she didn't go?

A devious one. Bloody devious.

Julia was just as bad. He was pretty sure that the only early invite that she had sent was to Poppy, knowing that she'd find something else to do.

'Women! You were better having your balls chopped off, mate,' he shouted to Dawkins.

The dog's long tail wagged.

The fact that his best friend hated his girlfriend, and his girlfriend was insanely jealous of his best friend, had turned his life into a minefield. Last week he'd actually found himself hiding at Mark's, afraid that if he listened to any more of their bitching about each other he'd kill one or both of them. That wasn't fair. Julia didn't bitch about Poppy. She just gave him guilt-inducing looks every time he mentioned her name. His life would be so much easier if they could just get on.

A sharp bend in the road took him by surprise.

'Crap!' The hedgerow hurtled towards him. He braked and spun the steering wheel. The tyres bumped off the tarmac and for a second he lost control. Wheels spun. Brakes screeched. And then, as if nothing had happened, the tyres reconnected with the road and the car was sailing once again.

Michael breathed out the image of his torn-up month-old driving licence, and breathed in week-old dog biscuit. Not again. He braced the steering wheel tighter as the poodle got more intimate with his ear than Julia ever dared.

'OK, OK! I get the hint. I'll slow down. Just get back on the seat.'

He reached down to turn on the radio, hoping some music would take Dawkins's mind off his ear. The speakers spat out three short beeps before the radio picked up the signal.

Dreary classical. No.

Drum and bass. No!

The news. Jesus! Was there nothing on at this time of the morning?

'The young woman's body was pulled from the lake at approximately five-thirty this morning. The police would not comment as to the circumstances of the death. I talked to a spokesperson for the John

Barleycorn Gathering—'

Michael's foot slipped from the accelerator to the brake. Dawkins growled. A horn tooted as a car flashed by. Michael turned up the volume.

'—one of the largest Pagan festivals held in the UK. He said that people were shocked and upset by what had happened. They will be having discussions as to whether the festival should continue. This is Sandy Wright in Scariswater, reporting for BBC Cumbria.'

The tacky breakfast show jingle echoed around his skull like a great big funeral bell.

Poppy.

The girl who found water irresistible.

No, it couldn't be.

He saw her face distorted by the dark waters. Her deep-set golden eyes hollow. Her coppery-blonde hair bound with lake-weed. Her mouth open. The last bubbles of air from her lungs breaking the surface.

A year ago she'd nearly drowned. Not that it had instilled in her any fear of water, not even a healthy respect. He reached a hand towards the mobile phone in the cradle on the dashboard. But that was no good. They'd discovered last year that her network didn't cover Scariswater.

Bile burned the back of his throat. He squeezed his hands back on the steering wheel, so tightly that his knuckles throbbed.

If she was going to die before her time, this was how

it would happen. In some bloody lake. Could that be it? Her life over before it had even got going, while she was still so caught up in what happened with her parents that she never really got a chance to live?

That wouldn't be fair. But life wasn't fair, was it? People died before their time all the fucking time.

Michael whacked the car into gear, yanked the steering wheel around and set off in the direction of Scariswater.

'It's all right, mate,' he said to Dawkins. 'She'll be all right. It won't be her. Poppy might be an awkward cow sometimes, but she wouldn't die on us.'

Would she?

CHAPTER FOUR

The slam of the ambulance door made Poppy jump. The arm that had held her steady for the last however long tightened around her.

He was a big man, a bit younger than Jonathan. He looked down at her with kind eyes and rubbed her arm, as if trying to get her circulation going, probably in the hope that she wouldn't notice his hands were shaking too.

Three police cars and a strip of blue and white striped tape were fending off the gathering crowd of gawping festival-goers. Police wandered around like out-of-place shadows – combing the pebbled beach. Her gaze followed one of them to a lumpy mound of damp red blankets; the only flash of colour in the now grey morning. It looked so innocuous; junk that had washed ashore. What lay beneath was anything but.

She shivered, and not for the first time since she'd been dragged from the cold clutches of the lake, she thought she might throw up. Poppy gripped her own red blanket to her chest. It did nothing to fend off the cold, shuddering nausea.

She stared at the blanket-covered body, hardly able to believe it was true.

The guy who'd helped her drag the dead weight

from the lake had tried resuscitation. He'd pounded her chest and done all the things you see people doing on the TV. But she must have been in the water too long.

The lake had won.

The sound of raised voices recalled her attention to the crowd of onlookers. A woman was arguing with the police. She pushed past them and ran to Poppy.

Mum fell onto her knees. 'Pops,' she murmured, grasping Poppy's face.

Mum's hands were warm and soft against Poppy's cheeks, but she could see the memories of the last time she'd been dragged from a lake, swimming like ghosts in her mother's bloodshot eyes.

Mum cocked her face to the side, silently asking if she was OK.

Poppy nodded and forced herself to smile. 'Don't fuss, I'm fine.'

'She wouldn't go with the ambulance,' said the guy beside her. 'She's freezing though. Could do with getting changed.'

'Thank you. Thank you so much for...' Mum's words trailed away. She shrugged and pulled Poppy into a hug. She could feel Mum's shuddering tears. They reverberated through her like shockwaves.

'Are you Poppy?' another voice asked.

Mum let her go, sat back, and wiped the tears from her cheeks.

It was a guy in grubby denim jacket and wrinkled shirt. He was a bit on the podgy side and needed a shave.

He held up an ID badge. 'DS Grant, Cumbria Police.'

'Any news on what happened to the other girl?' Mum asked.

There was a silence. 'Looks like she'd been dead for a while,' DS Grant said.

The Other Girl. It sounded so impersonal. So wrong.

'Beth,' Poppy forced out. The girl who she'd shared her biggest secret with. 'Her name was Beth.'

'You knew her?' It was her rescuer who asked. He loosened his hold on her and turned to face her.

His khaki shirt still bore the tidemark of the lake. She remembered his arms pulling her out, holding her while she coughed up sour-tasting water. He'd stayed with her while the paramedics had fussed over her.

His hair colour wasn't so much different from Poppy's – the kind of blond that could have been red if it had only tried a bit harder. And his face, though serious, had a kind of softness about it that reminded her of Dad. His steady gaze held hers, encouraging her to speak.

'We weren't friends or anything. I met her last night. She was hanging around on the bluff.'

'Do you know what happened?' Mum asked.

Poppy shook her head.

'I'm going to need to take a statement,' DS Grant said.

Mum sprang to her feet. 'Can't it wait?'

'Not really.'

'She's in shock and she's freezing. She needs to get out of her wet clothes. Christ, she's only sixteen, and she's just pulled a dead body from the lake, so why don't you give her some space?' Oh God, Mum had gone into six-armed warrior-goddess mode.

'OK,' the policeman said, taking a step back. 'Can you at least tell me where you'll be?'

Jonathan was slumped in a red and white striped deckchair in front of a rusted caravan painted with peace signs and demo slogans. When he saw Poppy, he leapt out of the sagging seat and hugged her so tightly the air was forced out of her lungs.

'What a terrible thing to happen. I'm so sorry you had to find her,' Jonathan said.

Poppy's head was so firmly pressed to his chest that his voice sounded distorted, like she was underwater. His heart pounded against her cheek just like Mum's had done. She pulled away from him as two policemen stepped out of the caravan. She glanced at Mum, who shrugged hopelessly.

At that moment, Bob appeared, filling the entire doorway of the caravan, looking like King Arthur with his red and black High Druid robes and flowing white hair and beard. He winked at her.

She grinned, flung her arms around Bob's thick waist and gave him a good squeeze.

'How are you feeling, our Poppy?' Bob asked, enfolding her.

'She's in shock, but won't admit it,' Mum said.

Bob tightened his grip. 'Not every day you find a dead body.' His big hand brushed the damp hair away from her forehead.

'I wish you'd put this blanket around you, you're going to catch your death.'

Poppy eased herself out of Bob's grip. Mum's face was grey and tired. Her arms were wrapped around herself and the blanket as if it was she who'd had a good dunking in the lake.

'I'm OK, Mum,' Poppy tried to say, as convincingly as possible. Mum's lips made a valiant attempt at a smile, but her eyes let her down on the follow-through.

'I think we all need a good strong cup of tea,' Bob said.

'I'll make it,' Poppy volunteered, desperate for a minute alone to get her head straight.

Mum shook her head. 'No. I'll do it.' Jonathan shot a concerned glance Poppy's way then followed Mum into the gloom of the caravan.

As soon as she was out of Mum's sight, Poppy felt the life go out of her like a rushing breath of wind. The bright paint of the caravan swayed in front of the dark spears of the fir trees and her knees sagged.

A hand grabbed her elbow. 'Come and sit down, lass,' Bob said.

Poppy sank into one of the deckchairs and squinted up through the pale morning sun at the concerned face staring back. She tried to ignore the sensation that a time bomb was ticking in her throat.

'I'm all right. I'm just tired. It's Mum who's freaking out!'

Bob snorted and collapsed into the other deckchair. She could hear Mum talking quietly to Jonathan, but not quietly enough.

'The thought of her being lifted out of the water like that. When they said a girl had died – it brought it all back. I thought I'd lost her this time.'

Bob caught her eye, his lips pressed together in what looked like a *hang-in-there-kid!* She felt sick and cold. Her eyes stung, but she wouldn't cry. That would only worry Mum more.

Police had cordoned off the lake and were wandering around the field in their luminous high-vis jackets. Three little kids kicked a ball about between the tents and yurts, their giggles the only music the gathering seemed able to produce.

Mum reappeared, followed by Jonathan, and handed Poppy a mug of tea. The heat nipped at her still-frozen fingers. She pulled the sleeves of her sweatshirt over her hands and used them like an oven mitt. Feeling

Mum's gaze on her again, she straightened up and forced herself to smile.

'They said you knew the girl,' Bob said.

For a second she saw Beth's face – the passion burning in her eyes. Then the fire faded and her face grew pale and waxy, dead and lifeless. She shivered and the image dissipated like ripples on water.

'Not really. I just met her last night. She was really nice.'

Bob shook his head. 'It's a flaming tragedy.'

'So, what'll happen? Will the festival go on?' Jonathan asked.

'That's what the fuzz were here about. I'll call the council together later this afternoon. But I reckon it'll be a good excuse to shut us down.'

'They won't do that, surely!' Mum said. She was thinking about the handfasting. Poppy got it – it was important to both of them. But a little niggling part of her was annoyed that they could even think about it. Beth was dead. It didn't seem right that life should go on like nothing had happened.

Before she could say anything, she was interrupted by a guy who couldn't have looked more out of place if he was dressed in a pink tutu and fairy wings.

'Pete! How are you, boy? I hear you're the hero of the hour!' Bob boomed.

Poppy's rescuer had changed into a blue check shirt, jeans and heavy-duty wellington boots. He looked even more out of place than Poppy did alongside all the hippy Pagan chic.

Pete shrugged and his cheeks glowed pink. 'Sally sent me down to ask after the lass. She'd come herself but she's about fit to burst.'

'Not long to go. When's she due?' Bob asked.

'Any day now.' Pete smiled at Poppy. 'Are you feeling any better?'

'Yeah, thanks.'

'No problem. Sally said to tell you that you're welcome up at the house whenever you like. I think she'd like the company, tell you the truth.'

'Tell her I'll be up to see her later,' Bob said. 'I'll bring her some raspberry leaf tea, that's supposed to help the baby along.'

'She'd like that.'

'Nice boy,' Bob said, as the farmer ambled away. 'His mum was a good friend to us when we first started John Barleycorn – letting us meet on their land. Had a lot of sympathy for the old ways. His father, on the other hand, was an old bastard, gods rest him.'

CHAPTER FIVE

There was a clatter on the caravan door.

'I'm looking for Poppy Sinclair,' a man's voice called.

'In here,' Bob said.

A man almost as big as Bob in a worn-out brown suit squeezed through the caravan door. 'DCI Hadley,' he said, in a thick local accent. 'This is DS Grant.'

The detective who'd been at the lake followed him in, ducking like he might hit his head even though he was a good foot shorter than his boss. Oh great, they were going to want her to talk about what happened and she really didn't know whether she could. She folded her arms over her stomach, hoping she could keep her internal organs from sloshing around.

The two policemen stood there, hunched like bald-headed eagles. Bob got up and motioned for them to take his place around the fold-down Formica table where Mum had forced gallons of chamomile tea down her, like *that* was going to help.

'Sit down, gentlemen. I'll make myself scarce.' Bob gave Poppy a quick reassuring wink before disappearing out of the door of the caravan.

The two policemen squeezed themselves onto the bench. Their jackets bulged over the edge of the fold-down table, and, in the case of the older guy, half his stomach as well. He rested his elbows on the surface – there was no room for them to go anywhere else – and sighed.

A shaft of light bled through the burgundy-coloured curtains, highlighting a column of swirling dust particles between them. The table was buried in stacks of books covering everything from ley lines to herbal medicine. One was entitled *The Peat Bog Bodies of the Northern Europe – Murder or Ritual Killing?*

'*Anti-Druid propaganda!*' she heard Bob growl in her head. She watched the old detective's eyes flit over the titles.

He grunted and then looked directly at her. 'You're Poppy?'

She nodded.

'And you are?' he asked, his gaze sliding to Mum.

'I'm Meg Donoghue. Poppy's mum.'

'Sounds like you've had a bit of a shock, Poppy, but would you mind telling us what happened this mornin'?'

She didn't want to talk about it. Didn't want to see lifeless eyes staring at her. She grabbed her mug of chamomile and wrapped her hands around it, trying to soak up the last of the warmth.

'What made you go out to the lake? Must've been quite early.'

'It was about half five. I couldn't sleep. Thought I'd go for a walk,' she said, realising how weird that sounded. She'd watched enough police dramas to know that the person who found the body was always a suspect. Wait until they heard about last night; that really would put her in the frame.

The man smiled, revealing tobacco-stained teeth. When he'd walked in the door she'd thought he looked like a farmer dressed up to go to a funeral. Now she was a murder suspect, he looked more like a sly old fox who'd had one too many full English breakfasts. 'I could never sleep in tents neither. Thought of all them creepy-crawlies.' He shuddered. 'And you headed straight for the lake, did you?'

'I suppose.'

'Did you see her right away?'

Poppy shook her head. 'Didn't know what it was at first. Just thought it was a shadow or something.'

'Is that when you called for someone?'

'I'm not sure. I think so. I don't remember. I tried to get her out but she was too heavy.' She could feel Beth's body limp in her arms. Except she hadn't been limp. That was why she couldn't turn her properly. She'd already started to freeze up. Did that mean she'd been dead for a while? 'Then Pete – the guy from the farm – and another guy helped.'

'Did you know her?'

Poppy nodded. 'I mean, no, I didn't *know* her. But I met her last night. We talked for a bit. Beth. She didn't tell me her surname.'

'What did you talk about?'

She shrugged.

'It would really help us to know what she was doing here, Poppy. She wasn't registered as a participant,' the younger detective said.

'She was looking for someone. A friend. She thought she might be here but I don't think she was.'

'What was her friend's name?'

Poppy tried to remember but the name was gone. She screwed her eyes shut, racking her brain. She saw Beth smiling up at the stars. Remembered the way she'd looked at her from under the long black lashes.

Flirting.

Beth had been flirting with her, it's just she'd been too bloody thick to notice until...

'Poppy?'

'I don't remember!' she blurted.

Mum squeezed her arm. 'It's OK, Poppy. I'm sure the policemen understand.'

The Old Fox exchanged a glance with his sidekick. 'What did she say about this friend?'

'She was in love with her.'

'*Her?*' the younger guy repeated.

Poppy could hear the titillation in his voice. Was that what Beth had had to put up with all her life? Sad blokes thinking that they were the one who could turn her, or hell, they wouldn't mind watching. 'Yes, *her*.

Have you got a problem with that?' She glared at the detective.

He shrank back into the bench and said nothing.

'And yesterday was the first time you'd met her?' the old guy asked.

'Yes.'

He nodded. 'Right you are. We'll need a formal statement, of course, but maybe we'll leave that until later. Until you've had time to think. Will you still be here?'

'I don't know,' Mum said. 'I think maybe we ought to go home.'

'No, Mum! Your handfasting. I'll be here.'

'Mrs Sinclair—'

'—Donoghue,' Mum corrected.

'Sorry. Mrs Donoghue, maybe you could come outside and give one of my constables your contact details, just in case you decide to take Poppy home.'

'Of course. Will you be OK?'

Poppy nodded and got up to let Mum out.

DS Grant watched his boss leave with Mum, but didn't move. He waited until they were out of the door before sitting forward and leaning his elbows on the table, just as his boss had done. It had been planned. Now the real questioning would start.

'Poppy, is there anything else you can tell us?' he asked.

Hold on, there was something. There had been

someone there before she got there. 'There was someone up on the bluff. This morning. At first I thought it might be Beth, but it wasn't. It was a bloke staring out at the lake.'

DS Grant scribbled something down in a notebook. 'You can't give me a better description?'

'No; it was sunrise. Just a shadow really.'

He pressed his lips together and nodded. 'You'd definitely never met Beth before?'

'Definitely.'

'Then how did you end up talking to her?'

'I was looking for somewhere quiet. I went up the bluff and Beth was already there. We just got talking.'

'Did you and she...'

'What?'

He smiled coyly. 'Hit it off?'

'We got on, if that's what you mean.'

He shuffled in his seat. 'Look, there's a young woman dead and we need to ask uncomfortable questions.'

Poppy couldn't help rolling her eyes. Even so, she felt her cheeks redden. 'I didn't fancy her, if that's what you're trying to ask.'

He nodded. 'What did you think of her?'

'What d'you mean?'

'Was she happy...depressed?'

'You mean depressed enough to kill herself? No. I don't think so.'

'Had she been drinking?'

'Yeah, but she wasn't drunk. Certainly not drunk enough to drown in shallow water.'

'What was she drinking?'

Poppy saw the glow of the sunset glint gold in the bottle. She blinked the image away. 'Jack Daniel's.'

'And how much had she had?'

'I'm not sure. No more than half a bottle.'

He bit his rubbery bottom lip and nodded seriously, like he'd worked it all out. 'That's a lot of Jack Daniel's.'

'She wasn't drunk. I'd have noticed.'

'I've seen it before. One minute they're as sober as a judge, the next they're off their faces. It's sad, but it happens a lot around here. It's a nice evening, they think they'll have a little dip in the lake to cool down. But they're drunk, they slip over, and that's it.'

Poppy watched the guy tell himself the completely made-up story of Beth's death.

'It didn't happen like that!'

'How do you know?'

'She was murdered!'

For the first time, the detective met her gaze. Ambition glinted in his sharp blue eyes.

'What makes you say that?'

CHAPTER SIX

When Poppy stepped out of the caravan, Jonathan reached out and took her face in his hands. He squished her cheeks and gave her one of his best therapist stares. 'OK?'

Poppy nodded as best she could with his hands clamped around her ears. His hands slipped away from her face and he backed off, allowing Mum to put an arm around her. She hadn't been handled this much since the divorce, when Mum had read some crazy manual that said that children of a broken home needed twice as much affection if they were going to grow up to be normal human beings.

'Do you feel like a lie-down now? And then Bob has invited us back for a late breakfast. If you feel like it. But if you just want to chill in the tipi – well, whatever.'

Mum didn't agree with being directive. Ever. Mum's liberal parenting, although the envy of all Poppy's friends, meant she felt left out when people start moaning about draconian restrictions. For rules and restrictions, she had to go to Dad. And these days he was too busy with his *mistress* to worry about her.

'Breakfast with Bob sounds great,' she said, leaning her head against Mum's shoulder.

The three of them headed back to the tipi. The festival had ground to an unscheduled halt. Most people seemed to be sat around outside tents, talking quietly. A couple wearing matching brown wool cloaks passed by like ghosts, chanting softly under their breaths. It was probably just their shopping lists, but if this kept up everyone would surely go home.

'Poppy!' a voice called as they were nearing the tipi.

Tariq darted between a gang of kids mucking about with wooden swords and stopped in front of them. He rested his hands on his hips as his chest heaved in and out.

'Thought – I – saw you,' he said, between gasping back breaths. He looked like he'd run a marathon so either he was even more unfit than she was, or he'd run a very long way to get to her. She preferred to think the latter.

Mum's arm tightened around her shoulder, but she smiled. 'Who's this?'

'Umm – Mum, this is Tariq. Tariq, this is Meg and Jonathan Donoghue, my mum and stepdad.'

Tariq smiled. 'Hey,' he said politely, but dismissively. His head tilted to the side as his dark gaze held hers. 'I heard you were the one who found the girl in the lake. Just wanted to check you're OK.'

He touched her arm and it was like dragons had breathed on her cheeks.

'I'm fine. A little lake water never did anyone any

harm,' she burbled, instantly regretting her choice of words. 'I mean—'

Tariq didn't seem to notice. He took a step forward, opened his mouth about to speak then, out of nowhere, two paws thumped into Poppy's shoulder, sending her reeling backwards into Mum. A tongue the size of a large trout slurped into her ear.

'Dawkins! What are you doing here?' she giggled, trying to regain her balance.

Hold on, if Dawkins was here that meant...

Poppy pushed down her crazy hound. There, sitting on the bonnet of his mum's brand new Prius, was Michael.

For a second she saw Beth grinning at the stars.

Love's a bitch that doesna let you go, Poppy.

Finding Meg and Jonathan's tipi could have been a hell of a lot more difficult than it was – the field was covered in conical white boils. But as it was, almost the first one he spotted had the telltale red stars around the entrance, and next to it was Poppy's rather more practical green igloo.

Michael pulled in next to Meg's silver Saab and trailer, and, leaving Dawkins in the car, jumped out.

'Poppy?' he called at the entrance of the tent. There was no answer. He moved to the tipi.

'Meg? Jonathan? Anyone home?'

A tight feeling settled in his chest and his mind

raced. He spotted a policeman and thought about accosting him, but then, between the tents he saw familiar strawberry blonde hair and a green sweatshirt pronouncing GOD IS DEAD, the one she only wore when she was particularly pissed off with the world. His shoulders slumped and for a second he was dizzy with relief.

He ran a hand through his hair and sighed. He was about to call her, when someone beat him to it.

A guy pushed past a group of kids and stopped in front of her.

He was a foot taller than Poppy – almost everyone was – and had the tight, muscled frame of a boxer although no one had seen fit to flatten his nose. *Yet.* The stranger reached out a hand and touched Poppy's arm. Wrong move. Poppy had a very strict sense of personal space. But she didn't give the guy the usual brush-off. Instead she gazed up at him, and – hold on a minute – *blushed?*

The hairs on the back of Michael's neck bristled. She'd only arrived last night and Poppy wasn't exactly a fast mover when it came to guys. Maybe she'd known him from before. He'd assumed she'd gone to the festival to avoid Julia's party, but maybe she'd had other reasons...?

Oh, that's just great! There he was driving halfway across the bloody Lake District, worrying she was dead, when all the time she was cosying up with some boxer dude.

Michael went back to the car, opened the door and let Dawkins loose.

'She's over there. But I warn you, it looks like you've got competition.'

Dawkins sniffed the air, and like a bloodhound, made a direct dart for Poppy. Michael slammed the car door and sat on the bonnet, folding his arms.

Poppy's giggle tinkled like a wind chime over the festival noise. 'Dawkins! What are you doing here? Tariq, I'll see you later.'

Michael stared at the churned-up mud. He took several deep breaths and tried to swallow the tightness that balled in his throat. *So what* if Poppy had other reasons for wanting to be at the festival? That was allowed. But it hurt to think that she might have been seeing someone without telling him. He was supposed to be her best friend.

'You know, dog-sitting usually involves actually staying put,' Poppy said.

He pressed his lips together and nodded. 'What can I say? I got bored of rifling through your cupboards.' He glanced up.

Poppy had her arms folded and she was trying to look put out, but there was a smile in the crinkles around her eyes. Her hair hung in damp snakes around her shoulders and she looked paler than normal, so pale that the freckles across her nose and cheeks stood out like a constellation of the stars she was so fond of.

'What are you doing here? Did you have an argument with Julia or something?'

He didn't smile. Didn't rise to the bait. For once, he really wasn't in the mood.

A crinkle appeared between Poppy's eyebrows, and she looked at him questioningly. She didn't get a chance to ask what was wrong because Meg and Jonathan had caught her up.

'Michael!' Meg said, hugging him and ruffling his hair the way she'd done since he was five. 'This is an unexpected surprise.'

He tried to smile, but his lips wouldn't cooperate. In the end he shrugged. 'They said on the news that a girl had been found dead in the lake. They didn't give any names.'

Meg nodded. Her gaze held his as if she too were remembering those agonising minutes on the shore of Lake Windermere, Poppy's lifeless body being worked on by the paramedics.

'Poppy found her,' Jonathan said.

'What?' Michael slid off the bonnet.

'Poppy found the girl. Tried to drag her out.'

'Jesus!'

'I'm fine! Well, I would be if people stopped fussing.' Poppy shrugged like it was no big deal. But it was.

Michael's heart was back in his throat. It was too close. He forgot all about the dead woman, and the fact that Poppy had been trying to help her. All he could think about was his best friend in another lake, risking everything. He squeezed his hands into fists. He wanted to shake her. Hell, he wanted to drown her himself.

'What were you doing in the lake?' he asked, through gritted teeth.

CHAPTER SEVEN

The police were still interviewing people when Poppy and Michael took Dawkins into the woods so he could run off some of his stupid.

Poppy watched as the giant ball of white fluff bounded around between the red trunks of the fir trees, scattering birds and chasing squirrels. She smiled. He was loving it. He'd have good dreams tonight.

What about her? What would she be dreaming about?

The shadow in the water? Beth's staring eyes? She felt the smile bleed from her face.

'You're quiet,' Michael said, breaking into her thoughts.

She shrugged. 'Dawkins behaving himself?'

'Don't change the subject.'

She forced another smile. 'Me being quiet – that's a subject now?'

'It's unusual.'

'Oh, I'm sorry. I suppose Julia's never short of something to say, even if it is about Max Factor's latest range of *wicked* nail varnish.' It was out of her mouth before she could stop herself.

Michael sighed. 'So this is what we're going to do? Well, fine, if picking an argument with me is going to make you feel better then let's do it. But can we not make it about Julia? Your material on that subject is getting old. How about we talk about your death wish?'

'I'm not picking a fight!'

Michael raised his eyebrows.

She suddenly felt washed out, like the lake had cleaned her out of comebacks. She flopped onto the ground, made soft by a covering of pine needles, and leaned back into the curve of the tree trunk.

She watched his walking boots kick up dried leaves and dust, stop, turn and point at her. She didn't have to look up to know what his expression would be. His jaw tight with frustration. His eyebrows raised, expectantly. She knew him so well. And he knew her.

'Sorry,' she muttered. 'I just... I don't get it. I don't understand how she could have drowned – she was so determined to find her friend. And the police – as soon as I said that she'd been drinking they just jumped to the conclusion that she must have been drunk and fallen in.'

'It could have happened that way.'

'She wasn't drunk. Yeah, she was drinking, but no way was she drunk. She was too focused to be drunk.'

'She could have had more after you left her.'

'She chucked the bottle away. And besides, you've seen the lake. You have to go miles out before it's deep enough to drown in.'

'You can drown in an inch of water if you're face down.'

Poppy picked up a brown and crumpled oak leaf and twiddled it around between her finger and thumb. 'You'd have to be unconscious first. It doesn't make sense. And he just brushed off the thing about the guy on the bluff like it wasn't important. What's the use of interviewing witnesses if they're not going to take them seriously? Why aren't they more bothered about this? Why doesn't anyone care?'

Michael slumped down beside her and pulled his knees up to his chest. Dawkins, clearly disappointed that the walking had ceased, shoved his wet black nose in Poppy's face. She tickled his ears, and feeling tears prick the corners of her eyes, buried her face in his fur.

There was a time not so long ago when Michael would have hugged her, but he hadn't done that for a while. It scared her, because it felt as if there was a barrier between them that was getting bigger and bigger every day. She blamed Julia, but what if it wasn't her? What if one day he didn't want to be friends with her any more? What if his relationship with Julia really was serious? What if he actually married her?

The questions swirled around her brain along with the image of Beth's blue face.

Sounds to me like you're in love with the guy, she heard Beth say.

Yeah, but what did it matter when he was in love

with someone else? Plus, you're dead, so stop bugging me! She immediately felt guilty for dismissing Beth's voice, which was totally stupid – it wasn't like it was really her.

Poppy sniffed and tucked her hair behind her ears.

Michael sighed. 'So what do you *think* happened?'

She turned to face him. His expression was expectant. 'The only way Beth could have drowned is if someone helped her.'

'You mean murder?'

'What else?'

His lip quirked as if he was about to smile, but then thought better of it. 'Who would want to kill her?'

'I don't know. But she was here looking for the girl she was in love with.'

Michael's eyebrows shot up. 'She was a lesbian?'

'Oh, get over it. I can't remember her name. It was something unusual. God! Why. Can't. I. Remember?!' Poppy growled and pounded the ground with her fist.

Dawkins sat up and whimpered.

'Y'know, it might help if you tried not to think about it for a bit. It might come to you,' Michael said. He leaned over and ruffled the dog's ears. 'Have you eaten?'

'How can you think of your stomach at a time like this?'

'Actually, I was thinking about your stomach. Maybe if you ate something you could think clearer.

62

And you might not be so arsey.'

That was just great. She'd just pulled a dead body out of the water and he was getting uppity about her being arsey? Fine. They'd go and get something to eat. And she knew exactly where from.

Zombified bodies wandered around the festival ground, speaking in hushed voices as if no one knew quite what to do. Poppy led Michael through the maze of caravans and tents towards the food vans; towards the chipped white van that had Radio 1 playing.

Michael looked at her. 'What do you want?'

She shrugged. 'Chips'll do.'

He took a deep breath, took his wallet from his back pocket and drew out a tenner. Then he turned to the guy in the serving hatch. 'Two chips please, mate.'

'Poppy, hi!' Tariq said.

Michael turned back to her and raised his eyebrows. He smiled knowingly, but there was just a glint of annoyance in his eyes. He was about to add something else to the order, but Tariq jumped out of the van and appeared at her side.

He might have Julia, *but look at the gorgeous older guy who's interested in me, MICHAEL!* She winced at her own behaviour. Why was she trying to punish him? It wasn't his fault he liked someone else.

'You're looking better,' Tariq said, leaning down to stroke Dawkins.

'I'm fine.'

Behind Tariq, Michael coughed.

'Oh, sorry, Tariq, this is my friend from home, Michael.'

Tariq bobbed his head in acknowledgement but made no effort to engage Michael in conversation. 'Have the police talked to you yet?'

'Yeah.'

'Did they say anything? Any idea what happened to her?'

Poppy shrugged. 'They haven't got a bloody clue. Don't even seem to care.'

'Poor cow. She was round here asking about some girl – Maya, I think.'

'Maya!' Poppy slapped her forehead. 'I couldn't remember the name, but you're right, it was Maya! Gotta go, I've gotta tell the police the name. Thanks, Tariq,' she said, setting off in the direction of the lake.

'But what about your chips?' Tariq called after her.

'I'll get them later.'

The festival had lost all the buzz of the night before. The seminars and workshops had resumed, but most people were sitting around in groups, talking quietly. The only music came from a guy sitting outside his sagging green tent, playing something that looked like a big recorder. The low, woody lament said it all.

Poppy stopped beside a patrol car and searched the

faces of the police officers, reluctant to go any closer. Michael stopped beside her and sighed.

The lake reflected the grey of the sky. Flat, silent and full of secrets.

'Poppy? Were you looking for someone?'

She turned to see DS Grant bent over, fussing Dawkins. Dawkins's tail flapped around, whacking against her legs.

'You, actually.'

'Aren't you gorgeous, hey?' the policeman crooned.

That was all the encouragement Dawkins needed. He launched himself at DS Grant. Resting his paws on the detective's shoulders, he was almost as tall as him. 'Whoa! You are a big girl!' the man laughed, allowing the dog to wash his face.

'Boy,' Poppy corrected.

DS Grant was finally able to push the hound down. 'Didn't think they allowed dogs at these things.'

'They don't. Someone's supposed to be looking after him.'

Michael grabbed Dawkins' collar and pulled him away from the policeman. 'I heard about the girl in the lake. Just came to make sure...'

'Ah. Right.' DS Grant nodded. 'Were you wanting to talk to the chief?'

'It's just I remembered the name of the girl Beth came looking for. It's Maya.'

'Right. That's helpful, thanks. We've found the dead

girl's car, by the way. And her parents have been notified, so we'll be releasing her name this afternoon.'

'Do you know who did it?'

'Did it?'

'Has to be murder, doesn't it? People don't just drown!'

'I'm afraid sometimes they do. It's for the coroner to decide now, but the boss is pretty satisfied it's accidental.'

For a second, Poppy imagined Beth on the postmortem slab, the cold silver blade cutting into her flesh until all her insides had been removed, slice by slice. Her face must have blanched, because she felt Michael's arm around her shoulders.

'But what about the guy on the bluff? The one I told you about. Maybe he—'

'—Was the guy who owns the land. The guy who helped you get the girl out.'

'Oh.'

DS Grant sighed. 'Listen, why don't you let your mum and dad take you home? If it were up to me I'd send the whole damn lot of you home. But the guv'nor doesn't want any accusations of religious intolerance. Get out of here, Poppy. You're gonna keep going over it in your head. And there's nothing you could have done.'

She shook her head. There was Mum and Jonathan's handfasting to think about. And she couldn't just walk away and forget about Beth. It would feel like she was abandoning her, just like Maya had.

She and Michael wandered slowly in the direction of Bob's caravan, where Mum and Jonathan had said they'd be.

As they walked, Michael's hand slipped away from her shoulders, leaving her feeling cold and alone.

'You know he's right,' Michael said, nudging her with his elbow. 'You need to get away from here. Why don't you come home with me? Your mum and Jonathan aren't going to want to get married now. They'll probably put it off. Come home. At least sleep in your own bed. Or stay at mine.'

Poppy shook her head. 'No. I can't. I've got to convince them.'

Michael stepped in front of her, forcing her to stop. His eyebrows were pinched together and his mouth was hard. 'No you don't. You're not the police. Why do you always have to get like this?'

'Like what?'

'Like everything is your responsibility. Like the world wouldn't fucking turn unless you were overseeing it! Jesus, Poppy!'

His words punched into her chest like bullets. She knew it, he was getting sick of her. The pain turned to anger. 'So I'm just meant to forget her, am I? If you don't like how I'm getting then you don't have to stay.

67

I don't know why you came in the first place!'

'I'm beginning to wonder myself.' Michael leaned down and attached Dawkins' lead. 'Maybe *Tariq* can talk some sense into you. Come on, let's go,' he seethed, and marched away, taking her dog with him.

CHAPTER EIGHT

'Where's Michael?' Bob asked. He was sitting alone at the Formica table in the dreary gloom of the caravan, surrounded by pipe smoke that hung over the piles of books like mist over mountaintops.

Poppy climbed up the metal steps and slid into the bench across from him, breathing in the sickly-sweet tang of tobacco. Bob puffed on his pipe and blew out a smoke ring. It wobbled over the table, like a UFO that was out of fuel. Poppy swiped a hand at it, dispersing the smoke into the atmosphere.

'I remembered the girl's name – the one Beth was looking for,' she said.

'Oh aye?'

'Maya.'

'That'd be Sandra Flynn's girl.'

'You know her?' Of course he knew her. Bob knew everyone.

Bob nodded. 'Sandra Flynn, Quincy Trevelyan, me and a couple of others set up John Barleycorn back in the late eighties. Sandra stopped coming years ago. But the last couple of times her Maya started coming.'

Immediately, Poppy's mind began turning over the possibilities. Beth's Maya. What if she really was here and Beth never found her? Or what if she did find her

– last night? 'What about this year? Is she here?'

'Aye, I reckon she is. Sam Wyatt said he'd seen her yesterday. She hasn't registered or paid, but that's not unusual. That girl don't think rules apply to her.'

'I should go and tell the police.'

'Or you could keep an old man company.'

'But—'

'—And leave the investigating to them that gets paid to do it.'

Bob sucked in his lips until they disappeared behind the long silver beard. His pale blue eyes stayed trained on hers, fixing her in the seat. She wasn't going anywhere.

'Fine.' Poppy sighed and flopped back against the worn-out cushions. She picked up a book on herb lore and began flicking through. The pages were filled with photographs of familiar hedgerow plants and their supposed medicinal qualities.

'Read that book you sent me,' Bob said.

She dumped the herbal on top of a three-inch thick tome on *Mysterious Britain*. 'Oh yeah? What did you think?'

The old man nodded thoughtfully and tapped his pipe against his bottom lip. 'Made a lot of sense. Course, it's only science catching up with what Druids have known for millennia. Ask any Pagan and they'll tell you that thought can affect the outcome of things.'

She might have known he'd say that. 'But don't you

get it? It's not a god, or goddess, or spirit. It's science. It's the way the universe works – quantum particles communicating with each other at a level we're not conscious of. There is no god or spirit – it's all rational and quantifiable. If we had the tools to measure it.'

Bob chuckled. 'You say potato, I say p'tar-toe.'

Poppy found she was smiling. She was never going to convince Bob – he was a lost cause. But that was OK; there were some things in life – some *people* in life – who weren't meant to change. They were meant to stay the same – like the cosmological constant. Change that and the whole universe would be thrown into a great almighty flux: up might be down, and gravity might disappear. Like her and Michael. Who knew what the quantum effects would be of them being anything more than friends? If they started going out then rivers might flood and a small Melanesian island might sink into the sea.

Bob clamped his pipe back in his mouth and puffed out a cloud of smoke.

'I know you're angry about your dad, lass. But that's no reason to turn your back on all that you've been raised to respect.'

'Why not? He has! But that isn't why I don't believe in...that stuff.'

'Then why?'

Poppy shrugged. She began straightening the piles of books. 'I suppose I just...'

'Saw the light?'

'Yeah.' Science was light. What had religion ever done except divide people? 'Yeah, I saw the light,' she said, defiantly raising her gaze to meet Bob's.

'And it has nothing to do with nearly drowning?'

'What? No!'

'Only to be expected,' Bob said, nodding. 'People thinks they know about nature – think it's all springtime and flowers blooming. All life and rebirth. Then there comes a time when they have to look the dark goddess straight in the eye and they don't like what they see. People think of Mother Earth as a gentle lady. They forget that she's also death.'

'I know that,' Poppy said, frustrated that he was treating her to a lecture from Paganism 101 when she'd grown up with the stuff. 'That's not why I don't believe in it any more.'

'Someone your age, not ready to die, well, it's only natural to be scared of that side of the goddess.'

'What had I ever done to her?' she blurted. It was out before she could really think about what she was saying. 'I mean – I – I don't mean her – I'm just—' She stared at the piles of books, searching for the words.

'Angry,' Bob said, gently. 'Aye. I was pretty fucking angry myself, tell you the truth. I'm angry about that lass dying too.'

Poppy looked up. The old man stared steadily back, took the pipe from his mouth and blew out a smoke ring. The circle of swirling smoke danced between them, as fragile as the circle of life he was so keen on.

'What makes you think she was murdered?' Bob asked.

Poppy shrugged. 'She wouldn't have killed herself. She was too worried about Maya.'

'From what I heard, they're sayin' it was an accident.'

'Crap. She was fully clothed. Who goes into the lake fully clothed?'

'You did.'

'I was paddling.'

Bob's face remained neutral. 'Maybe she was paddling and slipped over, hit her head.'

'She was murdered. I *know* she was murdered.'

'How can you know?'

'I just do!' Poppy said, her blood pressure rising.

'That your scientific opinion, or her quantum particles communicating with yours?' He chewed the pipe, trying to hide a self-satisfied grin.

She rolled her eyes. '*Ha-ha!*'

Bob chuckled. He leaned forward and for a moment studied her. Sometimes, when the old Druid stared at her, she could almost believe that he saw things that others couldn't.

'You should go and have your cards read,' he said, eventually.

What? She wasn't about to waste her money on... *Hold on a minute*. 'I thought you didn't like Tarot?

Thought you said it was misused by all and sundry?'

'Interesting lad, that Tarot reader. The one that's doing the workshop. Had a bit of a troubled past from what I hear. The craft set him on a different path though – changed his ways. Writes books now instead of burning them.'

'That's all very interesting but—'

'—Him and Maya – they were an item last time I heard.'

'Maya's boyfriend is *here*?' Poppy slid out of the bench. 'He's actually one of the workshop leaders?'

'Jonathan knows him from years back.'

'Sorry, Bob. I've gotta—'

'—Now hold your horses.'

'I've got to go and find him. He'll know where Maya is.'

'I said hold your damn horses!'

Poppy folded her arms. 'All right – horses bridled and steady!' she said, but her heart was skittering like a bucking pony.

'Word of advice from an old heathen—' He took down a tin from the shelf above him and took out some money and handed it to her. 'Don't go charging in there making accusations. Try for once to keep that tongue of yours from flapping. Listen to what the lad says. And for pity's sake, don't go lecturing him on physics.'

'Beth could have spoken to him. He might know

what happened. He could even be the killer. I mean, he couldn't have liked Beth showing up – not if she fancied Maya.'

'Boy's not a killer. Wouldn't let you go near him if I thought he was.'

'That based on careful psychological profiling, or his quarks communicating with yours?'

'Ha-ha!' Bob chuckled. 'You listen to the cards. Happen they might have something to tell you. And if Maya's with him – you be careful around that girl. She's trouble.'

CHAPTER NINE

Poppy scanned the marquee for someone who looked like a Tarot reader. The workshop had just about emptied out, but in the corner, beside a table piled high with books, a guy was holding court.

His head was shaved apart from one tuft at his forehead that was dyed green. His tanned, sculptured face was cocked to one side, listening to someone.

But hold on! She knew him. He was the guy who turned up last night, demanding to talk to her new stepdad. Bob had said they were friends, but Jonathan hadn't treated this guy like a mate, he'd treated him like a patient who'd overstepped one of his carefully maintained professional boundaries.

She watched the Tarot reader handling the crowd with all the skill of a snake charmer. Last night he had been as agitated as the lake in a gale, but now he was calm and in control. He was sort of handsome, actually. There was something about him that reminded her of an exotic bird, a kind of deadly beauty.

Several women in the usual Pagan garb flocked around him, emitting nervous giggles every time he opened his mouth. It was like a scene from a school disco – just with added juju. But it didn't look like any of them were *with* him. So where was Maya? Poppy sauntered over to the table and picked up one of the books. The front cover bore a Tarot card – the one with the world on it – and it was entitled *Tarot: A Road to Self-Discovery* by Kane Riverside.

'I feel like I've learnt so much!' one of the women was saying. 'Like I'm learning to read the cards all over again.'

'I'm glad the workshop inspired you,' Kane said. His voice surprised Poppy. It was soft, posher than she remembered, and totally clashed with his green-haired, tattooed persona.

At that moment, his gaze drifted over the heads of the women to Poppy. His expression didn't change, but the muscles in his neck visibly tensed. He stared at her, his wide eyes almost the same green as his hair, strange and unnatural. She knew she should look away, but he held her gaze like he had some kind of Superman tractor beam.

Poppy felt herself blushing. God, he was going to think she was one of his adoring concubines. She dropped his book back on the table and turned away – trying to find something else to focus on.

After a few more minutes of fan babble, she heard Kane excuse himself and a second later felt a presence beside her.

'Did you want to buy a book?' he asked.

Poppy bit her lip, felt in her pocket for the thirty quid Bob had given her and held it out to him. 'I was hoping that you'd do a reading for me.'

His gaze travelled down to her chest. She was about to be morally outraged when she realised that he was just reading the logo on her sweatshirt. GOD IS DEAD. Bugger! She probably should have changed into something that was a bit less in his face.

He smirked and started towards the marquee entrance.

'Put your money away,' he called over his shoulder.

'But...?'

'Come on. It's a long time since I did a reading for a signed-up sceptic.'

She followed him, almost having to run to keep up with his long strides. He led her away from the bustle of the tents, waving and acknowledging various people en route. They entered a small clearing on the edge of the lake where long twigs had been bent to form the skeleton of a sweat lodge.

For years, Poppy had been fascinated with all things Native American and had begged Bob's friend, a Lakota medicine woman called Mo Little Wolf, to let her join the adults in the purification rite. Not this year though.

Kane stopped a little way from the lodge and sat cross-legged on the grass.

'Take a pew, Sceptic,' he said.

Poppy kneeled a couple of feet away from him and watched as he produced a silk-wrapped bundle out of his jeans pocket. The sun was trying to break out from behind the clouds, but the heavy grey battleships were doing a good job of holding the line.

'I'm not a sceptic,' she said.

He unwrapped the cards and spread out the square of brilliant green silk over the ground, making the grass look yellow and dreary. The guy definitely had a green theme going on. All a bit predictable really.

'No?'

'No.' She tugged at her sweatshirt. 'Haven't you heard of irony?'

'Is that what it is?' He gave her a knowing look that made her wonder if he and Jonathan had talked about her. But Jonathan didn't do that with clients. Or at least he wasn't supposed to.

'So why do you want me to read your cards? What are you hoping to get out of it?' Kane asked.

She remembered the cover of his book. She shrugged. 'Self-discovery. Isn't that what Tarot is all about?'

'And she didn't even go to my workshop.' His eyes flicked up at her. Amusement danced in them. He wasn't her type – and he was *way* too old for her – but she could see what Maya saw in him. Something exciting and dangerous.

He handed her the pack of cards. 'Shuffle them well and try not to think too many negative thoughts, Sceptic.'

'My name's *Poppy*,' she said, shuffling the cards. She was dying to ask him about Maya and Beth but, remembering Bob's warning, she kept her mouth shut. She would play along with this charade. For a while.

'OK, that'll do. Now spread them face down over the cloth and pick six cards.'

She did as she was directed. Kane gathered the rest of the cards and put them to the side. He took the six cards from Poppy and laid them face down in a row.

'Pick a card,' he said.

Poppy looked at the row of cards, grabbed the one second from the right and handed it to Kane.

He looked at it and hesitated. He ran a hand over his mouth and blinked hard.

'What? What is it?' she asked, before she could stop herself. She didn't believe in this crap, but the way he looked at the card unnerved her.

Kane swallowed. 'This is you.'

He placed the card in the centre of the green silk. The picture showed a young woman bound and blindfolded within a cage of swords.

'Oh, great,' she murmured. 'That looks a bundle of laughs. What does it mean?'

'A number of things. I'd say that you feel isolated, but that isolation is of your own making or the result of a crisis in your life. It also means that you are the subject of much jealousy, or that you are struggling with jealousy yourself.' His eyes focused on her, as if he was waiting for her to confirm his totally groundless assessment of her character.

'What else?'

'That's not enough? Hand me the next card.' He took it from her and laid it next to the first. 'This is the problem.'

The card showed a black-haired woman, also blindfolded, kneeling and holding two swords crossed at her neck as if about to do away with herself. Behind her, a lake stretched out into the distance, flat and calm like Scariswater.

It's Beth. God, it's Beth!

'The Two of Swords. This card tells of violence, of trickery and deceit. Just what are you involved in, Sceptic?' Kane asked.

'I thought you weren't meant to ask questions,' she replied, not looking at him. 'Thought that would compromise the reading?'

He said nothing, so she handed him the next card.

'These are the options that face you.' He placed the card under the other two and held his hand out for the next. 'We're always facing forks in the road – this is the one ahead of you. Interesting.'

'Hmm?'

One card portrayed a knight on a galloping chestnut horse, holding aloft what looked like a club. The other was a king sat on a throne, holding a staff that was sprouting fresh green leaves, like a tree in spring.

'What's interesting?'

'The first two cards were swords – two women, yet

it seems your choice is between two wands – two men.'

'And what is that supposed to mean?'

'A dark-haired woman has brought you into conflict with two men? Does that ring any bells?'

'No,' Poppy said, quickly. Too quickly.

Kane's cheek twitched as if he was trying to stop himself from smiling. 'One of them is impetuous, the other thoughtful. One is ambitious and the other has a tendency to get lost. One represents all that is noble and honest, the other is more about immediacy and excitement.'

He was talking about Michael and Tariq. Shit. This was getting freaky. Or maybe not. Maybe it was some kind of quantum thing – he was just picking up on the stuff that was going through her head. Or maybe the stuff he was saying was so general that anyone would think that he was talking about a situation in their life.

'Next card, Sceptic.'

Poppy handed him another.

'This is what you need to make the right decision.' He turned the card over and for once it was one that she recognised, one of the major arcana.

'The Moon. Isn't that about imagination?' she asked.

He smiled, but his gaze was intense and searching – like it was him who was trying to get information out of her rather than the other way around. 'When did you lose your faith, Sceptic?'

'I never – I don't know what you mean.'

'The Moon is about more than imagination. You *know* what it's about.' He held her gaze and it felt like he could see through skin and bones – to what? Her soul?

'Intuition,' she conceded.

'That's right. The Moon governs not just the tides in oceans and lakes, but also the tides within us. The Moon reminds you that the only way that you will make the right decision is to trust in your intuition. Not to trust in your intuition could lead to…' His lip curled at the corner. '…*lunacy*. This card is urging you to trust in that which you don't believe, *Sceptic*.'

Her right leg had gone to sleep and something icy was slithering up her spine. She shifted and tugged her knees up to her chest, resisting the urge to shiver. 'What did you do before you started playing with cards?'

'I hated,' Kane replied, softly, as if he was telling her he'd worked in a pre-school. 'What happened to you to make you so angry, Sceptic?'

'What do you mean, you hated?'

'I was a Nazi. I used to beat up black people for fun. How did it happen, Poppy?'

'I have *no idea* how you became a Nazi. Maybe you had a troubled childhood?'

'That's not what I meant.'

She'd had enough of this charade. Time to get what she came for. 'Where's Maya?'

Kane's gaze dropped to the cards. He picked up the

Eight of Swords, the one that he said represented her, and stared at it – his green eyes suddenly sad. 'So that's what this is about. What did she do to you, Poppy?'

'Nothing. Beth, I met Beth.'

'Who?'

'Maya's best friend? Beth? Her body was recently pulled out of the lake by me, actually.'

Kane's gaze flicked back to Poppy. 'Beth was the girl in the lake?'

'Don't tell me you hadn't heard.'

'I hadn't.'

'You can't tell me that she didn't come to see you. She was looking for Maya. She knew she was most likely with you.'

'I never met Beth. I wouldn't know her if I fell over her.'

'But she was Maya's best friend!' The volume of her voice had risen to yelling. She swallowed and tried to rein in the frustration that was thrashing about in her chest.

Kane's eyes hardened. 'I never met the girl. Maya liked to keep us separate. Just one of the ways she manipulated everyone around her.' He gathered up the cards, wrapped them in the green silk and got to his feet.

'Hold on, where are you going?'

'Reading's over.'

Poppy pushed herself to her feet. 'You didn't finish.'

He walked in the direction of the canvas village. 'I don't need to see the rest of the cards.'

'Maybe I do! Kane, wait!'

He stopped but didn't turn around. Poppy ran in front of him and held out her hands to prevent him from leaving. He stared over her head, as if he couldn't bear to look at her.

'Is she here?'

His gaze stilled on the sky like he was reading the clouds, and spoke in a voice so far away it was almost as if he'd forgotten she was there. 'She disappeared, Poppy.'

'What do you mean? What happened?'

'We had an argument at last year's festival. She stormed off. I haven't seen her since.'

He was lying. 'But people have seen her.'

His gaze snapped down to her. 'Here?'

'Yes, *here*. So where is she?'

'Poppy, listen to me. Maya has a gift. Some people would call it charisma, but it's more than that. It's something darker and more powerful. She has you wrapped up in her web before you know what's happening and then it's hard to get away. Be careful, she'll have you dancing like a marionette.'

'I've never met her.'

Kane snorted. 'She doesn't need to be anywhere near you to work you. She doesn't need to be on the same plane to work you.'

'She's not *working* me. I just want to find out what happened to Beth.'

'I can tell you what happened to Beth – she got involved with Maya.'

Poppy's brow tightened. 'Are you saying Maya killed Beth?'

'She'd never do it herself. Never get her hands dirty – that's not how she works. It's just what happens to people who get involved with Maya.'

'But Beth was in love with her.'

'We all are. That's why she can do what she does. Leave it alone, Sceptic. Go back to your Richard Dawkins books and tell yourself that you could understand the world if only you could fit it in your test tube.'

How did he know about that? No, he was sidetracking her; trying to throw her off the scent by screwing with her head.

'What happened? What did you argue about?'

'Forget you met Beth. Forget it all and walk away while you still can. Don't mess with things you don't believe in; otherwise you really could wind up dead in the lake.'

Her mouth dropped open and for a long moment no oxygen entered her lungs. How did he know about that? Had Jonathan told him? Why would he do that?

Kane barged past her and marched away.

'Kane, wait!'

'No.'

'But you never finished my reading!' Poppy shouted after him.

'Death, Poppy. Your last card was Death.'

CHAPTER TEN

Agitated by the wind, Lake Windermere washed up against the sides of the yachts. Tackle clinked together like ghostly bells. On the far shore, wisps of grey cloud were rising up against the evening sky to join the heavy clouds that had collected over the hilltops.

The sky was working its way up to a storm, but Michael couldn't be bothered to move. He grabbed the bottle from his side and slugged back another gulp. The vodka burnt his throat but it didn't match the heat of the anger that burned in his stomach. He screwed the lid back onto the bottle and threw it onto the grass between him and the poodle.

He could just about pick out his yacht among the others that floated out on the lake, like a flock of seagulls taking refuge from the weather. He'd barely been out on it since the accident. If he were honest, he hadn't been able to stomach it now he knew how quickly things could go wrong. Poppy kept asking to go out, but there was no way she was ever going back out on that lake – not if he could help it.

That day, he and Poppy had gone out to Belle Island – something they'd done loads of times before. The lake was choppy, but not bad enough to keep them away. They mucked about on the island for a bit and then the rain started and they'd headed back to shore.

They'd rushed to get the sail up and neither one of them had put on their lifejackets. Stupid thing to forget.

They pushed off and everything was fine. They were almost back to the landing dock when some idiot in a speedboat got too close, sending a swell across already choppy waters. He heard a clunk and looked up in time to see Poppy slipping overboard.

He'd almost laughed. He wasn't worried. Poppy could swim like a fish – she was never out of the lake. He'd leaned over the side expecting to see her scowling back at him, annoyed, wet and cold – not injured. But when he looked overboard, all he saw was the constantly moving water.

'Poppy!' he'd called. No one had answered. He crossed to the other side of the hull – it would be just like her to swim to the other side to freak him out. Nothing.

His first instinct had been to go in after her, but he'd grabbed the radio and sent out a mayday message. Then he'd ignored the instructions of the coastguard and dived in.

Thankfully they'd been close enough in to shore that the lake wasn't more than ten feet deep. It was dark at the bottom, but through stinging eyes he'd spotted her. Her eyes were open, but she was making no attempt to swim. He'd grabbed her and swum to the surface. Then, at last, some of his training had kicked in, and he'd started rescue breaths. It made no difference. She was a dead weight in his arms.

Eventually, he and Poppy were dragged onto the coastguard's boat and they started resuscitation. For what seemed like forever there was no response. They cracked a rib trying to get her to breathe, but they were getting nowhere.

Her forehead was red with blood, but the rest of her face was blue with drowning. He'd felt like a part of himself was dying in front of him. He couldn't remember life before Poppy and he couldn't imagine navigating the rest of his life without her. She was like a sister to him. An infuriating, ridiculously bossy little sister.

And so he'd shouted at her. He'd promised her anything if she would just *wake up!* He'd got so damned hysterical that one of the coastguards physically restrained him.

They returned to shore, to a waiting ambulance. And then, just like that, she was coughing up lake water. She wasn't conscious, but she was trying to breathe again.

After a week in hospital, she was back to her old self. Except she wasn't. Nearly dying had changed her, had changed both of them. She'd come back to life but she'd left a part of herself – or at least a part of their friendship – in the lake. He'd thought for a while that she blamed him, but she swore she didn't.

And now this.

Another girl in another lake.

It was all too familiar.

His phone began to ring. He pulled it out of his pocket and looked at the screen. *Julia calling*.

Bugger – he was supposed to have gone round there. Why hadn't he?

He dropped the phone beside the bottle of vodka and squeezed his eyes shut against the pain that shot through his forehead.

CHAPTER ELEVEN

Death. She was surrounded by it. No matter what she did or where she went – death was there, haunting her, pursuing her.

Death, Poppy. Your last card was Death.

She dumped the book she hadn't been reading for the last hour and switched off the torch. A green glow shone through the nylon of the tent, marking the passage of the sinking sun.

Even if her last card had been Death, it didn't mean actual death. Kane knew that. Everyone knew that. It meant change in circumstance. Death of an old way of life, beginning of a new. It didn't mean actual physical death. Well, hardly ever. And even if it did mean death, it was all superstitious crap, right? But the way that he'd said it...

Poppy sat up, unzipped the tent flap and crawled out.

Jonathan was kneeling down, about to hit the peg holding the tipi's guide rope with an enormous hammer. He looked up and smiled.

'Hi Pops, how are you feeling?'

She'd always thought of Jonathan as harmless. Kind of like a hover fly – a bit annoying, but there was no sting in him. But the guy had clearly been talking about her to Kane, and she didn't like the thought of that at all.

'Where's Mum?'

'She's gone to the organising committee meeting. They're discussing whether in the circumstances the rest of the programme should go ahead.' He looked at her strangely. 'Are you sure you're OK? Do you want to sit and talk?'

No, she didn't want to sit and talk. He'd been doing quite enough talking about her to people who had no right to know the details of her life. On the other hand, there was stuff that she wanted to know.

Poppy folded her arms. 'That guy, Kane – the guy that was here last night.'

'What about him?'

'How do you know him?'

'Eventually you get to know everyone.'

She knew avoidance when she heard it. She was the mistress of avoidance. 'I got the impression that he was seeing you professionally, as a patient.'

Jonathan frowned. He dropped the hammer to the ground and stood up. 'Poppy, where is this coming from? Why do you want to know?'

'So he's a friend, then?'

'And again, I ask: why do you want to know?'

'I want to know why you would tell him stuff about me. I want to know if you've been gossiping about me and Mum to some mate over a beer, or if you're using me as some kind of psychological case study with your clients.'

Jonathan's brow tightened. 'What?'

'He knew stuff about me. It doesn't take a genius to put it together!'

'Poppy, why were you talking to Kane?'

If she told him why she'd been to see Kane, he'd tell Mum and then she would insist that they left. 'It doesn't matter. Just please don't talk about me.' Poppy turned to leave but in a second Jonathan was in front of her, blocking her path. She tried to step around him, but again he shifted to block her.

She looked up into his face and he stared steadily back.

'Poppy, I haven't told Kane anything about you. I wouldn't do that. But I am concerned about why you were talking to him?'

'He knew stuff. He *must* have got it from you.'

Jonathan shook his head, glanced away and rubbed the back of his neck. 'What is it that you think I told him?'

'You told him I was screwed up about what happened. And I'm not, OK? So will you stop telling people that?'

Jonathan swallowed and nodded, his eyes wide with understanding like she'd just revealed some big secret to him. 'I didn't tell him anything about you, Poppy.'

'Then who did?'

'Did you have your cards read? Is that what this is about? You know the cards most often reveal the things that are hidden in our own hearts. Maybe —'

'Don't!'

She turned to run but he grabbed her arm before she could get away. 'Poppy.' His voice was quiet, sympathetic. 'Why don't we go and get a drink and talk?'

'If you're not going to tell me the truth, then there's nothing to talk about.'

Poppy snatched her arm out of Jonathan's grip and made a dash for it. She stumbled between tents, fighting back the panic rising in her chest. Thoughts and feelings were flooding her skull like someone had opened a dam. If Jonathan was telling the truth, then how did Kane know so much about her? If he wasn't telling the truth, then why was her stepfather lying to her? It was too much.

She took a deep breath and tried to get a grip. She had to do something. Stop thinking. She needed distraction, now!

The scent of fried food carried on the breeze.

That was it.

She followed the smell of chips all the way to the warm glow of the burger van.

'What can I get you?' the guy behind the counter asked. He was about a hundred years old, bald, and definitely not Tariq.

'Er – I—'

'Hey.'

Poppy felt a hand on her arm. She turned to see Tariq. His hair had been mussed with wax, and it stuck out at odd angles. He wore a sleeveless black T-shirt that showed off the tattooed band circling his nicely formed bicep, which bulged because of the weight of the gym bag slung over his shoulder.

He smiled, and Poppy felt like a ridiculous teenybopper faced with her boy-band idol.

'Are you OK?' he asked, his wild eyebrows scrunched together in concern. 'I was just coming to look for you, thought you might need your mind taking off – stuff. But I didn't know whether that guy was gonna stay the night.'

Ah. She forced herself to say: 'Michael's just a friend.' After all, it was the truth.

Tariq's smile widened. 'Won't be a sec.' He disappeared up the metal steps into the van, exchanged a few words with the hulk who was on serving duty, and reappeared without the bag. 'Come on. Let's go and check out the stalls. I'll buy you an aubergine burger or something.'

The two of them wandered through the market that had sprung up some time that afternoon. There was a trend for hanging fairy lights and Moroccan lanterns from the awnings. The soft light from the coloured glass and the warmth of the evening made Poppy feel as if she'd somehow travelled to a distant land, and after half an hour or so, the thought of Beth's lifeless body was receding.

Tariq darted between the stalls, never standing in one place for too long.

'What d'you reckon?' he asked, pulling on a red and blue jester's hat.

'Kind of suits you, actually.'

'We need to find one for you.'

'We really don't.'

'Got it!' He spun around and in his hands he held a sparkly crown. He grinned and placed it on her head.

'Tariq!' she protested.

'A crown for the prettiest girl at the fair.' He leaned down and his lips brushed lightly against hers before he turned, dumped his own hat and paid the stallholder for hers.

Her breath caught. In her head there was so much noise that it sounded like a freight train was thundering through her brain. But she knew what she wanted to do.

As soon as Tariq turned back to her, she reached up a hand and slid it around his neck. His skin felt warm. And he smelled good, which surprised her. After he'd been working in the burger van all day she expected him to smell of chip fat. But no. He smelled of bergamot, jasmine and something else warm and inviting.

His arms looped around her waist. Warm breath

tickled her ear as he leaned in. 'Let's go somewhere quieter.'

He grabbed her hand and led her away from the campfires and fairy lights. The lake was the obvious place to go. Quiet. Romantic. And, er...hello? *Dangerous?* She was relieved when he led her in the opposite direction, down the track that led back onto the lane that counted as the main road in these parts.

For a second she hesitated. Was she really going to do this – snog some guy she'd just met when she was in love with somebody else? Yes, she told herself, that was exactly what she was going to do. *Michael has a girlfriend.* It was unfair to both of them for her to sit around moping over him. This was OK. This was what people did when they were single: they had fun and occasionally kissed gorgeous strangers at Pagan festivals.

Away from the fairy lights, the night was growing dark. Poppy looked up and saw the dim ghostly glow of the Milky Way: distant suns glinting away with nearer, brighter stars. To the north, Draco the dragon swooped across the sky. And one of those glinting tiny dots was the Cat's Eye nebula – a dying star emitting its last pulses of hot energy. At least when it died it would give birth to new stars. Maybe even new worlds. What purpose had Beth's death served?

Tariq pulled her off the track into the shadow of the

fir trees and, before she could do or say anything, he kissed her.

Hands cupped her cheeks, fingers tickled behind her ears and down the sides of her neck, and the crown he'd bought her toppled from her head.

His body seemed to be radiating heat. And she wanted that warmth. She wanted him to carry on kissing her because it was nice, so much nicer than all those fumbled nothings at school discos. Her heart pounded in her chest. But it was good – she felt alive, not dead.

Death, Poppy. Your last card was Death.

She broke from his lips and laid her head against his chest. Images spun in her head like water being dragged down a plughole: Beth's hands blue with cold; Michael's face before he'd stormed off and left her; the way the light had glimmered above her on the surface of Lake Windermere as she'd sunk, down, down…down.

Tariq's arms enclosed her.

'Are you thinking about that girl?' he asked, softly. She nodded.

'I'm not doing a very good job of distracting you, am I?

'That's OK.'

Tariq's hand slipped down her arm. He took her hand and led her back in the direction of the festival, stopping only to retrieve her crown from the grass. He placed it back on her head and smiled. 'So – where do you come from? I don't know anything about you.'

'Windermere. You?'

'Blackpool.'

Poppy snorted. 'Blackpool?!'

'Yeah – what's wrong with that?' he asked with mock haughtiness.

'I just didn't think anyone actually lived there. Thought it was all cheap B&B's and tacky fairgrounds. Although it explains the funny hat obsession.'

'It's not where I want to be, believe me, but at the moment it's where I need to be.'

'Why?'

Tariq glanced at her as if deciding what to tell her. 'It's a long story.'

'We don't seem to be doing anything else at the moment.'

He stopped abruptly, pulled her to him and whispered, 'We could change that.'

Poppy laughed, put her hand on his chest and gently pushed him away. 'No way. Not when it's just getting interesting.'

'Believe me, it's not interesting.'

She smiled at him until he rolled his eyes and carried on walking.

'Usual story: Dad did a runner, left us with no money so I had to get a job.' He sighed, ran a hand through his hair. His gaze dropped to the ground. 'I told myself it was just short term, y'know? But the problem is, you start to get ravelled up in things. I just don't know if I'll ever be able to undo it all.'

What a strange thing to say. She was about to ask him what he meant when the wind picked up, bringing with it the sound of drums and bodhrans beating a strangely militaristic rhythm against the backdrop of rustling leaves. Whistles joined in just as the breeze switched direction. Suddenly it sounded like the music was coming from behind them. She glanced over her shoulder, half convinced that she'd see a ghostly fairy army marching towards them. Of course there was nothing there...except...

She could just make out the curve of a shoulder and the glint of moonlight in long copper hair. It was a woman, standing in the shadow of the fir trees, watching them.

Poppy's feet stopped moving. She pulled her hand out of Tariq's.

'Poppy?'

'There's someone there,' she whispered.

Tariq glanced around. 'What? I don't see anyone.'

'She's right...' Poppy pointed to the fir tree, but there was nothing but shadows where seconds ago there had been flesh and bone. She hadn't imagined it. There had definitely been someone there.

'Where are you going?' Tariq shouted after her.

Poppy stumbled over the uneven ground to the place where she had seen the figure. There was a small gap between the swooping branches of the fir tree and a dense thorny bush. She pushed aside a branch and eased past, ignoring the sharp twigs that slashed at her arms.

Seconds later, Tariq burst through the bush, gasping and cursing. He stopped beside her.

'If this was some elaborate plan to get me somewhere—'

'—Shhh!' Poppy hushed him.

The darkness was thick with the smells of rotting bark and the fresh green sap of the fir trees. The breeze that had carried the sounds of fiddles and drums switched directions once again and they were left listening to nothing but the rustle of the air through leaves and the sound of their own breathing. Nothing moved.

'What exactly are we doing here?' Tariq whispered.

A sudden gust ripped through the fir trees, with the roar of waves crashing against rocks. Poppy's hair whipped into her face. She squeezed her eyes shut and for a second she thought she heard a girl's laughter.

The wind died just as suddenly as it had risen. She brushed her hair away from her eyes and looked from shadow to shadow. Nothing.

'I thought – I thought I saw...'

'Come on.' Tariq grabbed her hand and pulled her back the way they had come. He pressed his back against the bush to create a safe passage and helped her out onto the moonlit track.

Poppy turned on her heels, looking for any sign of the girl. But they were very much alone.

Tariq looked at her bemused. 'So what exactly was that about?'

It was a very good question and he was looking at her like she'd lost it. 'I thought I saw someone. Sorry.' Her cheeks filled with heat.

Tariq frowned and glanced back towards the bush. 'Who did you think it was?'

She ran a hand through her hair and realised she'd lost her crown. 'No one. Sorry – I guess this whole thing has me more freaked out than I thought.'

Tariq pulled her closer. 'Hey, it's completely understandable.' He hugged an arm around her while his other hand brushed down her back in long slow strokes, like she was a cat that needed taming.

'I don't understand how someone could kill her. How can people do that? Take a life?'

His chest rose and fell in a sigh. Eventually he said, 'Poppy, what did you tell the police?'

'What do you mean?'

'Before, when you went running off to tell the police about something.'

'Just that the girl Beth was looking for was called Maya.'

'You didn't tell them you got it from me, did you?'

103

She looked up and his arms loosened their hold on her.

'No. Why?'

He shifted. 'Nothing. Don't worry.'

She pulled away.

'It's nothing, Poppy. It's just I bought a consignment of oil that I suspect may have fallen off the back of a lorry. The last thing I need is the cops snooping around the van.'

'I see.'

'I don't normally do that kind of thing...but there was a guy and the offer was too good to refuse. Are you scandalised?'

She smiled, relieved. 'No. Well, I am, but...it's fine.'

'But this thing with the dead girl? Leave it alone, Poppy.' His voice was serious.

'What?'

'Don't get involved.'

'But I am involved.'

'You know what I mean. Don't ask too many questions. It'll only bring trouble.' For a second, she thought there was fear in his dark eyes. Catching her look of concern, he smiled. 'Sorry, I didn't mean to spoil the mood. I was supposed to be taking your mind off what happened, not bringing it all back.' Tariq took her hand and pulled her towards the festival ground. 'So come on, you were telling me about yourself before you dragged me into the woods to ravish me.'

'You wish,' Poppy snorted.

Tariq grinned.

'Actually, I think *you* were telling me about yourself. What were you doing before your dad left?'

'I was at Manchester uni.'

'That's weird. That's where I want to go. What were you doing?'

'Second year Law.'

She stopped and stared at him. So much for thinking that he wasn't into books. 'Tariq – that's like – you must have got at least three As!'

'It's no big deal.'

'You've got to go back.'

He shook his head. 'I don't know. Maybe.' He nudged her arm. 'So what do you want to do?'

'Astrophysics.' She saw Tariq's lip curl. 'Hey! What's funny about that?'

'Nothing. I don't normally go for science nerds.'

'Huh!'

'Hey, I know what it is, you just wanna get close to that guy off the TV, don't you?'

'No!'

'Oh come on! Physicist and rock star. Even if his band was crap, that's a pretty intoxicating mixture.'

'I want to go there because it's a good department.'

'If you say so.'

'I do,' she said, smiling despite herself.

'*Things, can only get better,*' Tariq warbled quietly.

'Hey!' She pushed him off balance.

He giggled and caught hold of her. He smiled down at her and pushed a lock of hair away from her face. 'That means I'm three years older than you. Does it bother you?'

For a moment she thought about going along with it. What he didn't know couldn't hurt him. But after how great he'd been, it felt worse than lying. 'Umm, four actually. I'm just about to start A levels.'

Tariq bit his lip and wiggled his eyebrows. 'Right. Poppy, you are sixteen, aren't you?'

She nodded.

Tariq wrapped his arms around her waist and pulled her so close that she could feel everything from the buckle of his belt pressing into her stomach to the ripple of abs against her chest and...*oh my God*... another part of him that was taut and ready for action. She felt jittery, light-headed and as if she wouldn't ever be able to breathe again.

'Just checking,' Tariq muttered before kissing her and stealing every last molecule of oxygen from her lungs.

CHAPTER TWELVE

It was too hot. No matter how he lay, or how many windows he had open, it was way too hot to sleep. But, if he were honest, it wasn't just the heat keeping him awake.

Michael rolled onto his back and stared at the dimpled ceiling. At the side of the bed, Dawkins was snoring.

'Glad you can sleep,' he muttered. Maybe he could have slept too, if his anger hadn't morphed into guilt.

He shouldn't have shouted at Poppy. She was his best friend and she'd had a crap day. But just recently not a day went by when she didn't do something that got under his skin. She'd gone from being the girl who was up for anything, to the girl who was intent on finding any reason to be mad at him. And it hurt.

For a while he thought it was because she was jealous of the amount of time he spent with Julia, but he wasn't convinced by that. But he'd done his best to keep up their usual routines even though it wasn't easy when the two of them couldn't be in the same room for more than ten seconds at a time without sniping at each other.

He screwed his eyes shut and rubbed his hands over

his face, wiping away the sweat that had beaded on his forehead.

And now there was the girl in the lake. Poppy wouldn't let it go. The girl was dead, but Poppy was acting like she could still save her. He'd seen it in her eyes – determination and desperation in equal measures. It was almost as if she felt guilty that she had survived nearly drowning and this girl hadn't. Some weird form of survivor's guilt? Maybe she was trying to save herself. Whatever the reason, she'd keep on about it until she got into trouble.

He sat up, flicked on his bedside lamp and grabbed his laptop.

Beside him, Dawkins grunted and shifted until his head was out of the light and firmly in the shadow of the bed.

He opened up Google and his fingers hovered over the keyboard. What the hell was he supposed to be looking for? He only knew the dead girl's first name, although the police had said they were releasing her name to the press. He typed 'Beth', 'dead' and 'Scariswater' into the search box, pressed return and up it came – an article from one of the local papers about the death of Beth Trimble.

OK, so the girl she was looking for was Maya, according to Burger Boy. He tried to ignore the scratchy feeling in his spine when he thought about the guy taking an interest in his best friend, and typed in

'Beth Trimble', 'missing person' and 'Maya.'

There were a couple of dead ends. Then he clicked on a link that took him to a missing persons' site. The photograph that slowly appeared in the top right-hand corner took his breath away.

The girl was the spitting image of Poppy.

Same strawberry blonde hair, same smattering of freckles across her cheeks, only the nose was slightly more pointed, more sculpted than Poppy's button nose. The eyes weren't quite as big as Poppy's, and they were blue rather than the golden coppery colour that he knew so well. The girl's lips weren't quite as full either. He'd always thought Poppy had nice lips. They were never cracked or pale like Julia's sometimes were, but always red and...

He blinked away the thought. The point was, there she was: Maya Flynn, reported missing almost twelve months ago by Beth Trimble. And she and Poppy could be sisters. That was more than a bit weird.

There was a mobile number and an email address for Beth, and a message asking anyone who knew the whereabouts of Maya to please get in touch. Then underneath there was a message from Maya's mum begging her to contact the police, just so she could know that her daughter was safe. There were no replies and no updates.

Maya was still missing. Beth was dead. And Poppy, the girl who didn't know when to stop, was probably investigating at that very minute.

But what if she was right and Beth had been murdered? How long would it be until Poppy asked the right person the wrong question?

With any luck, Poppy was holed up with Burger Boy, snogging the greasy face off him...even if there was something suspect about the guy, and he was way too old for her.

Michael grabbed his mobile. He'd just send her a text on the off chance it would go through.

CHAPTER THIRTEEN

Poppy gasped awake.

Arms were holding her fast. They had her locked against the ground. Dead arms. Dead hands. And someone was laughing at her.

'Get off me!' she screamed.

'Shush-shhhhh,' a voice whispered. 'You were dreaming, Pops.'

'What?' The arms released her and she rubbed her knuckles into her eyes, trying to clear the sleep from her vision. When she looked up again she saw the blurred outline of Mum.

Mum reached up a hand and smoothed down her hair. 'OK now?' she whispered.

Poppy swallowed against her dry throat and nodded.

'Come and have a drink,' Mum said.

'What time is it?'

'It's about four.'

'A.m.? Mum, just go back to bed. I'll be fine.'

'We're doing a swap,' a voice said from the open tent flap. In the torchlight she saw Jonathan clinging to the sleeping bag that was wrapped around his body. They hadn't talked since their argument earlier that night, but he obviously hadn't told Mum about it.

Mum's hand on her back urged her up. 'This is totally unnecessary.'

'Oh, believe me, it's necessary. If only to give me a break from a certain person's snoring.' She looked pointedly at Jonathan.

'Hey! I can't help it! It's the fresh air – opens up the tubes.'

'Please?' Mum asked.

Poppy sighed. There was no getting out of it. 'OK. Just tonight though.'

The sudden sound of a duck quacking made them all start.

'What the heck's that?' Mum asked.

Poppy grabbed her phone. 'A text. But I thought there was no signal round here.'

'What were you dreaming about?' Mum asked, as Poppy stood near the centre of the tipi, fiddling with her phone.

Poppy forgot about Mum's question the second she realised the text was from Michael. 'Aha! *Sorry about before*,' she read, '*shouldn't have lost my rag*. That's weird, I don't normally get a signal here.'

'It's been dropping in and out. I think it depends on the weather. Is it from Michael? Did you fight again?'

'It was nothing. He's just being a grouch at the moment.'

The tipi was alight with the soft glow of several

candles, all safely contained in lanterns. Poppy collapsed onto a pile of cushions. Mum handed her a bottle of spring water, and she screwed off the top and gulped it back. On the other side of the tipi, Mum dripped essential oils from small glass bottles onto a battery-powered burner. After only a few seconds the perfume surrounded her. She closed her eyes and tried to work out what the oils were.

At a guess, she'd say frankincense. Good for nightmares – so that would make sense. But there was something else. Something sweet and heady. She wasn't sure, but she thought that maybe it was ylang ylang.

'Why ylang ylang?' she asked.

'It's a good all-rounder. So nice they named it twice.'

Mum unrolled one of her treatment mats, threw a red chenille throw over it and motioned for Poppy to lie down on it.

She smiled and did as Mum asked. She lay on her stomach and rested her head on her crossed arms. Even through the thick mat, she could feel the unevenness of the ground. Someone had forgotten to scout the site for stones. Jonathan might be into all that *blokes running around naked in the wood* stuff, reclaiming their masculinity, but he had a lot to learn about camping.

Her hair was brushed away from her neck and then she felt the gentle pressure of Mum's magic fingers on her neck.

'Just as I thought,' Mum said, 'you're full of knots.

No wonder you were having nightmares.'

'Did I wake you?' Poppy asked, thinking about the half-dozen other bodies lying within a stone's throw of her tent.

'No. To tell you the truth, I couldn't sleep. I was thinking about Beth – about how her parents must be feeling.'

'Yeah.'

'And – well – Jonathan told me what happened.'

The knots in Poppy's shoulders tightened again.

'You know he wouldn't disclose information about you. Especially not to a client.'

'Kane's a client?'

'Yes. Has been on and off for years. I've got to say that I was surprised to hear you'd had your cards read.'

'I was just curious.'

'Did you get the answers you were looking for?'

Answers were in short supply. 'More questions than answers.'

Mum's hands slid down Poppy's back, massaging away the tension tied up in her muscles. For a while neither of them spoke. Only the strange night-time sounds of the campsite broke the silence. The sound of footsteps stumbling between the canvas. The hoot of a tawny owl. The occasional peal of drunken laughter. And there were other human sounds, that in previous years Poppy would have rolled her eyes at; but now they turned her mind to Tariq.

He hadn't done anything but kiss her, but for the first time in her life he'd made her think about doing... *it*. Weird. She hadn't thought about doing anything with anyone except Michael for a very long time.

As if her radar had picked up her thoughts, Mum asked, 'How was your date? It was a date, wasn't it?'

Poppy felt blood rush to her cheeks.

'He's a very good-looking young man,' Mum continued. 'I'm guessing he's a bit older than you?'

Poppy rolled onto her side and propped herself up on her elbow. Mum lay down next to her, mirroring her pose. 'So?' she encouraged.

'Do you think I'm too young to...y'know?'

Mum's face didn't change; didn't even flicker. She didn't reply either.

'I'm asking, Meg.'

'I think *you* need to decide that.'

'You *do* think I'm too young. I can tell.'

Mum smiled. 'Poppy, you have never once held back from doing something you wanted to do because someone asked you not to. So what would be the point in me asking you not to sleep with this boy? Am I to gather from this conversation that you're thinking about it – about having sex?'

'No, not really.'

'Tariq really is very good-looking. I could quite fancy him myself.'

'Ugh, gross! You're just saying that to put me off!'

Mum laughed. She reached over and caught hold of one of Poppy's auburn curls. 'You know you're the most passionate person I've ever known. Apart from your father.'

Poppy rolled her eyes. 'Oh, thanks!'

'Your dad's a passionate man. That's why he did what he did. He can't do anything by halves and neither can you. It's just not in your nature. So if now is the right time for you – and Tariq is the right person – then I can't stop you. But I do have one question.'

Oh, here we go… 'What?'

'How will it affect things with Michael?'

Poppy felt like a rock had been dropped onto her stomach from a great height. She rolled onto her back and stared at the conical wall of the tipi. 'I don't know what you mean.'

'Really?'

She didn't know what to say.

'Pops, your hormones may be screaming at you to sleep with Tariq. That's normal for someone of your age. And if your heart is telling you the same thing then maybe you're ready to take that step. But listen to your heart. If you don't, it'll be the thing that gets bruised along the way.'

Beth was floating on her back on a beautiful blue ocean. Her dark hair swayed about her like dancing black snakes. She splashed her hands, sending waves of white foam gliding towards Poppy, and laughed a full-throated laugh that wasn't at all choked by the long pink and silver scarf wrapped around her neck.

Love's a bitch that doesna let you go, Poppy!

When she woke this time, it was with a scream.

'It's OK, Poppy, wake up!' Mum said.

'The scarf!' she gasped. 'Mum, she had a scarf on when she was in the water.'

'What? Pops, I don't understand.'

'When they pulled her out there was a pink scarf around her neck. It wasn't hers. Beth wasn't wearing a scarf. Someone must have put it there!'

CHAPTER FOURTEEN

It was nine before any police showed up at the campsite. Poppy followed the blue and white striped tape they'd used to cordon off the shore of the lake. DO NOT CROSS, it demanded. Someone had ignored it. There, on the grey and brown pebbles, at the place where Beth's body had been dragged out of the water, was a homemade wreath of wild flowers; pink orchids and wilting cow parsley.

Poppy's feet stopped moving. *She* should have thought of that. She should have asked Mum to drive her into the village to buy a bouquet. How could she have been so thoughtless? Beth deserved flowers.

The clouds parted, allowing the sun to poke its rays through. Her gaze was drawn to the sparkles of sunlight that skipped over the dancing waters of the lake like tiny diamonds being tumbled on the waves. When she was little, Mum had told her that those little lights were water sprites that lived in the deepest depths of the lakes. Theirs was a world so cold and dark that when they saw the first hint of sun, they would dash for the surface where they would dance and skip, trying to warm themselves. If you listened really closely, you could hear them singing until they would eventually sink back below. But if a little girl happened to step into the water as the sprites were sinking, they would drag her down to their kingdom where she would stay a prisoner forever. There was even a song that she was supposed to sing to the sprites so that they knew she meant them no harm.

> *Children of the lake and sea*
> *Have nowt to fear from me*
> *So leave me be and I'll stay free*
> *To live my life 'neath sky and tree.*

It was a stupid song that tried too hard to rhyme, and she was pretty sure that it wasn't an old folk tale at all, and that Mum had made the whole thing up just to stop her from going too near the lake. It had worked for a while. She would see those dancing lights and remember that although the lake was beautiful, it was a world of cold and darkness where children were captured by sprites and never seen again.

Those were her nightmares now. When she dreamed about drowning there were always hands dragging her through the water and she would hear the distorted sounds of the sprites singing.

If she listened too hard, she would hear them now, strange watery voices mixed up with the whispers of the breeze through the fir trees. Had Beth heard their song? Were there hands that dragged her down into the water and held her there until she stopped struggling?

Were those hands human or did they sparkle and shine, beautiful but deadly in the moonlight?

'Hiya Poppy, you wanted to see someone?'

Poppy was so caught up in her own imaginings that the interruption made her jump. It was the short sergeant. He was sipping coffee from a cardboard cup and rubbing his bloodshot eyes like he'd just that second got up.

'Did you want something?' he repeated.

Poppy swallowed. 'The scarf around Beth's neck,' she said.

'What about it?'

'She *was* wearing a scarf? I didn't dream it?'

DS Grant screwed his eyes shut. '*What?*'

'She had on a pink scarf, right?'

'Yeah? So what?'

'She wasn't wearing a scarf.'

'What?' He looked at her like she was talking in a different language.

'When I saw her up on the bluff. She wasn't wearing a scarf. My God, are you even awake? No wonder there's so much unsolved crime.'

DS Grant scowled at her. 'Maybe she put it on after you spoke to her.'

Poppy shook her head. 'She wouldn't wear a scarf like that.'

'How do you know?'

'Isn't it obvious?'

'Clearly it isn't, otherwise I wouldn't be asking.'

'It's pink! Do you really think Beth was the kind of girl who wore pink? Didn't you see what she was wearing?'

'So you think that because she was wearing a scarf that didn't go with the ensemble she was...'

'Murdered. And have you found Maya? You know she's here?'

'Maya?'

'The girl Beth was looking for? The girl she was in love with? You are looking for her, aren't you? People have seen her but she hasn't registered for the festival. Don't you think that's a bit odd? A bit suspicious?'

'Jesus, it's too early for this. Poppy, thanks for telling me about the scarf. I'll definitely pass on the information.'

And that was it. He lolloped away from her like a podgy Labrador retriever.

Poppy followed. 'Is that it?' she demanded.

The detective sighed. 'What exactly do you expect me to do?'

'I expect you to investigate! Isn't that what the police do? Or is that only on the mornings you're not nursing a hangover?'

'Now, eh!' DS Grant said, spinning around and glaring at her. 'That's out of order! Do you have any idea how many cases we have open at any one time? It's not like the telly, y'know! We're short-staffed. I've got friends being made redundant and a tragic accident isn't exactly my number one priority. Now I realise that you're upset, but just let it go.'

'You said they'd have the postmortem by now.'

'Yeah, well guess what? They're short-staffed as well. Accidents happen, Poppy. Now if you'll excuse me, I have actual crimes to deal with.'

With that, he screwed up the empty cardboard cup, chucked it at the ground and stormed away.

'That's an offence, you know – littering!' she shouted at his retreating back.

Poppy didn't know whether she was more angry or upset. She ran a hand through her tangled hair and sighed.

'Poppy Sinclair berating cops? Bob *would* be proud,' a voice said.

The woman standing at her side had appeared with all the stealth of the wolf she was named for. Mo Little Wolf's dark eyes crinkled with held-in laughter.

'Mo!' Poppy threw her arms around the woman's neck and hugged her tightly. 'I didn't know you were here. I thought someone else was coming.'

Mo gave her a quick hug and then pushed her away, holding her shoulders and looking her up and down. She wasn't much older than Mum, but the years had etched her face like rock carved by water.

Mo nodded approvingly. 'You've grown. And are those...*breasts?*'

'Oh my God! *Mo!*' Poppy gasped, and folded her arms over her chest.

A wicked grin flashed across the Lakota medicine woman's face. 'You English, you're so squeamish. I love it. Hope you've drunk lots of water?'

'Huh?'

'You're sixteen. After all the years of bugging me, you can finally sweat with us. I've just seen your mom and she said it was OK.'

'Oh, wow…yeah, that's…' – the last thing she needed – '…great!'

CHAPTER FIFTEEN

The morning sun dipped in and out of clouds as Michael tried to avoid hitting any of the many craters and potholes in the track leading down to the festival site. His mum had already moaned to him about the mud splatters in the wheel arches. Thankfully she hadn't noticed the small scrape on the bumper from when he'd got a bit too close to a dry-stone wall. What did she expect? Lake District driving was an adrenaline sport at the best of times: add a few sudden downpours and a lot of surface water and it became a cross between waterskiing and downhill slalom.

Further down the track, a big black four-by-four with monster wheels and blacked-out windows was parked up. Two blokes were standing beside it talking.

Michael's foot slipped off the accelerator and the engine died.

'Fuck!' he hissed. 'Bloody stupid car!'

His hand went to the ignition but something made him stop. One of the guys standing beside the four-by-four was Burger Boy, the guy who was into Poppy. The other guy was tall, about forty, and wearing a slick grey suit that wasn't exactly suitable attire for a Pagan festival. Mister Slick opened the boot of the car and pulled out a black sports bag, the kind Michael used when he went to the gym, and handed it to Burger Boy. Burger Boy pulled a brown envelope out of his back pocket and handed it to Mister Slick, then the two shook hands. Mister Slick got into the car and Burger Boy strutted down the road like a guy who'd just won the lottery...or just done a very good deal.

Shit.

The black four-by-four sped towards Michael. Quickly he started the Prius and shot the car into gear. He hoped Mister Slick hadn't noticed he'd been stationary, but as the monster truck passed, it slowed. The Prius's engine died again. In the rear-view mirror, Michael saw the monster truck pull in behind him.

'Shit. Shit. Shit,' he murmured as the driver got out and walked towards the Prius. When he got to Michael's door, the guy leaned down and knocked on the window.

What the hell was he supposed to do? Get out? Just sit there, what?

He rolled down the window.

'You all right, mate?' the guy asked. His cockney twang seemed friendly enough.

'Yeah. Stupid thing keeps cutting out on me.'

'Thought about one of these. Do my bit for the environment, y'know – be a responsible citizen.'

'I think I'd prefer yours,' Michael said.

The guy glanced back at his dealer-mobile. 'Yeah, she's a beauty. And doesn't cut out.' The guy laughed at his own very funny joke. Michael laughed too, just to be on the safe side. 'You need a jump start?'

Michael tried the ignition. The car purred into action. 'Think I'll be OK. But thanks.'

'No problem.' The guy thumped his hand on the roof. 'Hope you've got recovery. Wouldn't wanna get stuck around here. Arse end of nowhere.'

Michael laughed along. 'I'm covered. Thanks for stopping.'

'Take it easy,' the guy said, and sauntered back to the dealer-mobile.

Michael sighed. 'Poppy, what the hell have you got yourself into now?'

CHAPTER SIXTEEN

The sweat lodge was no longer a skeleton of tree branches. It was a dome covered in animal skins and striped blankets that looked like they'd been stripped off a kid's bed. Between the dome and the lake, a group of women in shorts were collecting around the fire, rubbing their hands together and hopping from one foot to the other like it was cold. It was twenty-four degrees! What was that about?

Poppy sighed. She should have said no. Mo was cool, she wouldn't have held it against her, but after all that the woman had put up with from her over the years – all the begging to be let in on the ceremony – it would have seemed ungrateful. She tugged at the sarong that Mum had lent her, feeling this was like the worst sort of fancy dress party; one you were invited to by mistake.

A guy strolled across the grass towards the fire with long easy strides. The shorts and loose T-shirt looked so normal it was a shock to see the tuft of green hair. Kane. *Kane was sweating too?*

Poppy's whole body tensed.

'Hey, kid. What's up? You look like a scorpion stung your ass.' Mo winked.

'I thought sweats were single-sex. Isn't that the

tradition?' Poppy said, before she could stop herself.

'Normally they are. The guy leading the men's sweat is sick. They cancelled it. This guy asked if he could join the sisters. I told him to go jump in the lake, but he's persistent – a bit like you. I prayed about it and Spirit told me his need was genuine so I made an exception...so long as everyone agrees. But say the word, sister, and he's gone.'

The thought of sitting in a dark, confined, steamy space with Kane made Poppy want to turn and run. But from everything she knew about lodges and how they worked, people normally talked...told secrets. And Kane was keeping secrets she wanted to know.

She shrugged. 'I don't mind. But Mo? Don't put him next to me.'

Mo nudged her with her elbow. 'Kid, this is your first sweat. You're going to be right by my side.'

Poppy followed Mo over to the fire. When Kane saw her his jaw tightened and he looked away.

Death card. Ha! How about the pain in your ass card?

Litre bottles of water were passed out and they were all encouraged to drink as much as they could before entering the lodge. Mo gave out safety instructions. If you feel faint, you leave. If you have palpitations, you leave. If you feel claustrophobic, you leave.

'This isn't an endurance sport, people!' she barked. 'In this lodge we pray for Mother Earth, we pray for the brothers and sisters, and we pray for ourselves and give thanks to the Creator. Stuff'll come up. It's meant to. We all take baggage in there. Some of us take hand luggage; most of us take whole suitcases. Get it out and offer it to Spirit. But if at any time you need to leave, all you have to say is 'all my relations', and you can go.'

Kane was staring at his bare feet. It was weird seeing him without the combats and Doc Martens – like she was seeing him without his skin. He raised his head, caught her eye and quickly looked away.

The participants lined up outside the lodge. Some of the women crawled in backwards. When it was Kane's turn, he got down onto his knees and crawled in backwards too. Just as he was disappearing into the gloom, he glanced up. His bright green eyes connected with hers and for a second he stared at her. 'Have fun, Sceptic,' he said.

Poppy rolled her eyes and folded her arms.

Another woman followed him in and soon it was Poppy's turn. She forced a smile for Mo and crawled into the gloom of the lodge. Mo followed her in and settled herself between Poppy and the open flaps. Kane was almost directly opposite her, on the other side of the central pit dug into the earth. He looped his arms around his knees and stared at the ground.

Mo said a prayer and in came the first of the lava rocks that had been heated in the fire. Seven rocks in all were placed into the pit, then the flaps of the lodge were shut and they were plunged into almost complete darkness.

The temperature in the lodge began to creep up. Poppy could just pick out the outlines of bodies in the circle of darkness. At the centre, the seven rocks glowed orange, like they had been turned back into the lava that had formed them.

Something was thrown into the pit. Sparks jumped and danced, forming little fizzing lights between glowing rocks, and the air was filled with a bitter smoke that stung her nostrils and made her chest go tight. She began to cough and splutter.

Sage for purification – clearing the air...and apparently her lungs! Poppy slapped her chest to try and stop the coughing. A shadowy figure rose up and Poppy heard a splash of water. The hiss was so loud she thought the rocks were going to explode. Immediately the heat leapt up from comfortably warm to hot. Really hot.

Sweat prickled her armpits and she felt her brain begin to melt. She took a deep breath of muggy air. It didn't seem to want to go in her lungs. She felt dizzy, panicky. She wasn't going to be able to stand this for long.

Somewhere in the circle of shadows, someone began beating a drum in a heartbeat rhythm. And then Mo sang. It would never be a hit, and Mo's voice wasn't up to much, but the tuneless melody and occasional yips and shouts were strangely hypnotic, like Mo was transporting them all deeper into the earth. Poppy felt herself begin to relax. Maybe she could do this.

'For all the brothers and sisters!' Mo's deep voice rang through the darkness.

Poppy concentrated on breathing slowly. The heat in the lodge was choking. But despite the heavy hot air trying to squash them – or maybe because of it – the women talked. They talked about relationships that had gone wrong, men who they'd divorced, loves they'd lost.

Poppy stared out over the glowing rocks, waiting for Kane.

When he spoke, his voice quiet and strained. 'I loved someone. She – she's gone now. Except she isn't. Everywhere I look she's there. In crowds. Here, she's even here —' His words were choked off by what sounded like a sob.

Maya was here? Poppy thought back to when they were outside. Kane hadn't spoken to anyone. She assumed that all of the women in the lodge were just as much strangers to him as they were to her. He didn't mean the lodge then...he meant at the festival. So he had lied. Maya was here and he was hiding her.

Water splashed, rocks hissed and sizzled; and the air in the lodge went from hot to volcanic. Poppy's skin tingled like she was getting sunburn. It was unbearable. She sucked at the air but it scorched her throat and her lungs. She might be about to die – or at least faint – but that wasn't important. So many questions: Why was Kane hiding Maya? Was he protecting her? Could Maya have killed Beth? Did they do it together?

'She won't leave me alone,' Kane continued, his voice steadier. 'I wanted her so much...but I want her to go now. She has to go...before I—'

Before he what?! She wanted to leap over there and shake him. Before he killed her, like he killed Beth? What?

'Closing our hearts to people is one of the hardest things to do,' Mo said, gently. 'We're made to love, but sometimes it's not good for us. Lovin' people who'll never love us back is like throwin' our hearts on hot rocks over and over again.'

Poppy stared at the glowing rocks. In the faults and cracks she could see shapes and patterns. The heat from them burnt her eyes, but she couldn't look away, couldn't even blink back the blur of tears. Each rock was like a tiny sun that was dying right in front of her. She remembered Beth staring at the burnt-orange sunset – the pain and hopelessness of loving someone she knew would never love her back.

Poppy threw her head back. She was gasped, trying to find cooler air. And she did. She wasn't in the lodge any more, she was on the bluff beneath spinning stars that streaked the sky with glitter. Beth smiled at her, reached out a hand and trailed icy-cold water down Poppy's cheek.

'Love is like fire,' she whispered. 'Unless it's channelled it destroys everything. She wants to destroy you, Kane.'

Poppy blinked away the scene. It was a few seconds before she realised she'd said Beth's words out loud. She gasped. 'I'm sorry – I didn't mean to—'

There was the noise of movement.

'Ow!' someone cried.

'All my relations!' Mo shouted and the flaps were flung open just in time for Kane to stumble out of the lodge.

Poppy got to her knees, but Mo held her arm.

'Sisters, we'll resume this round in a moment. Take a minute to get some air.'

'I'm really sorry, Mo,' Poppy said, as the others made for fresh air.

'Take it easy, kid. What did you see?'

'Nothing! That's not it. Beth, the girl who died, it's what she said to me. I was just remembering it.' It must have been a memory. Her mind was playing games with her in the dark. 'I didn't realise I'd said it out loud.'

Mo grabbed a bottle of water, unscrewed the top and handed it to her. Poppy tried to take it but her hands were shaking. Mo steadied the bottle while Poppy took a deep gulp of warm, plasticky water.

'I should go.'

'No. You need to stay.'

Poppy stared up at the walls of the lodge. The fir branches that lined the walls were moving closer, pressing in on her. 'It's too hot. I'm – I'm going to be sick.'

'You walk out now and you take this with you. You stay, you leave it here. Understand?'

Poppy shook her head. She wanted to be outside. Hell, even the lake looked good to her right now.

Mo unhooked something from around her neck and put it over Poppy's head. She looked down and grabbed the pendant. In the shaft of light coming in through the open flaps, she could only make out what looked like a smooth black stone.

'What is it?'

'Apache's tear. It'll protect you.'

'Protect me from what?'

Mo reached into a bowl and then threw a handful of dried sage onto the rocks. Smoke filled Poppy's lungs.

'Mo! Protect me from what?' she gasped, amid coughs and splutters.

Mo shook her head and muttered something in her native tongue as her hands made a sign over Poppy.

Before Poppy could ask again what the hell was going on, an approaching body blocked out the light coming from the open flaps. Kane kneeled down and crawled back in. He took up his place without so much as looking at her.

The rest of the participants followed him in.

Poppy wanted out. But Mo was between her and the flap and the woman looked like she might rugby-tackle her to the ground if she tried an escape.

'The ancestors have deemed that we move forward to our last round. This time we give thanks to the creator for the blessings in our life, and we pray for ourselves, we pray for understanding.' All the time, Mo's dark eyes stayed trained on Poppy. 'And we will pray that our ancestors will keep us from harm.'

One at a time, seven more hot lava rocks were borne into the lodge on a long-handled shovel. Poppy watched hopelessly as the flaps fell closed and all the light in the world was shut out.

Mo threw more sage onto the rocks and then several cups full of water that bubbled and sizzled. The steam and smoke rose into the sweltering heat. Poppy's T-shirt was soaked through and the sarong clung to her legs. She was as wet as when she'd been pulled from the lake. The water that fizzed and hissed on the stones came from the lake. The same water that Beth had drowned in.

She tried not to think about it. She tried to listen to the women as they talked and prayed about their hopes and dreams, but all she could think about was Beth in the water all alone. No Michael to pull her out. Just hands holding her down until water filled her lungs. Hands that might have been Kane's. Or Maya's?

As hard as she tried not to, in her imagination she

saw Beth on the bluff, looking out over the lake. Moonlight painted her face in shades of blue and silver.

'The thing about shit is, eventually it floats.' Beth turned to her and laughed. 'Get it?'

'No,' Poppy whispered. 'I don't get it.'

Beth stepped closer. So close that Poppy could smell the Jack Daniel's on her warm, tickling breath.

'This isn't real,' Poppy said. 'You're not here.'

Beth smiled her red lipstick smile. 'Watch your back, Poppy. He's on to you.' She leaned forward and brushed her lips against Poppy's cheek. Her kiss wasn't warm. It was icy, wet. And she no longer smelled of Jack Daniel's but of rotting flesh. Beth stepped back, except it wasn't Beth, it was a corpse with long strawberry blonde hair. Poppy was looking at herself – dead.

She screamed.

'Shhhhh…' a voice hushed her, throaty and low. 'It's OK, kid. Breathe.'

Poppy's eyes flew open. The cold wet thing on her cheek was the wet towel that Mo was dabbing over her face. Mo's smile was one of relief. 'Welcome back.'

'Is she all right?' someone asked.

Poppy pushed herself up to a sitting position and saw that the person asking was Kane.

He's on to you, a voice whispered.

CHAPTER SEVENTEEN

'You sure you're going to be OK?'

Poppy nodded. 'I'll be fine.' She wanted out of there. Away from that stupid sweat lodge and away from all the crazy. She hadn't channelled the ancestors, for God's sake! She'd freaked out...or fallen asleep...or daydreamed...or something. It was more likely that she'd had a flipping mental breakdown than she'd channelled Beth's spirit!

'You know we need to talk about this,' Mo said.

'I can't. I need to see Mum,' Poppy said, knowing full well that Mum and Jonathan had gone to a meeting about their handfasting.

Mo Little Wolf frowned. The medicine woman wasn't stupid. She knew she was being given the brush-off. 'Anything like that happens again, you come to me or Bob.'

'Don't worry. If I have another freak-out I'll come and find you.'

'Wasn't a freak-out. It was a blessing.'

'Yeah, well, it didn't feel like it,' she snapped back. She took a deep breath and tried to get herself together. 'I'm sorry, Mo.'

'OK. Later. But promise me you'll keep the necklace on.'

She nodded, fingering the warm black stone that hung around her neck.

'Do you mind if I talk to your mom about this?'

'No!' Poppy gasped. 'You can't. I don't want you to. I've got to go. Thanks, Mo. I'll be fine, honest.'

The morning sun was unusually warm as she headed back to her tent; either that or the heat from the lodge was lingering in her body. Maybe the heat explained the heaviness she felt; like she'd picked up a hundred-litre backpack filled with lava stones that were all whispering in her ear about Kane and Beth and Maya.

He's on to you!

When Poppy reached her tent she flopped into one of the green canvas chairs Jonathan had set up outside the tipi. She didn't even have the energy to go for a shower or get changed. Her head buzzed with images of Beth on the bluff and Kane staring at her like she was the one tormenting him.

Life seemed to have returned to normal at the festival. The music of laughter and chatter drifted through the canvas village. People were walking with places to go and people to meet. How quickly they were able to shake off the presence of death.

Not her, though. Why couldn't she let it go?

Michael was right, she was treating Beth's death like it was her responsibility and it wasn't. She'd met the girl once. Yes, she should be sad that she died, and yes, she supposed it was natural to want to know why. But the way she was acting was crazy. She was letting her imagination get the better of her. And now Mo thought that she was some kind of sensitive! That was a joke. She was just stressed, over Beth…and Michael. She squeezed her eyes shut. *Michael.* God, what an idiot she was being. She had to talk to him – apologise.

She grabbed her mobile out of her pocket and looked at the screen, watching the signal dropping in and out. Maybe if she hit the button at just the right time, she could reply to Michael's text. She typed in:

Sorry I was such a cow. Put it down to hormones, or shock – whatever you like. I was a bitch and I'm sorry. Hope you and Dawkins are enjoying your boys weekend. X

Best to keep it short and sweet. The truth would only hurt them both. She took a deep breath, waited until the signal reached three bars, and pressed send.

'Are you wearing a skirt?' she heard a familiar voice ask. Great, she was imagining his voice now. 'Poppy?'

She looked up. Michael was standing there in a baggy white shirt and jeans. The sun cast a reddish tint on his dark hair and his eyes looked tired and sore. She sighed with relief. It was him. He was actually here.

She smiled. 'That's weird, I just texted you.' She glanced around. 'Where's Dawkins?'

'Caddying for my mother.'

'She's taken him to golf? Is that allowed?'

'I think she's pretending he's a guide dog or something.'

That was exactly the kind of thing his mum would do. 'I thought this festival had security – how come they keep letting you in?'

He held up his arm and pulled back his sleeve, revealing a wristband. 'I'm a fully paid-up participant.'

'Then you should probably go to a workshop. I think cleansing your chakras would be right up your street. Or how about—' She picked up a programme from where it had been dumped by Jonathan. '—Yeah, here you go: The Shaman's Way – discovering your inner animal. I'd say that you have a bit of a wombat vibe going on.'

'Why don't we just sit in your tent?'

Her tent was supposedly a two-man kind of thing, but actually was claustrophobic for one. She didn't fancy being that close; too dangerous. And given the amount of sweat that had poured out of her in the last couple of hours, she didn't think it would be pleasant for Michael either. 'Why don't we sit in the tipi? Mum and Jonathan have gone to sort out handfasting preparations, whatever that involves.'

'So it's going ahead then?'

'Yeah, this afternoon. Stay if you want. You know they'd love it.'

Michael nodded, but said nothing. She didn't like it when he was quiet – what followed was never fun. She pushed herself up out of the chair and slipped through the canvas flap of the tipi. Light flooded through the hole at the apex of the poles, shining a spotlight on the little altar of flowers and goddess and horned god statues Mum and Jonathan had set up. They were meant to be leading some kind of psychobabble workshop in there the next day and had gone to a lot of trouble to make the place cosy. There were enough rag rugs to almost cover the groundsheet. Large embroidered cushions were scattered around the edges. Mum had even bought some of those nice Moroccan lamps from the market.

Poppy slumped down onto a large faux velvet cushion, dreading what was coming. Michael chose another. He wrapped his arms around his knees and smiled.

'This is appropriate.'

'What?'

'Y'know – passing around the peace pipe and all of that.'

For a moment she was back in the smoky darkness of the lodge, her lungs full of sage smoke. She forced herself to return his smile. 'I'm sorry about yesterday. You were right, I was being arsey. As usual. My only defence is I had just found a dead body.'

'It wasn't just yesterday.'

Oh God! He hadn't come to make up with her. He'd come to break it off. She sat up onto her knees.

'Yeah, I know. And it's me. And I'm sorry, Michael. I'll be better. I'll stop being such a bitch, I promise.'

Michael squeezed his eyes shut and laughed. 'Don't make promises you won't keep.'

'I will! I mean, I'll even come back with you if you want. I'll go to Julia's flipping jelly and ice cream party. Whatever you want.'

'I don't want—' Michael still had his eyes shut, like he couldn't look at her. He swallowed. 'You don't have to do that. We don't have to like the same people to be friends. But we do have to be friends, Poppy. I don't want to lose you.'

'You're not dumping me?'

'What?' Michael's eyes flew open. 'Dumping you? You mean – no! I just don't want us to fight all the time.'

'Thought you liked it?'

'I do. *Normally*. But recently it's felt like you meant it. I know that you're upset about your mum and Jonathan getting married—'

'—I'm not!'

'Come on. You hate it.'

'I'm fine with it. Honestly. I mean, Jonathan's a fruit loop, and I'm not that keen on some of his friends, but Mum loves him.'

He smiled, but she could see disappointment in his eyes. Great – she'd upset him again. She just wished she knew how.

Silence followed, and not the comfortable kind. She had to say something – make some kind of joke to get them past this. She opened her mouth to speak and stopped when she saw how he was looking at her, like he was desperate to say something but didn't know how.

Eventually, he looked away and blew his fringe out of his eyes. 'Have the police said anything more about what might have happened?'

She sighed with relief. Safer territory. 'They're convinced it was an accident.'

Michael nodded. He picked up an oblong cushion that had tiny mirrors sewn into its red satin. Reflected dancing lights flashed on his face, and, for a second in her head, they were the sprites from the lake, come to take him away from her. She stiffened.

'I got to thinking about it last night. Maya's a pretty unusual name, so I did a quick Google search.'

'Did you find anything?'

Michael shrugged. 'I'm not sure. I didn't have a surname. But I did find a missing person called Maya Flynn.' He reached into his back pocket and pulled out a folded square of paper. Carefully, he opened it out and handed it to her.

The image was only a couple of inches high. A girl with startling blue eyes and long strawberry blonde hair smiled mischievously out.

Poppy touched her own hair, still damp with sweat.

'I thought she looked a bit like you. Not exactly, but the hair.'

Poppy remembered the girl watching her and Tariq from the shadow of the fir trees. The glint of moonlight on red hair.

In the photograph there was an arm around the girl's shoulder, but whoever it belonged to had been cut off. The arm was sheathed in black leather, and the hand that was cupped around Maya's shoulders bore long nails painted the colour of red wine.

Beth. Had to be.

'It's her,' she whispered.

'Are you sure? How do you know?'

'Because I've seen her.'

'You've *seen* her? When?'

CHAPTER EIGHTEEN

'We have to go to the police,' Michael said, as they pushed through the crowds of folk who'd been let out of the various seminars and workshops. 'Poppy!'

'The minute we do that, she'll be gone.' She ran her fingers through her damp hair. She felt better now that she'd showered away the sweat and sage smoke, even if the water in the Portakabin showers had been freezing.

'You honestly think this is a good idea?' Michael asked.

Before she could answer, she spotted someone waving at her. Tariq. *No! Why now?* She stopped and waited for him to catch them up.

'Hey, I was just coming to look for you.' He leaned down and kissed her. Today he did smell of chip fat and ten-day-old burgers. She felt cold. And as if he'd caught the chill, Tariq backed away. He glanced over her shoulder. 'Oh, it's your friend. Michael, right? Hi.'

Michael nodded. His smile was lopsided and forced, like it had been painted on by Picasso.

'Umm – Tariq, I'm kind of—'

'Don't mind me,' Michael said. 'Take your time. The longer the better, in fact.'

'Are you working today?' Poppy asked, forcing herself to touch Tariq's arm.

'Yeah. Yeah, I'm working.'

'What time do you get off?'

Tariq shrugged. 'I'm flexible.'

'I'll come and find you, if that's OK. There's just some stuff I've got to do.'

'Great.' Tariq's gaze drifted briefly over her shoulder again, then he smiled. 'I'll look forward to it.'

She felt his hand on her hip as he leaned down and pressed his lips to hers.

Kiss him! Kiss him, damn it! She placed a hand on his shoulder, all too aware of the toned muscle beneath her fingers, and quickly kissed him back.

It was enough. She felt his lips curve into a smile.

'Later,' he whispered. He nodded pleasantly at Michael, and took off.

Poppy sucked in a deep breath. Her heart was pounding so loud that it echoed in her skull. Michael's arms were folded and there were wisps of storm clouds in his eyes.

They started walking again.

'So, you and Burger Boy?'

'Don't call him Burger Boy like that's some kind of crime.'

'No, it's good. I mean, great that you've hooked up with someone who's got ambition and drive. I hear you can make a very good living from those kinds of small businesses. How old is he anyway?'

Poppy couldn't stop herself glaring at him.

Michael grinned. 'Oh, I see. You didn't get into particulars before you snogged him. That is, of course, if you did just snog him.'

That was it. She swung round. 'Don't!'

'What?' Michael threw up his hands, his mouth hanging open, all innocent. 'What's the problem?'

'Just stop it.'

'That's precious. You can say what you like about my girlfriend, but I can't poke a little fun when you pick up the guy from the burger van?'

Poppy groaned and carried on walking.

'So did you?' Michael asked, his voice carefully casual, as he fell into step beside her.

'What?'

'Sleep with him.'

'*What?* No!' Poppy's cheeks ignited. She glanced at him, expecting the full smirk treatment, but Michael wasn't smiling, not even a little.

'Good,' he said, shortly.

'What does *that* mean? And what kind of person do you think I am?' She shook her head. He knew she was practically a nun. So where was this coming from? 'You're supposed to be my best friend and yet you seem to be under the impression that I'm some kind of slapper!'

He bit his lip and looked away. 'I don't think that. But I do know you, Poppy. I know you're either in or you're out.'

It was just what Mum had said to her. She stopped. 'Hold on a minute. Have you and Meg been conspiring again?'

'Excuse me?'

'You and my mother. Have you been talking to her?'

'No. Why would I?'

It had started after the accident, when the two of them had tried smothering her in cotton wool. 'Don't come the innocent with me. I hear you, y'know, muttering in corners. Saying stuff you don't want me to hear.'

Michael stopped and turned to her. 'OK, yeah, I talked to Meg. Sue me.'

'What about?' She felt exposed, like they'd been picking through her drawers before she'd had time to tidy up. She folded her arms over her chest.

Michael swallowed. His gaze sank to the ground and he shrugged. 'I've been worried about you.'

'Why?'

'Look, I don't want to fall out and anything I say you're gonna twist until it sounds really bad.'

'I won't!'

'You always do.'

That was so unfair! She didn't twist things. Yeah, OK, sometimes she kept stuff from him, but that was different. She did it to keep them friends. She did it to stop herself from losing him. But look where it had got her. She was going to lose him anyway. 'Tell me. Come on, what've I done to make you so worried about me?'

Michael's mouth set into a hard line. He stared over her head and sucked in a deep breath. 'Do I really need to? Don't you know? Don't you see what you're doing?'

'What?'

'You're pushing me away.'

'I'm not! Michael, I know I've been—' Of course she'd pushed him away. Sometimes it hurt too much to be with him. Watching him with Julia near killed her.

He shook his head and turned his gaze on her. His blue eyes were hard and tension collected in the muscles in his neck, making them stick out. 'You're really gonna stand there and deny it?'

'Hello! GCSEs! Might not have been an important year for you, but it was for me.'

'During the summer?'

'I've been busy with Meg and Jonathan's wedding.'

Michael growled and glared at the sky. 'Stop it!'

Poppy swallowed. There were tears scratching to get out of her eyes but she wouldn't let herself cry. She didn't like lying to him but what choice did she have?

'For fuck's sake, Poppy, why won't you talk to me? It drives me mad that you won't talk to me. You used to tell me everything and now—'

'—We talk all the time!'

'About school. University. Parents. We don't *talk*

any more.' He rubbed his hands through his hair, making it stand on end. 'I miss you.'

She wanted to say that she missed him too, that she was sorry that she'd pushed him away, but if she let him get too close he was bound to see how she felt about him and then she'd lose him forever. She'd never felt less like smiling but she pulled out her cockiest grin and play-punched his arm. 'Are you sure you've got a Y chromosome?'

'What?'

'I'm not kidding – you're sounding more like a woman every day.'

'Oh thanks, that's nice.'

'Seriously, this carries on and you'll end up having periods.'

Michael snorted, shook his head and stared at the ground. 'You're the only person who can do this to me. Why is that?'

'Because I know all your deepest, darkest secrets?'

She just hoped he'd never find out hers.

Poppy had no trouble guessing which tent was Kane's. It was green and twice the size of all the tents around it – the kind of tent that people owned if they spent their lives hopping from one festival to the next. The flaps were fastened open with the thick gold-coloured ropes that grannies used to tie back chintz curtains, and there was a board with Kane's book covers pinned to it and a price list for readings. She peered at the opening. It looked like there was no one at home.

'You think she's in there?' Michael asked.

Poppy shrugged. 'She's got to be sleeping somewhere, and it's big enough to hide out in.'

'So what's the plan? We just going to knock on the door?'

'Unless you brought your invisibility cloak with you, I suppose we'll have to.'

Michael smiled. 'If I'm Harry, does that make you Hermione? Because I see a definite similarity in the hair.'

Poppy smoothed down her damp hair, sure to be drying into frizz. '*Excuse me.* Some of us didn't have access to a hairdryer. Or the half a gallon of product you use on your hair, *Michaela.*'

'Actually, I like the fresh from the shower look.'

She turned to him, hands on hips, waiting for the punch line. It never came and the look in his eye made her blink. He smiled and her stomach flipped like she'd just hit a speed bump at ninety miles an hour.

'Well, come on then, if we're going to do it, let's do it,' he said, wiggling his eyebrows. He grabbed her T-shirt and tugged her towards the open flap.

'Hello?' she called into the gloom. There was no reply. She glanced around. There were only a couple of guys chatting outside another tent, and neither of them seemed to have noticed her and Michael.

She looked at Michael, unsure.

He shrugged and strolled right in.

'Okaaay. But if we get done for breaking and entering, I'm telling the police it was your idea,' she said, following him in.

The main compartment was pretty sparse. In one corner there was a small fold-up table with two chairs tucked under it. In another, a red and blue striped blanket was spread over the grass. On it *An Introduction to Eastern Philosophy* lay open, face down, spine broken.

Michael was staring at something else.

On the back canvas wall there were three zipped-up doors, presumably leading to three different bedrooms. He went to the left-hand compartment and unzipped the flap. She followed him and peeped over his shoulder. Inside there was nothing but what looked like a few boxes of books.

She shook her head at him, and as he zipped up the flap, she unzipped the second flap and stepped inside. It was darker in this compartment, but in the dim light she could see that this was where the guy stored his junk. Michael followed her, in and looked around. There was a duffel bag open with clothes spilling out. A backpack filled with more clothes and a couple of CDs sticking out of the top. It was all guys' stuff. There were no hairbrushes, or girls' clothes – no sign at all that a girl was staying there.

Poppy nudged a few things and then sighed. 'She's not here.'

'But we don't know what's behind door number three yet,' Michael whispered.

Poppy winced. 'Did you take a corny pill with breakfast this morning?'

She followed Michael out and as he zipped up that compartment, she unzipped the last door.

The flap fell back and she gasped.

Before her was a girl with a pale face and reddish-blonde hair. She stumbled back, and so did the other girl. *What?* She blinked and realised that the girl in front of her was actually her own reflection.

The next second, Michael was at her side. 'Jesus!' he gasped.

A full-length mirror faced outwards, towards the door.

'What the hell kind of a trick is that?' he whispered.

She didn't quite know, but she had a horrible feeling she could guess. Poppy stepped away from Michael and edged around the mirror.

The air inside smelled stale, like the boys' changing room at school. In the centre of the compartment a sleeping bag lay flung over an air mattress. Beside it was an industrial-sized torch and surrounding everything was a circle of white powder.

Michael crouched down and touched the circle. He crunched the substance between his fingers and then licked his thumb. He winced. 'Salt?'

A circle of salt. She tried to swallow, but her throat had run dry. A circle of salt – she knew what that meant. Salt keeps out spirits. The spirits of dead people.

She's everywhere, she's even here, she remembered Kane whispering into the dark.

'What's going on? Why is the guy sleeping in a circle of salt?' Michael asked.

No, it was crazy. This was crazy. But the air wasn't just stale. It felt heavy as it settled in her lungs, like there was something dark here. Corrupt. Poppy felt the creeping sensation that someone was watching them. She spun around, half expecting to find Kane ready to charge at them, but there was no one there.

'What's wrong?' Michael asked.

'We need to get out of here,' she whispered, urgently. And even to her it sounded like begging.

Michael grabbed her hand and dragged her out of the salt-circled room, out of the tent. They didn't even stop to zip up the compartment. They headed to the nearby shelter of the woods.

Poppy leaned against an old oak tree and focused on the clean pine-scented air that was replacing the foul air from the tent.

Michael frowned. 'Are you OK?' he asked, keeping a tight hold on her arm.

She nodded, but she wasn't. She was shaking and she was cold, like her insides had been scraped out, put in the freezer for a couple of hours, and then dumped back inside her. If she believed in ghosts or atmospheres, she'd say that there was something wrong in Kane's tent. Very wrong. But she didn't believe in that rubbish, did she? It was the sweat lodge. She was dehydrated.

'We should go and find Meg,' Michael said.

'No. I'll be fine in a minute. I think I got too hot this morning at the sweat lodge.'

'Sweat lodge? I didn't think you were into that kind of thing any more.'

'*I'm not*,' she said, angrily, then shook her head. That's right, she *didn't* believe in all that crap. 'Sorry. Long story. I was kind of strong-armed into it.' She took a deep breath and forced a smile. 'Didn't look like she was there, did it? Guess I got that one wrong. Come on,' she said, stepping away from the oak tree. 'There's someone we need to find.'

CHAPTER NINETEEN

Michael followed Poppy, watching her strawberry blonde hair bouncing around her shoulders as she jogged through the crowds. She was moving surprisingly fast given the tonnage of secrets she was carrying around. He quickened his pace to catch up to her.

'Who are you looking for?'

Poppy stopped abruptly, making him crash into her, and then she ran.

'Where are you going now?' he shouted, but she didn't stop. What had got into her?

She darted between a couple of men, almost knocking one of them over. The guy had a hawk tethered to his arm. It flapped its wings and squawked its displeasure at being dislodged.

'Watch it!' the hawk man shouted.

But Poppy had gone. Michael gave a quick apology, edged past the sharp beak of the bird and took off after her.

He reached her just as she grabbed the arm of a guy Michael had never seen before.

'Is she dead?' Poppy shouted at the stranger. She looked wild.

The guy was six foot five at least. All his hair had been shaved apart from a green tuft at his forehead. He had on green combats and Doc Martens and looked like a member of the BNP or something. What the hell did she want with someone like him?

The guy looked down at her but he didn't reply.

'Maya!' Poppy shouted, drawing interested glances from the people walking past. 'Is she dead, Kane?'

'Yes,' the guy said, quietly.

'But I saw her!'

'I didn't say she was gone.' The guy said it so calmly that it sounded perfectly reasonable. But it wasn't. He was making no sense at all, and neither was Poppy. Michael edged forward, trying to get her attention before...

'Did you kill her?'

Oh shit! 'Poppy!' Michael grabbed her by both arms and pulled her back. 'What are you doing?'

Her cheeks were red and her eyes wide like she was on something. He shook her, but she wouldn't look at him – her gaze was fixed on the guy.

Kane took a step forward, closing in on her. Michael didn't like the way that the guy looked at her – like that hawk back there when it spotted a rat. He shoved Poppy aside and put himself between them.

'I'm sorry, mate,' he said, quickly. 'She didn't mean to accuse you of—'

'Murder?' Kane finished for him. His gaze drifted over Michael's shoulder to where Poppy was. 'This must be the King, Sceptic. Well, isn't he gallant?'

King? What the hell was he going on about? He turned. Poppy's cheeks had drained of colour.

'Ready to rethink that rationalism of yours?' Kane asked.

Poppy shook her head. Michael could see she was trying to act cool, but whatever this guy was going on about had freaked her out.

'If you didn't kill her, how do you know she's dead?' Her voice had returned to its normal pitch but her golden eyes stared at the guy, wide and unblinking.

'I told you the last time you questioned me,' Kane said. 'We argued. She stormed off. I never saw her again. Not alive, anyway.'

'What did you argue about?'

'Her father.'

'What?'

Kane glanced around, as if afraid someone might be listening. 'He had money and she wanted it. No, correction: she thought it was rightfully hers. She called herself a child of Lughnasadh. Said she was conceived at one of these gatherings so I assumed Daddy was someone here. And maybe he didn't want to pay.'

Poppy shrugged. 'That's all she told you?'

'Maya only ever told you what she wanted you to know. Do you do that with his majesty here?' Kane asked, nodding towards Michael.

Michael nearly laughed. The guy was talking crazy, but he'd got that right.

Poppy's brow furrowed. 'No. I'm not like her.' She said it like she was trying to convince herself as much as Kane.

'Really? I bet if we asked him he'd say different. I didn't kill Maya, Sceptic. I was in love with her, regardless of what she was. I feel her now. Smell her scent. Catch a glance of her in the distance. She comes to me in my dreams. She haunts me, Poppy. I think maybe she's haunting you too. She wouldn't like that you were alive – a pale imitation of her.' Kane leaned in to Poppy, and lowered his voice. 'And it's not just looks. You're almost as bitter as she was.'

'I'm taking it that was Maya's boyfriend?' Michael asked.

Poppy nodded but said nothing. He had no clue what half of that conversation had been about but it was clear she'd understood every word. At least now Kane had gone she wasn't looking quite so strung out. For a moment there she'd gone so pale he thought she was going to faint. But now she was looking better he was going to get answers. He was sick of being kept in the dark.

'C'mon,' he said, putting a hand on her back and guiding her through the crowds. Ahead was the main stage – like something you'd get at a music festival. By the number of people sitting on picnic blankets it looked like someone was about to come on.

'Do you want to check out whatever this is?' he asked.

She shrugged. She was back in her head. The barriers were up and she had no intention of letting him in. Well, tough.

'OK, talk to me. What *was* that? Maya's dead?'

She nodded.

'But you said you saw her.'

'I thought I did. It must have been someone else. It was dark, I must have got it wrong.' She didn't sound sure.

'And you think that guy killed her?'

'He's sleeping in a circle of salt. It's an old superstition that spirits can't cross salt. You heard him; he's got it into his head that she's haunting him. But how would he know she's dead if he hadn't killed her?' She hugged her arms across her chest and began to walk faster, as if she was trying to run away from him. Again, he speeded up.

'OK, calm down. If you seriously think that's what happened, we should go to the police.'

She looked away from him. 'I tried this morning; they won't listen to me.'

'And you're sure that guy killed her? Because I'm not sure he'd have said all those things if he'd murdered someone.'

Poppy stopped and turned to him. 'I don't know.' Her face crumpled and she rubbed her forehead. 'I don't know anything any more.'

He wanted to put his arms around her, comfort her, but he didn't dare. She was so jumpy at the moment and every time he touched her she pulled away. He took a deep breath and scanned the stalls, looking for something to distract her with. 'You know what my gran would say at a time like this?'

Poppy's face turned to him. 'What?'

'When you're handed lemons, make lemonade.'

She blinked a couple of times and then screwed up her face. 'That's totally random!' she said, shaking her head.

'Not random. It just so happens that there's real lemonade over there, made with real lemons, apparently.' He pointed to the trailer van. 'Come on, I'll buy you a real lemon lemonade.' He forced himself to smile.

He led her over to the van.

'Bet it'll be disgusting,' Poppy said, sounding more like her old self.

Michael shoved his hands in his pockets. 'So, err – what was that Kane going on about? All that stuff about me being the king. I mean, I'm not complaining. Being king of the universe is clearly my destiny.'

'Ha!'

'Had you spoken to him before?'

Poppy folded her arms. 'I went to have my Tarot cards read.'

He laughed. 'What? After all you've said about that kind of stuff you take part in a sweat lodge and have your Tarot cards read? Are you changing your mind about—'

'—It was research, that's all. Bob told me that Kane was Maya's boyfriend – he suggested going undercover.'

'So what did your cards say?' he asked in the spookiest voice he could muster.

'The usual crap. Y'know, you'll go on a long journey, meet a tall dark handsome stranger.' Poppy bit her lip and there was a distinct red tinge around her cheeks.

Michael felt his grin drain away. Tall, dark, handsome stranger – he supposed she thought that meant Burger Boy. He really wanted her to have someone. He'd even thought about trying to set her up with his friend Mark, who definitely had a bit of a thing for her. But Burger Boy was too old for her and from what he'd seen that morning he was definitely into something dodgy, even if he was wrong about it being drugs.

Should he tell her about what he'd seen? She was in a state already. Was it fair to push that on her too? The last thing he wanted was to give her another mystery to investigate.

Sod it! He'd tell her and deal with the consequences.

He'd just opened his mouth when he was interrupted by a guy with long curly blond hair wearing a hideous Hawaiian shirt.

'Excuse me, would you mind if I took a picture of you two for the festival archive?' he asked in a broad Aussie accent.

'Archive?' Poppy asked.

'Yeah, y'know, the one on the website. It's my job this year and I don't think I've got a picture of you guys yet.'

'How far back does it go?' Poppy asked.

The guy pulled a face. 'Uhhh...since the start, I guess. Can I take a picture? Do you mind?'

Poppy glanced at Michael.

He shrugged and pulled her to him. Immediately he felt her stiffen. Her discomfort hurt, but he pretended not to notice and forced a smile onto his face.

The guy took their picture, thanked them and moved on to his next victims. Michael let Poppy go and she jerked away from him, like he was radioactive. That was it. He couldn't keep ignoring it.

'Are you OK?' he demanded. But Poppy didn't reply: they'd reached the front of the queue.

Poppy's face creased with horror. Then she made gagging noises.

Michael laughed. The three quid was totally worth it just to see that face.

'You'd better drink it,' he warned. 'That's one pound fifty's worth of lemons in that cup.'

'Was there any sweetener back there?'

Michael sipped the lemonade. It was intense, and a bit sour, but not nearly as bad as she was making out. 'It's all right.'

'Then you can have mine,' Poppy gagged a few more

times, her face screwed up comically. She handed him her cup and fished her mobile out of her pocket. She pressed a few buttons and frowned. 'No signal. Again. Honestly, how hard would it be to put a mast up around here? I mean, it's not like there's loads of land or anything.'

'Who did you want to call?' he asked, and swigged back the first cup of lemonade.

'No one. I just wondered if I could get onto the festival website.'

'Why?'

'If there's photos going back to the beginning of the festival then maybe there's a picture of Maya's mum with her dad.'

'That's a long shot.' More commonly known as a wild goose chase.

She stared blankly at the sky.

'Does this mean that you think Kane is telling the truth? That Maya really was looking for her father?'

'Not really. But if he's right then Maya's dad could be here and maybe he'd know something. It's the only lead we have.'

At least she was saying 'we' now. Something inside him unknotted. He watched her thinking. Every thought, every emotion flashed across her face. He loved watching her. He'd never known anyone go through the whole range of human emotions as quickly as Poppy, and every one of them showed in her eyes.

Her gaze flicked around the festival ground, over the heads of the people sitting in front of the stage, back to where the wicker man's head reared over the tents and marquees. Her gaze stalled, and he thought he heard a sudden intake of breath.

Michael followed her gaze across the festival ground. Standing beside the lemonade stall, Kane was sipping from a cardboard cup and making no effort to disguise that he was watching them.

Could be just coincidence, Michael told himself. Or he could be following them. What if Poppy was right and Kane had murdered that girl?

'I'm going to talk to him,' he said, but Poppy's hand on his arm stopped him.

'I wonder if a different network gets better coverage around here,' she said, stepping in front of him, drawing his gaze away from Kane. Her grip on his arm tightened, making it clear she didn't want him going over there.

'What do you think?' she prompted, when he didn't reply.

'Doubt it. My phone reception's not too bad, but I've got no 3G. We could drive into the village if you like, it might be better there,' he said. And suddenly it seemed like a good idea. He wanted her as far away from that guy as possible.

Poppy shook her head. 'No, I've got it.' Her eyes narrowed with determination and Michael's heart sank. What now?

CHAPTER TWENTY

The rising humidity made the climb up the bluff to the farm property a real trek. By the time the barns and outbuildings came into view, Poppy was puffing and blowing like she'd run five miles. She glanced at Michael and was glad he looked just as out of breath as she was. He had no excuse: he spent every other weekend climbing mountains. She was glad to get away from the festival though. Well, glad to get away from Kane.

The farmhouse was built of grey stones that seemed piled on top of one another without any cement, as though gravity was the only thing keeping them from tumbling down. Poppy picked her way carefully across the uneven cobbled yard, afraid that if she took her eyes off the cobbles she'd go flying. She was relieved when they reached the gravel path that led towards the white front door.

'You can't just ask to use their computer!' Michael muttered for the tenth time.

She waved at him to be quiet, wiped the sweat from the back of her neck and knocked on the door.

For a very long time, there was no reply. She was about to give up hope when the door swung open and they were met by a woman whose face was as round as the pregnancy bump that was stretching her checked shirt.

'Yes?' The woman clutched the door like she was ready to slam it in her face.

'Hiya, I'm Poppy. Pete—'

'Poppy!' the woman gasped. Her eyes almost popped out of her face. It was like Poppy had just told her she was royalty or something. 'You're the girl who found the body!'

'Yeah.' Poppy glanced at Michael, who was looking more sullen than usual. 'I just wanted to say thanks to him – for all he did.'

'Come in, come in.' The woman beckoned, smiling. 'I'm Sally, Pete's wife. Pete's out seeing to a broken fence on the top field, but I shouldn't think it'll be too long before he's back looking for something to eat. I've just made some lemonade, if you'd like some.'

Out of the corner of her eye, Poppy saw Michael's down-turned mouth suddenly perk up. 'That would be great,' he said, eagerly. 'Poppy's a big fan of real lemonade. I'm Michael, by the way.' He offered Sally his hand and a disgustingly sweet smile.

She shook it and grinned. 'Both of you come on through to the kitchen. Don't mind the mess, will you?'

Poppy couldn't help rolling her eyes at him the second Sally's back was turned. His smile widened.

The kitchen was a mess, even compared to what Poppy was used to at home. Half-chopped vegetables were strewn across the kitchen table. Pots filled with liquids were bubbling on the range and there were heaps of laundry piled up in front of the washing machine. The air was filled with so many conflicting smells that it made Poppy's head spin. She suddenly felt woozy again.

'Busy time of year for us. And what with the baby due soon…' Sally smiled and tucked an escaped curl of blonde hair back into her ponytail. She poured out two large glasses of lemonade and handed them to Poppy and Michael.

Michael grinned. 'Thanks, that's just what we needed.'

Poppy couldn't help glaring at him.

'How are you, Poppy? Must have been a shock,' Sally said, nodding for them to take a seat at the table.

'Yeah, it was. But I'm OK, thanks.' She plonked down the lemonade as far away from her nose as possible and sat down in a slightly sticky chair.

'Pete said that you knew her – the girl?' Sally smiled prettily. Despite the roundness of her face, her features were small and a bit elfin. She reminded Poppy of Julia, which probably meant Michael was being nice to Sally because he fancied her.

'Not really. I met her the night before. We just chatted for a bit,' Poppy said, sounding a little more offhand than she'd intended.

'What about? I mean, do you think that she was

depressed or something?' Sally was trying to sound casual, but the hungry look in her pale blue eyes gave her away.

Poppy shook her head. 'I didn't think so.'

'So what did she say? Pete said she wasn't a participant. What was she doing here?' Sally smiled and looked down at the slate tiled floor. 'Sorry, you must think that I'm really morbid, it's just I feel like I've been locked up in this house for weeks. I'm so bored!'

Poppy smiled. She couldn't imagine what it would be like to live out here all alone. Especially when the poor woman was carrying a whale in her stomach. 'Isn't the baby due soon?'

'Last week!' Sally rolled her eyes. 'But nobody seems to have told him that. You know Bob, don't you? Well, he brought me this raspberry leaf tea concoction,' she said, holding up a red mug. 'It's supposed to bring on the baby but I think I've drunk a gallon of the stuff and the little sod still hasn't come out. Just hope he hasn't got too comfy in there.' She patted her stomach fondly. 'I was on the computer this morning to see if there was anything else I could do to help him along. I'm making a curry for tonight – that's supposed to be a good one.'

Poppy glanced at Michael. 'So you have internet access up here?'

'Broadband, would you believe. I'd have gone mad if not.'

'My phone signal's useless – I was trying to look up something from the festival website but couldn't get on.'

'Go on Pete's computer if you want.'

Score! 'That would be great. But are you sure you don't mind?' It was a struggle to keep the excitement out of her voice.

'Of course I don't mind. Come through to the office.' Sally got up slowly, using the chair arms to balance out the bump. Michael rushed over to help her.

'Eh, you've got a good one here, Poppy,' Sally said with a wink. 'Not many men with manners these days. Mind you, even the good ones you have to watch. Always on the look out for a better offer. Ruled by your pants, you lot.'

Michael laughed. Poppy's cheeks started to burn. She was about to correct Sally's assumption when Michael butted in.

'She doesn't know how lucky she is. Don't forget to bring your lemonade, Pops,' he said, with an innocent smile. 'You wouldn't want to forget about it.'

She was *so* going to make him suffer when they got out of there. Poppy grabbed the glass of lemonade, and Michael's – he wasn't getting away without drinking the horrid-tasting muck – and followed him and Sally through the house to a study that looked a bit, but not much more, organised than the kitchen.

The walls were covered in bookcases filled with

box files and lever-arch files that had dates and codes on the spines.

Sally went behind the desk and typed something into the computer. 'There,' she said, picking up a few stray used mugs from the desk and heading for the door. 'You go ahead and do what you need to do.' There was the sound of a door slamming. She smiled. 'That'll be Pete. I'll go and tell him you're here.'

As soon as Sally was out of the room Poppy darted to the computer. She opened the search engine and typed in

John Barleycorn Gathering.

Michael followed her around the desk, grabbed the back of the chair and leaned down so that his face was right next to hers.

'This could take hours, Poppy. Do you even know when she was born?'

She could smell the lemons on his breath and the forest-smelling shower gel he used religiously. She caught her breath. His closeness made her feel dizzy and slightly crazy – like she might do something stupid.

'She can't be that much older than us,' she said, swallowing hard and trying to concentrate. 'I'll try the early nineties.'

The archive turned out to be huge. And not all the photos had labels.

'This is no good,' Michael said. 'You're not going to find anything this way.' He batted her hand away from the keyboard, opened a new window and clicked on 'image search'. 'Let's try *John Barleycorn* and... what's her mother's name?' He looked away from the screen, right at her. She could feel his gaze burning into her cheek.

He was so close. So close that if she turned her face they'd be millimetres away from kissing. A voice in her head told her to do it, and to hell with the consequences. That voice, it was Beth's.

Have you kissed him? Have you tried? What'll happen if you do nothing? Say nothing? Watching him with someone else, it'll eat you up, Poppy, until there's nothing left.

She held her breath and squeezed her eyes shut. *Go away!* she screamed silently.

Love is like fire. Unless it's channelled it destroys everything.

'Poppy? Poppy, are you OK?'

She heard the worry in his voice. Felt a finger brush a strand of hair behind her ear. When she dared open her eyes at last, Michael was perched on the edge of the desk, staring at her with a worried expression.

'We should leave this,' he said. 'You're not well.'

She tried to swallow back the queasiness that had lodged in her chest. 'I'm fine. Just a bit of a headache.' Before he could object, she typed in *Sandra* and pressed return.

There were ten or twelve results, and from the

thumbnails she could tell that all the photos featured the same woman. She had waist-length straight blonde hair, so white that it must have come out of a bottle.

Michael stopped frowning at her and shifted so he could see the pictures. 'Any names?'

Poppy glanced from one to the other until she saw someone she hadn't expected to see. And there he was again. And again.

'Bugger!' she whispered.

'What is it? *Oh!*' Michael said, catching on.

He'd barely changed. Same long grey hair and beard. Same Druid robes. The beer belly was smaller and the face was a little thinner, but there was no doubt who it was. And he was kissing Sandra – Maya's mum.

Bob?

'Nice to see you, Poppy,' a voice said from the door.

Both she and Michael jumped away from the computer like they'd just been discovered looking at porn.

'Hiya, Pete.' Poppy jabbed a finger at the mouse and closed down the search engine.

The farmer ran a hand through his gingery hair and shrugged. 'Sorry about the state of me,' he said, glancing down at his mud-splattered jeans and work shirt. 'Those damn sheep are escape artists. I'm constantly mending fences. Nice to see you, though. How are you feeling?'

'Fine,' Poppy said. She attempted a smile. And it

was true. She was fine apart from the fact that her heart was trying to beat down the wall of her ribcage and her head was filled with a swarm of angry bees that were making so much noise she could barely hear what he was saying.

'Any news from the police?'

'They're pretty convinced it was an accident.'

Pete nodded seriously. 'Does seem likely. Poor lass. So,' he said, perking up. 'You're the lucky lad who's Poppy's boyfriend, eh?' He shot Michael a laddish grin.

'I'm not sure lucky is the word,' Michael said, and slipped his arm around her shoulder.

At his touch, the hairs on Poppy's neck bristled and her shoulders tensed. Michael must have felt it, because his arm tightened and he frowned down at her.

Through the open window came the sound of a hunting horn.

'Oh heck, sounds like something's afoot,' Pete said.

And there was something afoot. Something important...somewhere she was meant to be. *Bugger!*

Poppy jumped up. 'Mum's handfasting. I've gotta go!'

CHAPTER TWENTY-ONE

Poppy sprinted over the cobbles, ignoring Michael's calls for her to wait for him. She was going to be late for Mum and Jonathan's handfasting. She skirted the bank of trees, running full out. Then, just as she reached the bluff where she and Beth had talked, the glint of sunshine reflected off the lake flashed in her eyes, blinding her. It felt like someone had grabbed her ankles. Her feet stopped moving and she toppled over.

Poppy cried out as pain reverberated through her hip and spine.

She pushed herself to a sitting position, brushed the grass and mud from her hands and looked out over the festival ground. Below, people holding multicoloured streamers and flags had gathered, forming a large circle around the wicker man.

There was no air. She couldn't breathe.

Michael kneeled beside her and grabbed her arm. 'Are you OK? Is your ankle hurt?'

She shook her head, pushing down the panic. She couldn't talk. If she did she would scream. It was all too confusing: Beth, Kane, Maya, Jonathan and now Bob?

Michael's gaze held hers. 'What's this about, Poppy? Really? You only met that girl once but you're acting like she was your best friend in the world.'

Beth's face flashed before her. 'That girl?' The words flooded out of her mouth. 'She has a name, y'know! Don't you think she deserves justice?'

'Of course I do, but that's not what this is about. Talk to me!'

'She loved Maya so much that she died trying to find her. And Maya didn't even love her back. Have you any idea how horrible that is? To love someone who doesn't love you?'

Michael's face softened. He let out a sigh. 'Your dad loves you, Poppy. He didn't leave because he didn't love you.'

'I'm not talking about Dad! I'm talking about—' She shook her head as tears started to drip down her cheeks. 'Just forget it.'

Michael was holding both arms now, so tight that it hurt. 'No. I won't forget it. You promised that you'd talk to me, and then half an hour later you're shutting me out again.'

'I'm not shutting you out!' It was a flat-out lie, but how could she tell him the truth?

'You think? You haven't been the same since the accident. When we're together you can barely look at me. You're meant to be my best friend but it feels like you don't even like me any more. So yeah, Poppy, I have a pretty good idea what it's like to love someone who doesn't love you back!'

His face was inches from hers, his blue eyes so full of pain and anger. She hadn't meant to, but she'd hurt him. Beth was right: her feelings for him were destroying them both. It was madness. It had to stop.

'I do love you!' she blurted. 'Don't you get it? I'm *in* love with you, OK? Happy now?'

Michael's hands released her. He let go of her like she'd burnt him.

Oh God, what had she done?

'I didn't mean...' She took a deep breath and wiped the tears from her eyes. 'I meant to say...' There were no words. No lies to cover up the truth. No excuses. No jokes. Only the realisation that it had finally happened. The secret that had lived inside her for years had finally exploded like a supernova and there was no going back.

She dared a glance at him.

His cheeks had paled and his mouth was open in shock. But it was his silence that damned her. He just stared at her and said...nothing.

She scrambled to her feet. 'I've gotta go – Mum's thing – can't...'

She ran.

No footsteps pursued her. He didn't call for her to stop. Only a lonely silence followed her from the bluff. And the knowledge that she'd screwed up everything. But maybe that was inevitable.

Poppy stumbled through the canvas village, tripping

over guy ropes and bags of rubbish as she went. She headed towards the wicker man, trying to ignore all the panicked thoughts that were thrashing around her head.

The circle of people was at least thirty deep and she couldn't remember where Mum had said to meet her. She tried standing on her tiptoes, but everyone had been sleeping in growbags and she couldn't see a thing.

Not knowing what else to do, she pushed her way through the crowd, but some people weren't keen to lose their spot and it was like swimming through concrete. A hand on her back propelled her forward.

'Scuse us!' a voice shouted. It was Mo Little Wolf. The woman parted the crowd with a few well-placed glares and pushed Poppy to the front.

Mum and Jonathan were standing in the centre of the circle, holding hands in front of Bob. She darted over to them. She was so breathless that she could barely utter a 'sorry'.

Mum rolled her eyes, but looked relieved to see her. Jonathan forced a smile onto his face, and in his eyes there was what looked like an apology.

'Nice of you to join us, our Poppy,' Bob said, raising laughs from the crowd. 'Poppy might not be a believer, but she does live on Pagan Mean Time.' There was more laughter.

'Anyway, as I was saying,' Bob continued. 'Having been joined together for a year and a day, Meg and

Jonathan have decided that this handfasting will see them bound together, not for another year, but for all eternity. This is a serious commitment that must only be undertaken by those who have tested their love for one another and believe that they are truly soulmates. Eternity is a long time, but not to those that love.'

Poppy gasped back breath after breath. From the edge of the circle, Kane was watching her. His eyes were sunken. And he looked thinner, almost as if something was eating away at him from the inside. Something, or someone? He thought Maya was haunting him. But if he was so certain Maya was dead, why the heck hadn't he been to the police? There was only one answer that made any sense. He killed Maya, and if he killed Maya that meant he killed Beth too.

A shuffling of the crowd drew Poppy's attention. Someone was pushing through the bodies. Only when he reached the edge of the circle did Michael look up. He stared at her and after knowing him just about all her life his face was unreadable to her. A total blank.

'Meg and Jonathan, do you promise to be there for each other, no matter what the future brings? Do you promise to always tell each other the truth, and practise kindness towards one another? Do you promise to love each other, now and in eternity?'

'We do,' Mum and Jonathan said together.

Michael's gaze fell to the ground. It felt like he'd let

go of her hand and she was sinking down to the bottom of the lake. Slowly he turned and excused his way out of the circle. She wanted to cry out for him to stop. She wanted to tell him it had been a joke. Anything that would fix this.

As she lost sight of him, the circle started to spin. The faces and streamers became nothing more than blurs of light and colour. She blinked hard, trying to make it stop, but she couldn't. In the blur pictures formed: Beth laughing at the sunset, and Maya – her dead double – grinning like she knew; like she knew that Poppy had screwed up everything.

'And so I bind your hands together, Meg and Jonathan, sealing your destinies for all eternity. May your love for one another bring you, and all whom you love, great joy!'

The crowd cheered. Poppy put her hand to her head as bright lights flashed before her.

'You may now jump the bride. I mean, the broom!' Bob's voice boomed.

There was another cheer and somewhere music started to play.

'Poppy? Poppy, are you all right?' Mum was asking.

She took a deep breath and looked into Mum's face. She looked so filled with happiness that she seemed to glow with it. Poppy forced herself to smile.

'Oh, Pops, are you crying? And I thought I'd never see the day when you'd cry at a wedding!'

Poppy was dragged into a fierce hug. Mum's hair tickled her nose; her arm crushed her neck, and yet Poppy felt more alone than she'd ever felt in her life.

When Mum was done hugging her, Jonathan took his turn, whispering to her that he was sorry they had fought, that knew he would never replace Dad, but he'd always be there for her – whatever she needed.

Poppy nodded and congratulated him, and then found herself face to face with Bob.

'Aww, Pops, come here and give your old uncle Bob a hug.' He grinned and held out his arms to her.

Poppy swallowed.

'What's the matter?' Bob asked, frowning.

Mo pushed between them, blocking out Bob. 'She looks kinda pale to me. Think maybe she's dehydrated after the sweat.' Mo hooked an arm around her back. 'Come on, let's get you a drink.'

Mo waved away a confused Bob, and pushed Poppy through the partying crowds and the outer obstacle course of tents. Poppy realised where they were heading when the sweat lodge came into view, squatting by the lake like an overgrown toad.

She put on the brakes. 'No! No, I don't want to go back there!' she gasped.

'There's nothing there that isn't in here, Kid,' Mo said, tapping her chest. 'Like I'd let you sweat again anyway,' she snorted. 'Not letting you anywhere near my lodge again until you can handle yourself.'

'I'm sorry I made such a mess of it.'

Mo's face creased into a smile. 'Nothin' to be sorry for. Not your fault the ancestors are playing games with you. Now come sit on the grass and chew the cud with me. I think there are some things you should maybe tell me.'

They found a spot partly shaded by an old oak tree and Mo went to get a bottle of water from a stash next to the lodge.

'Drink up,' she said, handing it to Poppy.

She unscrewed the top and downed several gulps of the cool water. It didn't make her feel any better. Dehydration wasn't the real problem. The inability to keep her mouth shut was the problem. Her temporary insanity was the problem.

Mo kneeled down and settled herself opposite her. 'What happened?'

Poppy shook her head. 'I wish I'd never come. Wish I'd just gone to Julia's stupid party and then none of this would have happened.'

'Julia?'

'Michael's girlfriend.'

'And Michael would be?'

'My best friend. Or at least he was before I went and told him I was in love with him. What was I thinking?!' She dumped the bottle of water on the grass. Balled up her fists and pressed them into her eyes before the waterworks could start again.

'That's pretty heavy stuff.'

Poppy nodded.

'What did he say?'

She saw his shocked face. Heard his silence. 'He didn't say anything.'

'How long have you…?'

'I don't know.' And it was the truth. She couldn't remember when she'd started to love him. Maybe she'd always loved him. 'What does it matter? He has Julia. I think he's in love with her. I shouldn't have told him. I've no idea why I did. I just lost it and it was out before I could stop myself.'

'Like in the lodge?'

'Yeah – no – I don't know.'

'What do you know about the girl you found?'

Poppy couldn't help the growl that escaped her throat. 'I don't believe in ghosts…or ancestors…or whatever. I don't believe in this stuff, OK?'

'Just because you don't believe in something, don't mean it don't exist. There were two spirits in that lodge, battling for your attention. Thought I was going to have to kick some serious dead ass. But you went and passed out before I could get things straight. I thought one must be the girl from the lake. Who was the other?'

'I don't know.'

'Don't mess with me, child. You brought those spirits into my lodge and I'm betting you took them out with you. Those spirits are messing with your head.

You tell me exactly what shit you've got yourself involved in otherwise I'm going straight to Bob, and he can sort you out.'

CHAPTER TWENTY-TWO

Flames leapt and danced through the torso of the wicker man. Poppy jumped every time the sculpted twigs cracked and sent plumes of black smoke up to the dark grey clouds that hovered in the sky like a constant threat to the celebrations. No one else seemed to have noticed. The music from the band playing on the main stage was loud enough to fill the whole festival ground with toe-tapping Pagan tunes. And just about everyone seemed to be dancing and drinking, despite the sticky humidity.

Jonathan twirled Mum around, sending her long red dress spinning around her. Mum giggled, stuck her hand in the air and yelled 'Olé!'

Poppy couldn't remember Mum ever looking so happy. She had always seemed so thoughtful, so serious. But there she was, dancing with her new husband like there was nothing in the world that could make her sad.

Poppy tucked her knees beneath her chin and hugged her legs to herself. Her thoughts turned to Michael. She waited for the tidal wave of pain, but it never came. In fact, she couldn't seem to feel anything. It had all happened so quickly that it didn't feel real.

But it *had* happened. It was real. She'd made an idiot

of herself and probably lost her best friend as well as the guy she loved. Why the hell did they have to be the same person?

'Mind if I sit down?'

Poppy looked up to see Bob staring down at her. He had his serious face on, which probably meant that Mo had talked to him. She shook her head, but her insides were tense.

Groaning, Bob eased himself towards the grass. He landed on his backside with a grunt and flashed a smile at Poppy. 'Don't ever get old, lass.' Bob stared at Mum and Jonathan. 'She looks happy, doesn't she?'

They were doing something that looked like the tango crossed with limbo dancing without the pole. 'Yeah, she does.' Poppy grinned as Mum held out her skirt like a cape while Jonathan did his impression of a bull.

'You don't look happy.'

'I'm fine.'

'Only two women ever looked at me the way you looked at me this afternoon. The first was my mother when I told her I weren't going in the police like my old dad. The second was the ex when the doc told us I couldn't have kids.'

Poppy's head snapped back to Bob. 'You can't have kids?'

'Not with the ex, not with any woman.' Bob shook his head. His hair swayed like a silver mane, but his gaze stayed trained on Mum and Jonathan. 'The nearest thing I have to a daughter is dancing over there. And the nearest thing I have to a granddaughter is sat right here. What the hell made you think I was that girl's father?'

Poppy sighed. Mo had talked to him. 'I found a picture of you and Maya's mum on the festival archive.'

Bob snorted like an old horse. 'Me and Sandra had a bit of thing after the divorce. Didn't last. Sandra's what you call a free spirit. If you'd looked a bit harder you would have seen pictures of her with a different bloke damned near every year. That's what upset you?'

'Sorry. I've got everything wrong today. Should have just stayed in my sleeping bag.'

Bob shifted so he could hug an arm around her. She settled her head against his shoulder and put an arm around his beer belly.

'What else did Mo tell you?'

'That was it. And she only told me that so as I could set your mind at rest. Bloody woman's better at keeping secrets than MI5. She did tell me you needed keeping an eye on. But am I to gather you had a brush with her medicine while you were in the lodge?'

She shrugged. Medicine? Was that what it was? 'Bob, why didn't you tell me that I look like Maya?'

He nodded. 'Suppose you do have a bit of a look of Maya. But you're not anything alike.'

She turned her face up to his. 'You turning into a sphinx or something? I look like her, but I don't look like her. What the hell kind of logic is that?'

Bob grinned. 'You've heard that old sayin' about eyes being the windows of the soul? Well, I reckon that's true. When we look at people we see more than just their bodies, we see who they are. When I look at you I see this lively and interesting spirit. A good soul. You've always had a good soul. But Maya...' He shook his head. 'Maya's different. There's a darkness in that girl. Don't know whether it's anger or hatred, but there's so much of it in her that it calls to the bad stuff. Kind of sucks it into herself. I suppose you think I'm talking a load of old nonsense?'

She thought of Kane's hollow eyes, like all the things he'd done were still inside him – eating away at his... *soul?* She shook her head. 'I think I get it.'

Bob looked at her strangely. He didn't say anything, but she thought that perhaps there was a small smile of victory on his face as he turned his gaze back on the burning wicker man. He probably thought that after a year's aberration she believed again.

Did she? Did she really believe that what had happened in the lodge was supernatural? No. She wasn't going down that road. She was finished with Beth and Maya...the whole thing! If they were hanging around haunting the place they could go and find other minds to screw with.

She leaned against Bob. 'I think you'd have made a great dad,' she whispered. 'But I'm glad we got you instead.'

As Bob hugged her tightly, she squeezed her eyes shut, tried to block out the guitar strumming and drums, and tried to find somewhere quiet inside herself. But everywhere there was noise.

An hour later, Mum and Jonathan were still dancing. They had tried persuading Poppy to join them, but she'd experienced enough public humiliation for one day.

She took a deep breath of sticky, smoky air and scanned the other revellers. Just beyond the light of the Big Willy bonfire, she spotted Tariq talking to some guy. They seemed to be arguing about something.

The old guy, whose thinning, straggly grey hair was covered mostly by a bandanna tied like a woman's headscarf, pointed a finger at Tariq's chest. An unhappy customer, maybe?

Tariq's hands were waving about defensively, clearly trying to calm the old guy down. Eventually the old guy shook his head and stalked away. Tariq ran a hand through his hair and glanced around. His gaze met hers. He hesitated and then walked in her direction.

'I though you were going to find me this afternoon,' Tariq said, collapsing on the grass beside her.

'Sorry, I got caught up in things.'

Tariq nudged her with his elbow. 'Hey, what's wrong?'

'Nothing.'

'I don't believe you.'

'What were you arguing about with that guy?' she asked, more to distract him than because she was curious.

'What guy?'

Poppy raised her eyebrows.

'Oh…him. It was nothing. Why so interested? You want me to hook you up or something?'

Poppy smiled. 'Oh, thanks. That's a lovely image.'

Tariq leaned closer. 'Why don't I give you something to replace that image?'

Her chest tightened and her pulse ticked in her throat. But she wasn't sure whether it was because she wanted to kiss him or because she wanted to run away as fast as she could.

She forced herself to look at him. 'You gonna strip off and dance naked under Big Willy there? That would just about do it.'

Tariq smiled and pursed his lips, as if he was actually considering it. 'I don't mind dancing naked but I'm not that keen on a big audience. If you want to go somewhere quieter, I'll show you my cancan.'

Poppy struggled against it, but she felt her lips curve into a smile.

'That's better.' Tariq's grin grew cockier and he

settled on the grass like he meant to stay. 'So what's up? You not keen on your new stepdaddy?'

Poppy groaned, annoyance flaring again. 'Why do people assume that I'm not OK with Mum marrying Jonathan? I'm happy for her. Why wouldn't I be?'

Tariq sucked in a deep breath and raised his eyebrows. '*Sorry.*'

She sighed. 'No, I'm sorry.'

'So what happened to your dad? Was there another woman?'

'Not exactly. He's training to be a vicar.'

For a second Tariq nodded seriously. Then he burst into laughter.

Poppy laughed too. 'Yeah, I know. Both my parents are religious crazies.'

'Is that why he left?'

'No. I blamed it for a while; it all kind of happened at the same time. Even thought I'd get back at him by calling the dog he bought me after an atheist. But I think really they just fell out of love.' She watched Mum and Jonathan swirling round like they were dancing on ice. 'I think Mum's happier with Jonathan.'

Tariq jumped to his feet and held out his hand to her.

'What?' she asked.

'Dance with me.'

She stared at him in horror. 'I can't dance to this. It's *folk* music.'

'Of course you can dance to it.' He grabbed her hand and before she could argue, he'd yanked her to her feet. He lifted both her hands around his neck. 'They go there, and mine go round here.' His hands slid round her back, tickling her ribs as they went. They locked her in a tight grip. 'Now we sway. See? Easy.'

'Who do you think you are – Fred Astaire?'

'Who?'

'Old Hollywood star? Danced with Ginger Rogers?'

'Oh, right, yeah, sure,' Tariq said, but she could tell he didn't have a clue what she was going on about. Michael would have got it. They went through a phase in junior school of watching old black and white movies from his gran's collection. Most of them had been musicals. She would wrap one of Mum's scarves around her waist so that it hung like a long dress, and Michael would borrow his dad's fishing hat and they would dance together like Fred and Ginger. In a flash she was back there. Michael holding her hand. Spinning around until she was dizzy and they both collapsed on the floor in giggles.

Tariq's lips on her neck woke her to the darkness, the flickering bonfires and the guy she was dancing with who wasn't Michael.

'Don't you care that my mum's over there?' she asked, squirming, trying hard not to push him away.

'Is she watching?'

'Not yet.'

'Then I don't care. *Yet.*' He blew a raspberry into her neck that tickled and made her giggle.

One song finished and another began. Everyone around them cheered. Tariq glanced from side to side and back at Poppy. 'Am I missing something?'

'It's *John Barleycorn.*'

'Who?'

'The song, it's called *John Barleycorn.* It's the old folk song that the festival was named after.'

Tariq nodded and listened for a minute.

There was three men come out o' the west their fortunes for to try,
And these three men made a solemn vow, John Barleycorn must die,
They ploughed, they sowed, they harrowed him in, throwed clods upon his head,
And these three men made a solemn vow, John Barleycorn was dead.

'Cheery,' he said eventually.

'It's about the harvest. Barleycorn is the crop. It's about life, death and rebirth.' Life, death and rebirth. On and on. Except where was the rebirth? All she saw was death. 'I have to go,' she said, pushing him away.

'Why?'

'I can't – can't do this.'

'Do what? Poppy, we're just having fun.'

'I nearly missed Mum and Jonathan's handfasting because I was too busy screwing up things with my best friend. I thought I could work out what happened to Beth, but I can't cos I'm hopeless. And being here with you is just making things worse!'

'Hey.' Tariq brushed his thumb against her cheek. 'You're not hopeless. Don't say that.'

'I am! And if you knew what was good for you you'd get as far away from me as you could.'

He pressed his lips together and shook his head.

'I'm serious, Tariq. Everything I do goes wrong.' She felt panic rising. Michael was gone. Her dad was gone. She'd accused her stepfather of breaching his professional ethics. She was no closer to finding out who killed Beth. Everything she touched... 'I can't even deal with my own life. How on earth did I think I was going to help anyone else?'

Tariq leaned in and kissed her. She tried to turn away, but his hands slid up to her face and cupped her cheeks, holding her steady.

It was like he'd injected her with a crazily strong painkiller. Suddenly she didn't care about anything. Thoughts floated away like dandelion clocks scattered to the night. And all those whirling emotions were driven away by just one incredibly strong desire.

She almost didn't notice the rain.

But the cold sharp splashes brought her to her

senses. She pushed him away. 'I can't do this.'

Tariq blinked. 'Poppy? What's wrong?'

'I can't *do* this!'

A guy who had been hovering a few paces away tapped Tariq on the shoulder. 'Hey Tariq, can I—'

Tariq spun around. 'Not now, OK?' He turned back to Poppy. 'What's wrong? Why can't you do this?'

'There's someone else.'

The hovering guy tapped Tariq on the shoulder again. 'Hey, man. I just wanted – I thought you were the guy to see.'

Tariq's face tightened, like he was going to explode. He squeezed his eyes shut. When he opened them again he grabbed Poppy's hand.

'Just give me a minute to get rid of this guy. Please don't go.'

She nodded.

'I didn't mean to disturb your evening,' the guy said, as Tariq tried to steer him away. 'All I wanted was some pot.'

He was a dealer. Tariq was a flaming drug dealer.

Poppy's mouth fell open. It was still hanging open when Tariq turned and saw her staring at him.

The band struck up a new number – a frantic reel that filled her head so that she couldn't think straight. Beth was dead, and Maya was nowhere to be found. She'd messed things up with Michael. Someone at this festival was a murderer. And the guy she'd been fooling around with was a drug dealer.

As Tariq started towards her, she turned on her heel and ran.

CHAPTER TWENTY-THREE

The moon and stars danced on the swaying waters of Scariswater. The festival had packed up and left, so, apart from the celestial bodies, they were alone on the bluff.

'Any minute now.'

'But this isn't right. There's weeks before they're due.' Poppy held the astronomy book right up to her face, squinting to read the tiny print by moonlight. 'It says here that the Perseid meteor shower reaches its peak on the thirteenth.'

'Exactly. It reaches its peak. Not everything is about the big climax, Poppy. And how about showing a little respect to your elders and betters? Let alone the dead.'

Poppy turned to Beth. 'But you're not dead, are you? You're standing right there.'

Beth took a swig of Jack Daniel's and shuddered. 'There's no denying that the afterlife bears an uncanny resemblance to the before life.'

Poppy turned back to her book and began trying to read it again. 'It says—'

'—Oh, for fuck's sake.' Beth grabbed the book and chucked it over the bluff.

'Hey! Now I won't know where to look!'

'Sure you will. You just need to trust your gut.'

'My gut gets me into trouble.' Poppy sighed and stared out into the starry sky.

Something caught her eye – faint movement. A sudden breeze set the fir trees whispering like an excited audience awaiting the beginning of the show.

'This is it!' Poppy said. She stared at the vast purple night.

'Twinkle twinkle, little star. How I wonder where you are...' Beth whispered.

'I'm here, my darling.'

Poppy glanced to her right.

A more beautiful version of herself stepped closer. 'Maya?'

She felt the other girl's hand slide up her back.

'I'm right here,' Maya whispered. 'I've always been here.'

Before Poppy knew what was happening, she was falling over the edge of the bluff and tumbling down... down...down...

Poppy jolted awake, the sound of splashing water echoing in her ears. She tried scrambling to her feet before realising that she was in a tent and standing really wasn't an option. She felt for her torch and flicked it on. The light banished the pictures from her dream, but she could still hear water splashing. No, it was OK. It was just rain beating against the nylon tent.

Her face was cold with sweat and tears and she

couldn't breathe. She put her hand to her throat. There was something missing. The apache's tear – it was gone.

She grabbed the torch and shone it at her sleeping bag until she found it nestled in a crease. Shakily, she retied the leather lace around her neck and held the black stone to her throat.

Eventually, the images from the dream floated away to the edges of her mind. Poppy rubbed the smooth stone between her fingers, and found herself feeling strangely glad she had it.

She sighed and shook her head. What was she doing? It was a dream, her subconscious playing games with her! Next she'd be sleeping in a circle of salt like Kane.

Kane.

The guy could have murdered two girls, and he was out there. Poppy groaned and flopped back onto the ground mat as her mind began churning through every detail of everything he'd said, trying to think of something she might have missed, something that would give him away.

CHAPTER TWENTY-FOUR

Sound exploded in his ear.

'What the...?' Michael felt around until he found his mobile lying next to him on the pillow. He'd left it there in case Poppy called.

He grabbed the phone and bolted upright. 'Yeah?'

'Is that Michael Quinn?' a voice asked. Deep, local. And definitely not Poppy.

He swallowed the bitter taste at the back of his throat. 'Yeah, who's that?'

'This is Detective Constable Johnson, Cumbria police. You're a registered participant at the John Barleycorn Festival, is that right?'

Michael shoved his knuckles into his eye. 'No... I mean, yeah. Yeah, I am.'

'We're asking all participants to gather in the main marquee at eight a.m.'

'What? Why?'

'It'll be explained when you get here.'

'But it's my girlfriend's birthday today. I'm supposed to be helping with her party.'

'Then I suggest you get here as soon as you can, so you can be interviewed and get back to your party preparations.'

The line fell dead.

Jesus. Poppy had been right: that girl Beth had been murdered.

Michael ran a hand through his hair and squeezed his eyes shut against the pain in his forehead. Going back to the festival meant seeing her. He knew it was wrong to have buggered off like that yesterday, but she had kind of dumped it on him. What did she expect him to do?

She was in love with him. He flopped back onto the pillow and stared at the ceiling. Poppy was in love *with him*.

He pulled the duvet over his head and slipped down into the warm cocoon. A memory formed in his head. He was running up a sand dune under a blue sky. The breeze coming off the estuary was almost tropical and did nothing to alleviate the heat beating down out of the clear blue sky. Poppy was ahead, her bare feet kicking up sand as she ran between the clumps of shore grasses. The rays of the sun caught in her hair and for a moment she looked as though she was trailing red and gold flames behind her, like she was some sort of magical fire creature. Michael doubled his efforts, but she was fast and it was only when she slipped and tumbled down a particularly steep dune that he caught up with her. She tried to get away from him, but he grabbed her wrists and wrestled her to the sand.

He kneeled over her as she lay on her back, laughing so hard that she couldn't speak.

'You stole my ice cream!' he said, unable to keep the grin from his face.

She wriggled, trying to get away. One of the straps of her vest top slipped off her shoulder, revealing an unexpectedly lacy bra. 'I think it's back there if you still want it,' she giggled.

But he didn't care about the ice cream; in that moment there was only one thing that he wanted – her.

He wanted to trail his fingers down her long pale neck, to feel the curves that had softened her body into something new and exciting. And God, he wanted to kiss her. She must have seen it in his eyes that he wanted to kiss her.

He hadn't, though. He'd waited because she was his best friend and he didn't want to screw things up. Then the accident happened and just when he'd been about to say something she'd pulled away so completely that he'd thought it was her way of telling him it was never going to happen. So he'd dated other people, tried to ignore the ache in his chest any time they were close. And now he had a girlfriend who he liked. He even thought that he might be starting to love her. He'd accepted that Poppy was never going to be anything more than his friend. He'd moved on... hadn't he?

And now this.

Michael glanced at his watch and groaned. Seventen. He felt dizzy at the thought of seeing her. What did that mean? Had he just kidded himself that he was over her?

There must be eight hundred people registered at the festival. Maybe he could sneak in at the back without seeing her. But he knew that wasn't going to happen. Life was crueller than that.

After having to prove who he was to three different policemen, Michael found a place to park on the opposite side of the camp to where Poppy's tent was. It was true, he was being a wimp, but he just couldn't face her until he'd thought of something to say that wouldn't come out like a pathetic rant.

With his head down, he traipsed across the boggy field, glad he hadn't spent the night in a leaky tent. Hundreds of sleepy campers were stumbling their way towards the main marquee, like ants finding their way home after an attack by a stampeding anteater. The market stalls were empty. Metal poles were hanging down at odd angles, and the tarpaulins were billowed with puddles of water. The storm must have been pretty bad round here. No wonder everyone looked comatose.

The marquee hadn't escaped the ravages of the weather either. The whole of the front panel of canvas had come down, so that he could see the gathering crowd inside.

'Michael! Michael – here!' he heard someone call.

He turned to see Meg waving from behind a group of people. She dodged around them and ran to catch up with him. She hugged him and through her brown curls he spotted Poppy trailing behind with Jonathan. She folded her arms and kept her eyes fixed on the ground.

Michael swallowed back the sick feeling and pulled away from Meg. 'Congratulations on your hand-thing,' he said.

'It's a shame you missed it!'

'Sorry about that. I had to go.'

'So they called you back too?' Jonathan said, clapping a hand on his back. 'Wonder what's going on.'

'I can only think they've figured out Poppy was right – about Beth,' Michael replied.

Poppy didn't look up. She just tilted her head forward so that her hair hid her eyes.

He caught Meg glancing between them. 'Riiiight,' she said. 'Maybe we should get inside.'

A desk had been set up on the makeshift stage and there were at least thirty uniformed police standing around the marquee's edge. Michael didn't think he'd ever seen so many in one place before – there wasn't much call for riot control in Windermere, although things could get a bit heated on a Saturday night when the Kings Arms emptied out.

The air smelled of heated damp earth and wet sheep – probably all those woolly jumpers this crowd liked to wear. Poppy kept her distance, staying on the other side of Jonathan. She hadn't even bloody acknowledged him. This was excruciating!

The thump of a microphone being tapped echoed over the mumbled chatter of the crowd.

'This thing working?' a gruff voice asked.

'Yes!' the crowd called back.

A big guy in a brown suit lumbered onto the stage. 'Good mornin' everyone. I'm Detective Chief Inspector Hadley. Thanks for your cooperation. I'm sorry to report that we are now calling the death of the young lass found in the lake *suspicious*. We'll be asking each of you to make a statement as to your whereabouts on Thursday night, and asking you whether you heard or saw anything that might shed light on this tragedy. Officers are stationed at the entrance of the marquee and they'll be giving you a time at which you are asked to come back here and give your statement. We've got a lot of folk to get through, so please be on time. We're asking you not to leave the site until you've given your statement. I'm sure that all of you are just as anxious as we are to get answers for the lass's parents.'

The detective handed the mike to one of the uniformed officers and climbed down off the stage.

So Poppy had been right. He leaned forward so he could catch a glimpse of her. She was still staring at the muddy, trampled grass, obviously determined not to look at him.

'Right, well, we'd better go and get our appointments sorted out,' Meg said.

Michael nodded and followed them to the already hideously long queue.

'Do you want to come back for some breakfast?' Meg asked him, when they'd each been issued a reference number and an appointment card.

Poppy's gaze was fixed on the card she'd been given. She turned it over and over in her fingers like she was trying to hypnotise herself. He touched her elbow and she jerked away from him.

'What?' she asked, accusingly.

Michael took a deep breath. 'Can we talk?'

'Let's go and get breakfast started!' Meg said breezily. She dragged a protesting Jonathan in the direction of the tipi, leaving Michael and Poppy in a lonely bubble, within the milling crowds.

'I don't think there's anything to talk about,' Poppy muttered.

Nothing to talk about. *Was she kidding?* 'So that little bombshell you landed on me yesterday, that's the end of our friendship, is it?'

She shrugged.

He couldn't believe her. 'Look, I'm sorry I left yesterday. But you caught me off guard.'

'I'm sorry it horrified you.'

'It didn't horrify me. I just—' Frustration threatened

to choke the words before he could get them out. 'God, you keep pushing me away and then you're telling me you're in love with me. What was I supposed to do?'

'I'm sorry,' she whispered.

Michael ran a hand through his hair. God, this was confusing. He loved her, he knew that, he'd always known that, but he was in love with Julia too, wasn't he?

'Don't be. I don't want you to be sorry. I really don't want you to be sorry.'

He'd just reached out to take her hand when he spotted Dealer Boy heading in their direction. He snatched his hand back.

Tariq stopped almost on top of her. 'Hey, can we talk?' he asked, quietly.

Michael took a deep breath. Seriously? She told him that she was in love with him yesterday and she was still seeing this guy?

'Not now,' Poppy said.

Tariq wasn't taking no for an answer. 'Please, Poppy.'

She shook her head, frowning with impatience. 'Look, I'm sorry about last night. I'll find you later, all right?'

Tariq nodded, glared at Michael and stormed away.

Last night? Michael's whole body tensed. 'What happened last night?'

CHAPTER TWENTY-FIVE

Michael was looking at her like she'd cheated on him. Then he bit his lip and glanced away. 'I'm sorry. I didn't mean it like... I just meant, are you OK?'

She nodded. How could she begin to explain? 'It was nothing – I—'

'—Poppy!'

She turned to see Mum a few feet away.

Mum's head cocked to one side. 'The police want to see you.'

Poppy turned the appointment card over in her fingers and looked at the time written on it. 'But my appointment's not until ten-fifteen.'

'They're at the tipi. They want to see you now.'

'You'd better go.' Michael touched her elbow so quickly she thought she might have imagined it. 'I've got my appointment anyway. I'll find you when I'm done.'

'Right.'

She watched him walk away, more confused than ever.

Mum slipped her arm around Poppy. 'Everything OK?'

'You remember DS Grant, Poppy,' Mum pulled her

down onto one of the big red fluffy cushions. Poppy knew she'd done nothing wrong – apart from a bit of breaking and entering – but she couldn't help feeling guilty at the sight of the policeman.

'Yeah, I remember him,' she said. 'What's going on?'

His podgy face remained neutral. In fact he looked a bit like a jeans-wearing Buddha, sat cross-legged on one of Mum's cushions. 'Coroner thinks someone might have hit Beth over the head before helping her into the lake. And there are some other things.'

'What other things?'

'I'm not at liberty to tell you. But I hear you've been pursuing your own investigation.'

'What's he talking about?' Mum asked.

Poppy picked at a nail. 'I might have asked a few questions. Someone had to. You lot were busy with other more important cases, remember?'

Mum buried her face in her hands. 'Poppy! You could have got yourself into trouble.'

'I didn't. I was careful!'

'Anyway, is there anything you found out that we should know?' DS Grant asked.

'Oh, so you're finally willing to listen to me now?'

'Willing and eager.' DS Grant blew out his cheeks, making him look a little bit like the pet hamster she'd had when she was in junior school. 'The coroner thinks there might be something ritualistic about the killing.

Now you didn't hear that from me and so help me, if I hear it from anyone else I'll know it came from you and I'll have you for interfering with a police investigation. Are we clear?'

She nodded. 'What do you mean, ritualistic?'

'I can't go into details. But what you said the other day about the scarf, turns out the coroner agrees. There's something called the threefold death that Pagans used when they killed ritual sacrifices. The coroner thinks the murderer used it to...' He cleared his throat. 'Also, there was a drug in her system that could have been recreational, but could have been used to sedate her. Can you tell us anything?'

Shit! Drugs? Was that why Tariq had been so keen for her to stop asking questions about Beth? Because he'd sold her something?

'Poppy? Can you tell us anything at all?'

She ran a hand through her hair. 'Beth was here looking for Maya Flynn. She was in love with her, right? But Maya was going out with Kane, the Tarot card reader. So I went to see him, but he swears he hasn't seen Maya since the festival last year. And then Michael found Maya listed on a missing persons website and I remembered what Beth said that night on the bluff. I look a bit like Maya, right? And when she saw me she said that she thought she was seeing Maya's ghost. And—' Poppy swallowed. This was where she was going out on a limb. '—It hit me that she was being literal. She thought that she wasn't going to find Maya because Maya's dead!'

'*Whoa!*' DS Grant said, holding up a hand. 'What are you telling me?'

'It's not one murder.' She stared at the detective, willing him to believe her. 'It's two. No one's seen Maya Flynn since last year. Not alive, anyway. Kane said that she was going after her father's money. And her father was someone here. Y'see, she was conceived at this festival. At first I thought it was...'

She was about to say 'Bob' when she saw that Mum was staring at her open-mouthed.

'Who?' the detective prompted.

'Err – just one of the old guys who comes to the festival, but then I realised that it wasn't him. It had to be someone else, and then everything went wrong...and I mucked things up...'

'What went wrong?' DS Grant asked.

She turned to Mum, desperate now to tell her. 'I think I've ruined things with Michael, Mum. I said – I told him I—' A tear trickled down her cheek.

'What? Who's Michael?' the policeman asked.

Mum waved him away and squeezed Poppy's hand. 'We'll talk about it later, OK?'

She nodded, sniffed back the tears and took a deep breath.

'Michael is Poppy's best friend from home, Sergeant,' Mum said, before he could ask again. 'It's got nothing to do with your case.'

'Right. OK. So, Poppy, am I getting this right? You think that Beth came here looking for Maya, but actually found out that she was murdered by someone, and that person realised that she knew, and murdered her too?'

'Yeah. I think so.'

'And this Kane guy...?'

Poppy hesitated. Was she sure? She had no real proof. But she'd been keeping so many secrets for so long that she just wanted to get it all out of her. It was up to the police to figure out if she was right or not. 'I can't prove it, but how could he know for sure if he didn't do it?'

'Why didn't you tell me any of this?'

'I did try! Remember?'

The detective nodded and avoided her gaze. 'Right then, I'm going to send for the boss and then I want you to go through all of that again, *slowly*. And then I need you to promise me that you won't ask anyone any more questions.'

As soon as the detective left, Mum turned to her.

'What happened?' she asked.

But before Poppy could answer, the flap opened, letting in a flash of light, and Michael popped his head in. 'How did it go?'

Mum smiled sadly. 'Should I leave you two to talk?'

Poppy could do no more than shrug.

Mum got to her feet and waved him in. 'Come in, Michael, before the police get back.'

'They're coming back?'

'Don't act like you weren't listening out there,' Poppy said.

Michael smiled. 'I would have, but I had to go and be interviewed.' He slumped down onto the ground mat and waited for Mum to leave.

Poppy wrapped her arms around her legs and rested her chin on her knees.

'I'm sorry I left like that yesterday,' Michael said.

'No, I'm sorry.'

'Are you?' The shaft of light from the tipi's oculus cut across his face, making his eyes appear unnaturally blue. They stared steadily back at her, refusing to look away.

'I'm sorry it upset you.' He'd never know how sorry. 'I'm sorry if I've wrecked things.'

'Why did you wait until I was seeing someone? You must have known that—'

'—Must have known what? That it was a monumentally bad idea? Yeah, I've got that now.' Poppy focused her eyes on a clump of grass someone had trodden in. She wasn't going to cry. She *refused* to cry.

'*No!* You must have known that *I liked you*. That I waited... *Years,* and you never showed any interest in being anything more than friends. You were always going on about the guy from the newsagents, or the guy from the garage. Meanwhile I couldn't get past first base with a girl because they all assumed I was going out with you!'

What? She must have misheard... Her head snapped up. Michael stared back at her. His face was tight, as if every muscle was stretched to breaking point but his gaze was soft, like he was willing her to believe him.

'But – Julia?'

'Julia only went out with me because I got drunk and moaned to her about you treating me like your annoying younger brother!'

'But you're older than me.'

'I know! A year and two fucking months older!' Michael's face broke into a smile. 'Do you really think that you could wind me up like this if I didn't care about you?'

Poppy shook her head. She couldn't think, couldn't breathe. All this time he'd wanted her too?

A bleeping noise sent Michael searching his pockets for his phone. He looked at the screen and frowned.

'Who is it?' she asked, knowing full well what the answer would be.

Michael raised his gaze to meet hers. 'I'm supposed to be helping set up the party.'

'Right.' She bit her lip and nodded. 'Julia.'

'What do you expect me to do? Tell her I can't go to

her eighteenth because I'm here having a heart-to-heart with you?'

'Of course not.'

'You think I should dump her on her birthday? When this could be a three-minute wonder?'

'What do you mean?'

'You. You spend a year making me feel like you don't want me near you, and then you say you love me. How do I know that this is what you really feel? Are you even sure yourself? I mean, God, Poppy, you dumped this on me and then spent the night with that guy.'

'I didn't spend the night with him!'

'OK. But you do know what he is, what he does?'

'How do you know...?'

He swallowed and kneaded his hands. 'I saw him the other day – looked like he was meeting his supplier.'

'And you didn't think to tell me?'

'I didn't want you to think I was trying to break you up. And then you landed your bombshell and it didn't really seem like the right time.' He rubbed his forehead. 'Look, I'm sorry, but I don't think I can do this right now.' He got to his feet and pushed open the flap of the tipi.

'Are you leaving again?'

'I just need some space. And so do you. I'll give you a ring next week some time.'

Next week? She'd never gone a week without talking

to him since they started secondary school. What was she supposed to do? It was the summer holidays. And he had her dog!

'What about Dawkins?'

'I'll get Mum to drop him round.' With that he slipped through the flap and was gone.

CHAPTER TWENTY-SIX

Poppy stood at the bottom of the wobbly metal steps and watched Tariq. She should have known he was too good to be true. He'd fed her a line and she'd swallowed it, hook, line and sinker. She was so naive. Just like she'd been with Michael. For two whole minutes in the tipi she'd thought it might all be OK. And then he'd left. And now she had no idea what was going on.

Tariq was too busy furiously scrubbing the stainless steel worktop to notice her. A deep line cut between his wild eyebrows and he was holding the Brillo pad so tightly that his knuckles shone pale.

Even if he was a dealer, he was a darned cute one. A part of her couldn't believe that he was even interested in her. Maybe seducing innocent schoolgirls was a bit of a thrill. Well, after spending another hour and a half in the company of Detective Sergeant Grant and his boss, she'd picked up a few interrogation techniques and she had some questions for Tariq.

Tariq straightened up and flung the Brillo pad at the worktop, cursing under his breath. Just then he saw her. He spun around, his mouth hanging open with not so much as a hello.

'Thought you might want to buy me an aubergine

burger,' Poppy said. 'Your treat, seeing as you can afford it.'

She walked away and left him fumbling with his apron strings.

In thirty seconds he was there beside her. They walked among the falafel and crepe vans. Poppy didn't speak. That would make it too easy for him and she wasn't in the mood to make life easy for any guy. Instead, she pretended to take great interest in each and every one of the menu boards. Tariq didn't speak either, he just followed her around like a lost puppy. Eventually, after she'd spent a good five minutes umming and ahhing over the menu of Al's Jamaican-Continental Diner, Tariq stepped between her and the chalkboard.

'Look, I'm sorry!'

'Are you trying to get out of me buying dinner? Man, that's cheap for someone who earns...what? What does a dealer earn?'

Tariq glanced around nervously. 'OK, I deserved that, but can you keep your voice down?'

'Why?' She carried on her journey down the food aisle. 'Maybe that's what you're lacking – a really good marketing strategy. I mean, if you're gonna do good business, people need to know that you're the guy with the high. That's it! We could paint a new sign for the burger van. Tariq – *The Guy with the High!* I think it's catchy.'

A hand grabbed her wrist. Hard. And before she could object, she was being dragged towards the woods.

The afternoon sun had waned. It would be dark in the woods. Lonely.

She tried to yank out of his grip but he had tight hold of her and he wasn't letting go.

'Get off me!' Suddenly she was frightened.

He stopped abruptly. She bumped smack into him.

'You obviously have things to say,' he said quietly, 'which is fine, but do you mind if we go somewhere a bit more private so when you bawl me out the whole festival doesn't hear?'

He let go of her wrist and she rubbed the throbbing indentations he'd left behind.

Her heartbeat slowed to a normal rhythm and she was about to tell him where to get off, when she noticed that he was staring at her wrist. His cheeks reddened. He hadn't meant to hurt her. He took a tentative step towards her. His hand reached out towards hers.

'Poppy, God, I'm—'

'—Whatever,' she muttered.

She headed into the shadow of the trees. Immediately the temperature dropped by several degrees. She couldn't stop herself from shivering. She was aware of Tariq's footsteps behind her and the voices of the food sellers on the vans. As long as she could hear them, they'd hear her, she told herself. Even if Tariq was unlikely to hurt her, she wasn't totally stupid. She stopped and turned to face him, folding her arms, and giving him a 'So?' look.

Tariq shoved his hands in his pockets. He didn't look at her. He kicked at some rotting pinecones from last year's drop.

'I told you I wasn't doing what I wanted to do,' he muttered.

'All that stuff about you being a law student, about your dad leaving, was that all lies?'

He shook his head. 'That was all true.'

'You needed money so you thought you'd try your luck on the other side of the law, huh?'

He sighed. 'Yes. But I didn't exactly plan it. There was a guy. He—'

'—And you couldn't get a job in McDonald's like everyone else?'

He looked at her from beneath his heavy brow and his lip curled in an unwilling smile. 'In case you haven't noticed, I did that too.'

'Are you taking drugs?'

He glared at her. 'Do I look like an idiot?'

'But it's OK to push the stuff to other people?'

'I'm not a pusher!' He shook his head in denial. 'I don't force anyone to take anything. I sell to adults who are entitled to make their own decisions. In some countries you can buy what I sell in pharmacies!'

'We don't live in those countries.'

Tariq rolled his eyes. 'You really want to stand here

and debate the Controlled Substances Act?'

'No. I want to know what you sold to Beth.'

That had his attention. He rubbed a hand over his top lip, then stepped closer and lowered his voice as if the trees might be listening. 'Poppy, I didn't...'

'That's why you've been so worried, isn't it? That's why you didn't want me asking questions. You were worried that your merchandise might have killed her.'

Again, he stepped forward, closing the gap between them. He was so close, his eyes so dark, so serious.

Poppy's pulse ticked in her temple. Her throat ran dry and for the first time she was aware of how much stronger he was than her. If he did want to hurt her he could do it. Hell, if he wanted to kill her, all he'd have to do was squeeze.

'You have no idea what you're messing with.'

'Then you'd better tell me.'

His chest rose and fell with increasing speed, but still he said nothing.

'That's the trouble with drugs, isn't it? Most of the time it's fine. People have their little trips and they come back down to earth safely.' Beth's face floated before her. Drowned and dead. 'But *sometimes* they end up in the lake, don't they? You have no clue what you're buying – what you're selling on to people.'

Tariq stared at her, silently.

'If you don't tell me, I'm going straight to the police.' She almost meant it.

'No you're not.'

She held his gaze. 'Watch me.'

He looked away first. 'OK – OK! I sold her an E. What do you want me to do? You want me to go and hand myself in?'

She sighed, not knowing whether she was relieved or sad. All she knew was that she felt washed out. 'No. I don't want you to hand yourself in.'

'Was it...did it kill her? Is that what they're saying?' His eyes were wide and panicked.

'It wasn't your fault, Tariq. They found the drugs in her system, but that wasn't what killed her. She was murdered.'

He rubbed his hands over his face and blew out a long slow breath. 'You're sure?'

Poppy nodded.

He put his hands on his hips and squeezed his eyes shut. 'Thank fuck for that. I thought maybe...'

'You don't have to worry about it. But they're going to be looking for whoever sold it. Maybe you should do yourself a favour and get out of here.'

She turned to leave.

'Wait! Poppy – I know I'm not what you thought I was, but I'm not a bad guy. All that stuff I told you was true. And I like you.' He stepped closer. His hand slid into her hair. 'A lot.'

'It's not what you do that's the problem – I mean, it is – but...'

She didn't get a chance to say anything else. His mouth was on hers, preventing any sound from getting out. He kissed her until she stopped struggling, then he nipped her bottom lip just hard enough to make her gasp. As he turned his attention to her neck, she couldn't stop her hands from sliding into his hair.

Her heart was beating so hard, her stomach so squirmy and her legs so jittery that she almost didn't stop him from one-handedly unbuttoning her jeans and pushing the denim over her hip. But his warm touch to the bare skin of her back was like a bucket of cold water over her head. She got both hands on his chest and shoved him away.

'No way!' she gasped.

He gave her a slightly confused, slightly amused look.

'You think you can distract me like that?'

'Seemed to be working,' he said, moving towards her.

Poppy held out a hand to prevent him from picking up where he'd left off.

He sighed. 'It's that guy, Michael, isn't it?'

'No!' She'd had so much practice that the lie slipped out easily. She took a deep breath. 'Yes, it's Michael.'

'It's pretty obvious he's in love with you.'

'He's got a girlfriend.'

Tariq narrowed his eyes at her. 'Were you using me to try and make him jealous?'

'Of course not!'

'Well, it's worked. I'm surprised he hasn't punched me yet.'

'Michael's got a very beautiful girlfriend. And I don't think he really does love me. I mean, I know he loves me. But I'm not sure he loves me the way I love him. Maybe he did at some point. But I think I blew it.'

'I wouldn't bet on it. He's spent a lot of time driving over here to see you.'

'He's like that.'

'If you say so.'

'What does that mean?'

Tariq shrugged. He was right on top of her again. His arms slipped around her waist. He smiled wickedly and kissed her cheek.

'Don't you care that I like someone else?' she gasped.

'You might be in love with him, Poppy, but you fancy me,' he whispered. 'And I'll take what I can get.' His hot breath tickled her ear. Damn her stomach, and legs, and every other part of her that was tingling. She kept her gaze averted. She wasn't going to be drawn into this madness by beautiful almond-shaped eyes with irises the colour of rich chocolate. Damn it, she wasn't this easily manipulated!

'Poppy? *Poppy?*' His lips quirked to one side into the cutest darned lopsided grin she'd ever seen.

'Tariq, don't...' As his lips brushed against hers and turned her legs to water, there was the crack of a tree branch snapping. She pushed him away and spun around. 'What was that?'

'What was what?'

'Police!' a voice called from the darkness.

CHAPTER TWENTY-SEVEN

Poppy glanced at Tariq. His cheeks had paled and his mouth hung open like he was about to start singing a few verses of *Jail House Rock*.

He leaned into her. 'Did you...?'

'No, of course not,' she whispered back.

From the gloom between the trees, two burly policemen in flak jackets lumbered into the clearing.

One held up his warrant card. 'Can I ask your names, please?'

Was she about to be arrested for illicit snogging? 'Poppy Sinclair. What's going on?'

'Tariq Nasheed.'

'Have either of you seen this guy?' The taller policeman held up a picture of a guy with a shaved head and a smooth skull-like face. There was no green tuft, and there was a hardness in his eyes she'd never seen before, but it was definitely Kane.

Her heart leapt into her throat. 'What's happened? Where is he?'

'We want to talk to him but he seems to have left the site.'

'You mean you don't know where he is?' Poppy's stomach lurched. Kane was out there. And if he'd run, that meant he was guilty, right?

The policeman's radio buzzed. He took a step back and spoke quietly into the receiver.

'Have you seen him?' the other cop asked.

'Not today,' Poppy said.

Tariq shook his head. 'I've seen him around, but don't think I've seen him today.'

The tall policeman turned back to them. 'Did you say your name is Poppy?'

'Yeah.'

He smiled. 'Your mum's looking for you. And Mr Nasheed, we have a couple of questions for you.'

'I've spoken to Sergeant Grant and he thinks it would be best if we went home.' Mum was stuffing the contents of the tipi into bags like they'd just been told a hurricane was coming.

'What?'

Mum glanced up, a worried frown creasing her forehead. 'Poppy, he's gone missing. He'll know it was you who put the police onto him. We can't stay.'

'But...'

Mum stopped shoving cushions into bin bags and turned to her. 'What?'

'I just...' Poppy sighed. 'Nothing. You're right. It's time to go home.' Except it didn't feel like time to go home. It felt like everything had been stirred up and now she was leaving before getting to understand what had actually happened here. 'I should go and say goodbye to Bob.'

'Can't you wait until Jonathan comes back and I'll come with you?'

'Oh, come on. I'm only going to Bob's caravan. Have you seen how many police there are around here? If Kane's got any sense he'll be halfway to London by now.'

'Jonathan's talking to them now, to see if he can help find him. Kane's got a record, y'know?'

Poppy swallowed a groan. 'I'll go straight there and straight back.'

'Hmm...'

'I'll be ten minutes.'

Poppy gave her mum a quick hug before she could reply, and slipped out of the tipi. The light had begun to fade because of some whacking great clouds that were crowding the sky. She could taste the rain like a threat from above. As she started out across the festival ground towards Bob's caravan, she reached into her pocket for her mobile. She had to tell Michael what was going on. She was pulling up his number when it hit her: she couldn't phone him. She couldn't text him.

Michael didn't want to talk to her. Her best friend – no, she had to stop calling him that – the guy she was in love with was at his girlfriend's eighteenth and wouldn't want to talk to her. Tears clouded her vision.

In an hour or so she'd be back in her room at home. If she opened her window she'd probably be able to hear the sounds of the party coming from Julia's.

She sniffed back the tears and tried to get herself together. She didn't want Bob to see what a pathetic mess she was. She'd say a quick goodbye to him, and go back to the tipi via the burger van. She at least needed to find out what had happened to Tariq. It wasn't as though she could ask the police if they'd arrested the festival dealer.

Bob was standing outside the multicoloured caravan talking to a policewoman and Pete from the farm. Bob was gnawing his bottom lip like he was chewing a wasp and Pete didn't look too happy either. Bob spotted Poppy and motioned for her to join them.

'Your mum found you, then?' he asked, putting an arm around her. She smiled up at him.

'Hello, Poppy,' Pete said. It looked like his mouth was trying to smile but the farmer didn't really look at her, as if he was still mulling over what they'd been talking about before she arrived.

'Anyway, thanks for your help,' the policewoman said brightly. 'I'll get back to you when we have more details of the press release.'

Poppy thought she felt a growl rumble in the old druid's chest.

The policewoman smiled, seemingly oblivious to the waves of hostility rolling off Bob. 'Er, could I have a quick word with you?' she asked Pete.

'What?' A sullen, wary look crossed Pete's face. He

seemed as fed up as Bob. 'Oh, yeah, OK.' He shrugged and followed the policewoman over to one of the marquees the force had commandeered.

'Press release?' Poppy asked, squeezing Bob.

Bob nodded and his arm dropped from around her shoulders. 'They can't wait to tell the world that a ritual murder happened at a Pagan festival. By morning there'll be television crews and protesters. After everything we've worked for – all that time trying to educate folk that Pagans are just normal people. Once the tabloids get hold of this they'll turn us into a freak show. We'll have to move the festival next year...and that'll hurt Pete. That family relies on the money we gives 'em.'

'I'm sorry.'

'I know.' Bob cupped her face with his big paw of a hand and rubbed her cheek with his thumb. 'So you're going home, then?'

'I feel like we're abandoning you.'

'Don't be daft. I don't want you here while Kane's...' He sighed. 'I should never have sent you to see that lad.'

'I'd have found him myself, Bob. You know me – dog with a bone.'

He smiled down at her fondly. 'In't that the truth.'

Dog with a bone, except she was about to walk away from it all. She was leaving Bob to deal with the media backlash, she was leaving Tariq to God knows what fate, and Beth – she was leaving Beth. And there were still so many questions to be answered.

'Bob? There was something he said – Kane – he said that Maya was looking for her dad. Do you know who her dad was?'

'Ye gods, Poppy!' Bob exclaimed, shaking his head. 'It's a good thing you're going home.'

'She's not found any more bodies, has she?' a voice asked. It was Pete, stood behind her with his hands shoved in his jeans pockets. He was smiling, but Poppy could see he was making an effort. Losing the income from the festival had to be pretty bad news.

'Not through lack of trying.' Bob hugged her. 'Thinks she's a sleuth from an Agatha Christie novel.'

'I do not! And I've got to go. I promised Mum I wouldn't be long.' She kissed Bob on his scratchy whiskered cheek. 'Will you call in on your way home?'

'Aye, reckon I might.'

She turned to Pete. 'Thanks for everything.'

Pete shrugged. 'You too – I mean, take care.'

She felt bad for him. It was rotten news, especially with a baby on the way. 'Say goodbye to Sally for me.'

She set off in the direction of the tipi. As soon as she was out of sight of Bob, she switched directions and headed towards the food vans. The market stalls were nearly empty, everything sold or packed up. The tarpaulin roofs sagged with rainwater and filled black bin bags lay in piles. A sharp-toothed creature had mauled one of them, and the contents had spilled out over the sodden grass. Without fairy lights and the bustle of people, the stalls looked like nothing but piles of rusting bones. The magic was gone.

A cold gust of wind shuddered through the stalls setting metal poles clanging and ruffling the tarps. Poppy pulled her hoodie tighter around her. Her gaze was drawn to the tops of the fir trees on the fringe of the festival ground. They were all leaning to the left, bowing down as if to appease the storm that was brewing. The wind was really getting up. Mum would freak if it started raining when she was halfway through packing up.

Poppy picked up speed as she worked her way between the abandoned stalls. She was just about to step over a dropped veggie burger and fries when her eyes caught a movement between the stalls.

She turned, expecting to see another festival-goer, but there was no one there. Must have been a bird or something. As she turned to go, there was a flash of brown, so fast she didn't have time to make out what it was. She whipped around.

She was alone in the metal forest of poles. The only people she could see were a couple of distant figures walking between the tents and caravans on the opposite side of the market. A little voice in the back of her head told her to turn back – go and help Mum dismantle the tipi. But that would mean not saying goodbye to Tariq, not knowing what the police wanted from him.

She took a deep breath and carried on walking, absently fingering the smooth black stone hanging around at her throat.

'Poppy!'

She stopped. She didn't breathe.

'POPPY!' a voice half whispered, half shouted.

She whirled around, searching for the person – if it was a person – who was haunting the empty market. Her gaze skipped from one market stall to the next, from shadow to tree to...*movement!*

Someone was there. Coming towards her.

Poppy edged away, thinking hard, trying not to panic. She was midway between Bob and Tariq, but what if Tariq wasn't there? If the food vans had closed down like the market she'd be stuffed.

'*Poppyyyyyyy!*' the voice hissed.

Her feet made the decision for her. She sprinted for the food vans. A figure lunged out from behind a sagging tarp right in front of her and she crashed into it.

Strong hands grabbed her shoulders and held her in place.

'Shhhh!' Kane whispered, pressing a finger to her lips.

CHAPTER TWENTY-EIGHT

The music pounded through the house.

Michael held the same can of Red Stripe he'd been clutching since mates from school began flooding the house.

Julia was loving every minute of the attention. At that second she was dancing with a group of her friends – one of those slinky kinds of dances, totally out of time with the heavy beat of the music. Her long arms were in the air, her blonde hair swishing around her bare shoulders, and her silver sequinned dress clung tightly to her jiggling hips.

As if sensing him watching her, she turned and, with a seductive finger, beckoned him over.

He smiled, but shook his head.

Her pale pink lips puckered into a pout that made him laugh. Realising that the mountain wasn't going to go to Mohammed, she danced her way across the room. At that moment, a few of the other guys from school showed up with bottles of what looked like vodka. Julia waved excitedly at them, but didn't stop her journey towards him.

She stopped in front of him. Her big blue eyes were shining with mischief. She flicked her hair over her shoulder and Michael couldn't help glancing down at her shimmering form.

Without a word, she pressed her lips to his.

She tasted of the sweet white wine she'd been drinking since about five that evening, and of something else...perhaps a promise of something more to come? Her parents had cleared out for the night so they pretty much had the house to themselves.

She pulled away, linked her hands behind her back and swayed from side to side, looking pleased with herself.

Michael was aware that the whole room was staring at them. Every guy was wishing himself in his place, and all the girls in school wanted to be Julia, not because she was kissing him, but because she could have whoever the hell she wanted. All the girls he knew were locked between being jealous of Julia and being in awe of her. Except for Poppy.

He wondered what Poppy was doing. He wanted to call her, but he had no idea what to say. He'd bottled it again. He should have stayed and talked to her – tried to work out if she really knew what she wanted and maybe even work out what he wanted.

Julia cleared her throat. 'Hello? Earth to Michael?'

He blinked.

'What's wrong?' Julia asked, raising her voice over the music.

'Nothing.'

She ran her hand over his chest. 'Dance with me?'

He shook his head. No matter what she said or did, he wasn't dancing with her or anyone else. He couldn't dance – couldn't seem to get his legs and his arms to do what they were supposed to do. Poppy always said he looked like a creature from one of those build-a-monster flip books – the wrong legs on the wrong body.

A finger poking his ribs brought him back to the party. Julia was frowning.

He shrugged and smiled. 'Sorry, it's the beer,' he said, holding up the can.

She narrowed her eyes. 'Don't drink too much. You have to be sober enough to give me my birthday present.'

'But I've given you...your...'

Julia grinned and her cheeks glowed red. She leaned forward and whispered. 'You *have* brought you-know-whats, haven't you?'

CHAPTER TWENTY-NINE

Poppy tried to shove Kane away but the hands gripping her shoulders felt like they were made of iron. Panic flooded through her and she hit out, punching and kicking. He loomed over her, his green eyes staring into hers from his skull-like face. He pulled her back to his chest and two arms wrapped around her, fixing her in place.

'Let me go!'

'I need to talk to you.'

'No!' she screamed.

His hand clapped over her mouth, trapping the sound inside her. The arm around her chest tightened its grip. Shit! Her gaze darted from stall to stall, hoping someone was close enough to realise what was going on, but tears blurred her vision until she could see nothing but watery shadows in the fading light.

Kane leaned his head into hers. Hot breath grazed her cheek.

'I won't hurt you. You just need to listen to me.'

She didn't believe him. He was going to kill her. Like he'd killed Maya...and Beth.

He started moving, dragging her backwards. He was taking her to the woods. *Shit-shit-shit!* Once he got her in the woods it was game over. She was dead. In the shock of realisation her entire body sagged. Kane swore as he lost his grip on her. He yanked her to her feet and for just a second, his hands loosened.

She kicked back as hard as she could, heard a satisfying thunk as her heel made contact with his shin. Kane gasped in pain. She shoved him away and ran.

Heavy footsteps thundered after her. Despair flooded through Poppy as she realised she wasn't fast enough; she wouldn't have been fast enough even if her legs hadn't turned to shaky rubber.

A hand grabbed her arm and she screamed.

As his grip tightened, she swung her elbow into his chest. Kicked, scratched, anything she could do to hurt him before he hurt her.

'She wants you dead, Poppy!' he shouted. 'I'm trying to help you!'

What? Suddenly, Kane's hands on her shoulders were the only things keeping her on her feet.

He stared at her, his eyes pleading. 'You *have* to listen to me! She'll kill you. This place – it was in her blood. You have to leave. Here she can get to you. You need to get away, Poppy. She'll kill you like she's going to kill me. I've seen it in the cards. Death. Always Death.'

He let her go; she stumbled, nearly fell, then backed away, her heart thudding painfully. Had she got it wrong? Was he really trying to help her?

His eyes were so wide they looked like the eyes of a

corpse, as if he was dead already.

A voice called out. Someone was running in their direction. She turned and saw Tariq and another guy. Kane heard them too. His head swung one way and then the other, like an animal being baited.

He stumbled back and pointed a finger at her. 'Get out of here. Go and never come back.' Then he turned and ran.

'It's him!' someone shouted.

Poppy watched Kane escape through the metal bones of the market stall, towards the centre of the festival ground. Out of nowhere, three or four figures gave chase.

A hand grabbed her arm and she gasped.

'It's OK, it's me,' Tariq said, his face scrunched with concern. 'Are you OK?'

'Umm —'

'— Poppy, did he hurt you?' Tariq asked, urgently.

Poppy shook her head. 'Something's not right.' Something bad was going to happen to Kane.

The sun hung low over the hillside, bleeding red light through the black spikes of the fir trees up on the bluff. Before she knew what she was doing, she was running too, joining the hunt. Her legs kept pumping the ground, but Kane had disappeared into the canvas village.

Police were shouting directions to each other, like they were trying to flush out an animal. And then he appeared again, his shaved head pale against the dark of the landscape, running up the steep bank that led up to the farm. Black shadows swarmed after him, spreading out, creating a net in which to catch him.

Adrenaline finally kicked in and Poppy picked up speed, ignoring Tariq's calls. She attacked the hill, using the solid rocks that stuck out of the gravelly earth to propel herself up. When she eventually reached the top she skidded to a stop, almost crashing into a stationary policewoman.

The policewoman turned and frowned. 'You need to get back down the hill, now!' she said.

But Poppy's eyes sought out Kane as she struggled to catch her breath.

Kane had taken a wrong turn and ended up trapped, thirty feet away, on the rocky outcrop of the bluff that hung over the lake. Or maybe he hadn't taken a wrong turn. Maybe this was where he'd wanted to lead them.

The police were standing, spread out in an arc, their arms outstretched like they were playing a game, and behind Kane, thirty feet below, the lake shone red with the sunset. Kane seemed to have shrunk in size, or maybe it was just that he was hunched over, cowering like a wounded fox faced with a pack of hounds.

'Poppy, are you OK?' a breathless voice asked behind her. It was Tariq.

'Yeah. But Kane—'

'—Don't worry, they'll get him,' he whispered.

That's what she was afraid of.

Death. Always Death.

Kane had come here to die.

Just then, the police officer who was talking gently to Kane took a step forward. Kane edged further towards the edge. His foot slipped and he only just managed to stop himself from falling.

'No! Poppy screamed.

Kane's face snapped up. His eyes connected with hers and his cheek twitched in what could have been the beginning of a smile, but sadness and fear got the better of it.

'I didn't kill Maya, Poppy,' he called over to her, his voice trembling and thick with fear. 'She killed me.'

With that Kane took a step back and slipped from sight.

As Poppy screamed, the dream came back to her. Maya pushing her. Falling...falling...falling...

She wasn't even conscious that she had run to the edge until she was staring down at Kane's contorted body, broken on the pebbles below. One leg had gained another joint, bent the wrong way, and his face stared up at them – seeing or unseeing, she couldn't tell. As if to finish off the job, a tide of red lake water rolled over him.

'She pushed him – she pushed him!' Poppy heard herself shouting.

Arms folded around her and she was enclosed in a

tight hug as she gasped for breath.

'Come away.'

It was Tariq. His fingers tried to brush her hair away from her face, but it was stuck to her cheeks by tears and sweat. It was in her eyes, in her mouth, but she could do nothing other than cling to him and take in deep shuddering breaths of air.

'Get an ambulance,' someone was saying, 'and get down to him, check if he's alive.'

Tariq squeezed her tightly. 'It's OK, Poppy. It's OK.'

But it wasn't.

The tipi was packed with people. Mum, Jonathan, DS Grant, the policewoman she'd seen talking to Bob and Pete earlier. Bob and Mo were outside, *giving them space*, but not willing to leave entirely. Even Tariq was sat by the flap, looking like he'd rather be anywhere else on earth.

She shot him a quick smile. He couldn't be finding it easy, being surrounded by all these coppers.

Tariq lifted his eyebrows in a question. 'OK?' he mimed.

She nodded. And she was OK now. Everything was fine as long as she didn't think too much...and as long as she was surrounded by ten or twelve people.

As the conversation between Jonathan and the policewoman dwindled to a pause she could hear the bark of police dogs and the hum of engines.

She couldn't stop her mind from replaying the scene. Over and over like a YouTube clip on repeat. Her imagination had even added a soundtrack. Now she didn't hear the shouts of the police officers calling for him to stop, instead she heard the sickening thud of Kane's body as it had tumbled down the sharp incline of the bluff, and the splash as he'd landed head first into the shallow waters below.

'There's still a chance he'll make it,' DS Grant said, catching her eye.

It had taken twenty-five minutes for an ambulance to arrive. But he was still breathing when they'd loaded him into the back. Just.

'I think he's ill. I don't think he wanted to hurt me.' She didn't quite know why she was defending him. He'd killed two women. Or at least she'd thought he had. But he'd been scared and confused and she couldn't rid her head of the thudding noise, nor the feeling that somehow Maya had killed him, just like he'd said she would.

A hand rubbed her back. She looked up. Mum's face was surprisingly calm, like she'd managed to fit in an hour's Zen meditation since her initial freak-out. Mum leaned over, kissed her forehead and then pressed her face against Poppy's so that she was surrounded by Mum smell. It wasn't just the scent of the oils she used in her massage, but that special something in her DNA that always made Poppy feel safe and at home.

There was a buzz of static from a radio.

'Excuse me a minute,' DS Grant said, getting to his feet and slipping out of the tipi.

Mum's shoulder shifted beneath her head. Poppy sat up and looked at her.

'I'm going to call Michael,' Mum said.

'What?' Poppy's stomach twisted. Michael was the one person she wanted most... but she couldn't have him. Especially not tonight. 'No. You can't. It's Julia's party. I don't want you to call him.'

'He'd want to know what's happened,' Mum said.

'No! I'm fine. There's no reason for you to call him. I'll speak to him in the morning.'

'You should call him,' a voice said from the opposite side of the tipi. Tariq's gaze held hers. He smiled, but there was a frown mark between his eyebrows that told her he wasn't joking. 'It's going out on the news. If my best friend was involved I'd want to hear about it.'

Mum squeezed her shoulder. 'I'll just tell him that you're OK. I don't want him hearing about it from somewhere else and driving over here if he's been drinking.'

CHAPTER THIRTY

The soft glow from Julia's bedside lamp did nothing to disguise the pinkness of the room. Pink fluffy pillows. Pink flowery bedspread that looked like something his gran would choose. And then there was the teddy collection. Hundreds of them. Everywhere he looked there were fuzzy pink and brown noses, glassy eyes... all staring at him.

Were they gonna watch?

Behind him the door clicked shut. He turned to see Julia dragging over a chair to prop underneath the handle, the way that they did in films. A gang of her friends was downstairs still drinking cocktails with no names, listening to husky-voiced women singing out of the iPod speakers, and slagging off all the blokes they'd ever known.

A girly sleepover, that's what she'd told her parents. He couldn't believe they'd fallen for that old chestnut.

Happy that the chair would stop any unwanted visitors disturbing them, Julia turned and smiled.

'Should I put on some music?' she asked.

Michael shrugged. 'OK.'

She went over to a white chest of drawers that was covered with twenty or so bottles of perfume and began fumbling with the stereo. After a minute she sighed.

'Bloody thing won't work.'

He gently budged her aside. She hadn't flicked onto the right function. He pressed a couple of buttons. 'Remote?'

'Here,' she said, holding out the small black plastic remote.

As he took it, he noticed her hand was shaking. A nervous shiver worked its way up his spine. He took a deep breath, pushed the play button and chucked the remote on the side.

Over the course of the evening her eyeliner had smudged. She'd tried to fix it, but it was industrial-strength stuff. She always wore a lot of make-up when they went out. He preferred her without, but now probably wasn't the time to tell her.

She took a step forward and slipped her hand into his hair. And she stared at him. Her wide eyes were as shiny as the hundreds of glass eyes watching them.

'I love you,' she whispered.

She'd said it before, but this time it set bugs crawling through his veins.

Did he love her?

He liked her. He thought she was sexy. But he loved Poppy. He was in love with his best friend and had been for as long as he could remember. Was it possible that he could love them both? He felt paralysed standing there in Julia's bedroom with all those accusing glass eyes staring at him. All those bears, they knew.

Shit! This was confusing.

Julia pulled down his head to kiss him. Her lips were soft and inviting. She wanted him, for definite. There was no confusion in her kisses and it felt good.

She guided his hands to the zip to her dress. It got caught and there were a few moments of nervous giggling from both of them. Then it was free and Julia, this girl who he'd fancied since they were both gawky and twelve, was practically naked. She was beautiful and she'd been more of a friend to him than Poppy for the last six months. And he did love her in some way.

'Are you sure?' he whispered.

'Yes,' she replied.

His brain left the planet and all he was left with was wanting.

They landed on the flowery bedspread and the teddies scattered. She pushed off his shirt and then they were flesh on flesh.

Ring-ring!

God, it was so good that there were bells.

Ring-ring!

Bells? There were bells? No, it was a phone.

Ring-ring!

Her fingers were on his belt, trying to undo the buckle.

Ring-ring!

'My phone,' he muttered, pulling it from his back pocket.

'Ignore it,' Julia gasped.

'Yeah, I—' He was about to reject the call when he saw the screen: *Meg calling*. The moment froze. *What the fuck am I doing?*

Julia grabbed the phone from him and threw it on the bedside cabinet.

'No! Hold on.' Michael untangled himself from Julia, grabbed the phone and hit *Answer*.

'Meg?'

'Michael. Sorry to call so late. I know you're at a party—'

He squeezed his eyes shut. '—It's OK, what's wrong?'

CHAPTER THIRTY-ONE

Poppy lay with her head in Mum's lap, and a big chenille blanket wrapped around her. The constant stroking of Mum's hand against her hair was hypnotic and Mum had turned out most of the torches in the hope she would fall asleep. But she couldn't. And so she drifted. Not really awake, not really asleep. Thoughts flitted through her head, some of them so quick she couldn't grasp on to them. Others lingered and then were gone, forgotten like a dream.

Love is like fire, Poppy; unless it's channelled it destroys everything.

Everything and everyone. Beth had lost her life to love. Tariq had abandoned his dreams for love of his family. And Kane...

'Kane was a fool for love,' said a voice she didn't recognise. Someone laughed.

Poppy gasped and sat up. 'Who said that?'

On the other side of the tipi, Jonathan, Mo and Bob were talking in hushed voices. All three of them stopped and turned to her.

'Who said what, Poppy?' Mum asked.

'About Kane. Who was laughing?'

They all looked at her like she was mad.

'No one was laughing.' Mum pushed Poppy's hair

away from her face. 'You must have been dreaming.'

Right...dreaming. She blinked and rubbed her eyes.

'Err – excuse me. Can I come in?' DS Grant's face appeared through the flap.

'Of course, Sergeant,' Mum said, beckoning him in.

The detective settled himself on a cushion and took up what was becoming his familiar Buddha-like pose. He kneaded his hands together and stared at the ground. He looked whacked, like he'd been chased by a pack of dogs. He glanced up and their eyes met. He held Poppy's gaze.

'What is it?' she asked, her stomach already tensing up.

'I'm afraid Kane died on the way to the hospital.'

CHAPTER THIRTY-TWO

After hours of darkness, when it felt like the night would never end, Poppy stood at the edge of the lake and watched as the sun steadily crept into the sky, sending ribbons of pink and gold light weaving through the sharp peaks of the fir trees and hills in the distance. The rosy light danced on the rippling waters of the lake as if the water sprites were celebrating the return of the sun.

'It's a beautiful morning,' Mo said, beside her.

Poppy nodded. It *was* beautiful – the sky, the lake, the trees. Postcard pretty.

But what was that old saying? *Red sky in the morning, shepherd's warning*. A cold shudder worked its way up her spine. In a flash, where there had been beauty she could see only danger. The trees were too jagged and the lake too red...blood-red. Poppy tore her gaze away and looked instead at the mottled-grey pebbles beneath her feet.

'Are they gone now?' she asked, quietly.

'Is who gone?'

Poppy turned to Mo.

The faintest of smiles carved a way through the medicine woman's solemn features. Mo wasn't even pretending not to know what she was talking about.

But she was going to make her say it anyway.

'Maya, Beth. Whoever it was in my head.'

Mo's dark eyes reflected the glow of the sunrise, as if they could filter out the pure light of the morning from the blood and horror of last night. She nodded, considering Poppy's question.

What did she need to consider? Kane was dead. The police had found a notebook in his pocket complete with mad rantings about Maya that had convinced them that he'd killed her and Beth. They were even going to begin the search for Maya's body. Poppy had worked out what had happened to them. She'd done all she could do, hadn't she? 'Why the hell would they still be haunting me?' she blurted.

'I don't know.'

'What do you mean, you don't know?' The panic she'd been so careful to keep under control broke free. 'I can't take them home with me, Mo. I can't handle them screwing with me any more.'

'Maybe they still have something to teach you.'

'I don't want any more lessons.'

'Or maybe *you* haven't let them go.'

'Me? Are you saying it was all in my head?' Poppy ran a hand through her hair and laughed. Just two days ago, if the roles had been reversed, she'd have told Mo to book herself in for a few sessions with Jonathan.

'Doesn't matter what I think,' Mo said, gently. 'Only matters what you think. Whether they're spirits or memories, the best medicine is to let them go from your heart.'

Michael had said something about her needing to learn to let things go. It was true. If she'd have let go of Michael rather than chasing after him, maybe they'd still be friends. If she'd stopped searching for Beth's killer, maybe the police would have found Kane before he ended up dead in the water.

'How do I do it, Mo? How do I let them go?'

'I'm sorry, no more questions today,' Bob said, waving away the gaggle of journalists holding out Dictaphones and scribbling in notebooks. 'Go and find yourself a nice celebrity scandal to fill your pages.'

As he stalked away from them, a couple of women police officers stopped the news hounds from following.

'Got your own bodyguards now?' Poppy asked, smiling.

Bob glanced over his shoulder. 'Aye. Nice girls. One of them was telling me that her old gran used to read the tealeaves. Happen even the police aren't immune to the Old Ways. Let's go and make her a cuppa, hey? Put her to the test.'

Bob's arm clamped firmly around Poppy's shoulders and he led her to the caravan.

Once inside the darkened tobacco-smelling cave, Poppy slumped down at the fold-down table where the police had interviewed her after finding Beth. Was it really only a couple of days ago? It felt like weeks. On the table were the usual mountains of books as well as a couple of business cards with the phone numbers of various police officers. That had to be a first. Usually, Bob was trying to evade the police, not contact them.

'New friends?' Poppy asked, holding up one of the cards.

Bob chuckled. 'Have to admit, they've been pretty decent,' he said, pouring boiling water into a teapot. 'We've even been allocated a family liaison officer to help handle the press. All part of their community relations programme, apparently.' He snorted. 'Could have done with some community relations the last time they hauled me off the bypass protest.'

Bob dumped two steaming mugs of builder's brew on the table and slumped down opposite her.

'Thought you were making tea for your bodyguards.'

'In a minute. Why don't you tell me what's on your mind first?' He scratched his beard and raised an expectant eyebrow.

Poppy picked up one of the mugs of tea and wrapped her hands around it. 'Mo says I need to let go of what's happened.'

Bob nodded, but said nothing.

'She said I could leave offerings to their spirits. Parting gifts. She said it's normal, it's what people are doing every time they leave flowers on a grave. I didn't want to ask Mum and Jonathan, they'll only want to make a big deal out of it and I don't want to talk about it, or work out what I think happened, I just want to do it. Will you help me?'

Bob grabbed his pipe, shoved it in his mouth and reached for the matches. 'What do you need?'

It took nearly an hour to select three gifts. It was worse than buying birthday presents for people she actually knew.

Bob stuffed everything into a cloth bag and handed it over to Poppy. She took it and hugged him. His arms encircled her and leaned down and kissed the top of her head.

'I should be at yours before dark,' Bob said, 'so tell that mad dog of yours that I'll be requiring my usual armchair, and there's only room for one of us.'

'I'll do my best.'

Bob let her go and stepped back. 'Are you going where I think you're going?'

Poppy nodded.

'Could you do me a favour while you're up there?'

'Of course.'

Bob grabbed one of the books from the table, opened it up and took an envelope from between the pages. 'Could you put that through the door of the farmhouse? It's just a thank you. They got more than they bargained for this year.'

'No problem.' She grabbed the caravan door and

yanked it open. Light flooded into the gloom.

'Pops?'

She stepped down onto the wobbly metal step and turned back to Bob. 'Yeah?'

He shoved his pipe into his mouth and chewed the end. 'I meant what I said the other night. You're a good soul, lass. None of this was your fault.'

People were starting to pack up. She wandered through the cars and VW vans that were being piled high with camping equipment, towards the food vans. She knew she didn't have long to get up the bluff and back before Mum started looking for her, but there was someone else she needed to talk to first...if he hadn't cleared off or been arrested.

Thankfully, the chipped white van was still there – open and doing some last-minute business. When she got to the hatch she was relieved to see Tariq in his clean white apron, putting away sauce bottles into the lockable cupboards.

'Hi,' she called.

Tariq stopped and stared. 'What are you doing here?'

'Oh, that's nice.'

He disappeared and she heard his quick footsteps clanging on the metal steps. He reappeared at her side. There were little worry lines around his dark eyes that made him look like a proper grown-up who'd always been too old for her. 'I didn't think your mum would let you out of her sight for the next ten years.'

'So you were just going to disappear without saying goodbye?'

He smiled. 'I thought that's how you'd want it.'

'That's not how I wanted it. I wanted to say goodbye and, well, say sorry,' she said. Her cheeks filled with heat, but she was determined to say it. 'I think maybe you were right. I was using you. I didn't mean to. But you were right – that stuff you said about Michael.'

He shrugged. 'That's OK. I was just trying to get you into bed – or at least a sleeping bag.' He smiled, and it was such a sweet smile that she knew he was joking. Whatever he was, he wasn't *that* guy. 'Has he come to his senses yet?'

'Who, Michael? I don't know. Maybe it was a stupid idea. Maybe you can't be...*more*...when you've been friends as long as we have.'

He squeezed her shoulder. 'Don't give up before you've even tried. But if you do – give me a call?'

He leaned down and kissed her. It was gentle and lovely and made her want to kiss him back, but that would be wrong on so many levels. She pulled away.

Tariq cleared his throat. 'Yeah. Sorry – bad idea.' He punched a fist into his other hand. 'Thanks for coming to say goodbye. I'll see you around, Poppy.'

'Yeah, see ya.' She gave him a last smile and started walking in the direction of the bluff. She stopped and spun around. 'Hey, Tariq?'

He turned to look at her.

'I think you should go back to Manchester. Finish your degree.'

He nodded. 'You never know, maybe we'll be there at the same time,' he said with a faint smile.

The bluff seemed steeper than before. The sky over the lake was a sheer blue but the air was hot and sticky like it was about to storm. Poppy pushed herself up the slope, not daring to stop in case her feet wouldn't start moving again. Every muscle in her body ached like she'd climbed a mountain already that morning and her head was clouded with tiredness.

By the time she reached the summit the ground seemed to be moving of its own accord and she honestly thought that Cumbria might be experiencing an earthquake.

After taking a moment to get her breath back, she wandered slowly towards the crumbling edge of the bluff. As she did she was bombarded by memories, so many that they made her dizzy – the desperation in Kane's eyes before he stepped over the edge and slid from view; Beth's too-red lips singing the name of her murdered love.

Mayaaaaaa...

Poppy stopped, squeezed her eyes shut and pushed the images away. They were just memories. Surely she could choose not to see them. It was her brain, for heaven's sake!

She opened her eyes, forced herself forward, as close to the edge as she dared, and dropped to her knees. When Mo had told her to say goodbye, she'd known it would have to be here. At the place where it started... and ended.

Below, the choppy grey waters sloshed up against the pebbles where Kane had fallen. The warm breeze pulled at the fine hairs around her face, tickling her nose and eyes. Poppy brushed them away, pulled the cloth bag off her shoulder and felt inside for the three gifts she'd managed to find from among Bob's stuff.

The first was a Tarot card. It wasn't from a normal deck, not the kind that Kane read; instead it was from a set of Druid cards that depicted animals rather than human figures. This one had a picture of a blackbird, its beak open in song. Bob had explained to her that the blackbird was the guardian of the forge – the entrance to the underworld, where people were transformed and made new. It seemed appropriate somehow.

Next to the card she placed a tealight. A candle to burn for them: Beth, Maya and Kane.

Poppy took a box of matches out of her pocket and lit one. The small flame was too weak and easily extinguished by the breeze. Poppy sighed, dropped the match and tried another. This time the flame took hold. She carefully cupped her hand around the tealight and held the match to the wick until it caught fire.

For a moment she watched the flame dance, felt its heat against her skin. As soon as she took her hand away the candle would be extinguished, but this was all meant to be symbolic, right?

Poppy removed her hand and let the breeze consume the flame, leaving only a wisp of smoke to rise into the atmosphere.

The last gift was a miniature bottle of whiskey. She took it out of the bag and smiled. 'Have a drink on me, Beth,' she whispered as she set the bottle on the grass.

Crystal clear, as if she'd known the girl her whole life, an image of Beth formed in her head. Her glossy hair, the fire in her eyes.

Poppy took a deep breath and tried to compose herself. She should have asked Mo how exactly she should do this. But it was too late now. She'd just have to wing it.

'I'm leaving today, Beth.' She felt stupid saying it out loud, but she preferred to think that even if there was some kind of afterlife, the dead couldn't hear every thought that passed through her head. 'I suppose you'll know about Kane. And I'm sorry, I really am. You shouldn't have died; it wasn't fair. Life's a bitch, hey? I just hope you found Maya and you're happy.' Poppy shook her head at her own lack of eloquence. If anyone heard her, they'd think she had cracked...

talking to dead people. Maybe she had.

'I guess I just wanted to say that I won't forget you.'

Poppy ran her fingers over the small square bottle and in her head she saw Beth smile.

She was done. It was time to leave.

'See ya,' she whispered.

As she got to her feet her phone buzzed. She pulled it out to see who was texting her.

It was Michael. *Crap!*

All thoughts of gifts for dead people disappeared. Her heart thundered like the hooves of a runaway horse. She clutched the mobile tighter. It was just a text message. Nothing to be afraid of. Except it could say that he'd had enough of her, or that he and Julia had decided to leave school, get married and have lots of babies. Could she handle it if he was telling her that he never wanted to see her again? She went to shove the phone back in her pocket but stopped herself. She was being a wimp. She'd caused this situation: it was time to face up to the consequences.

She took a deep breath, opened the message and read the contents.

Sorry had 2 leave yesterday. Am arse. Do over?

An apology. She felt sick with relief, and then doubly sick at the thought of talking to him again, but she didn't have much choice if they were ever going to get back to the way things were. She typed in:

I'll text you when I get home.

Poppy hit *send*. Almost immediately, her phone buzzed again.

Am arse of EPIC proportions. The Ben Nevis of arses.

She smiled and texted back:

True.

She waited, and sure enough, her phone buzzed again.

But u know I hate it when u figure something out b4 me.

The breath caught in her throat.

What did I figure out?

Silence. Poppy stared at the phone, willing another text message to appear.

What do u think?

She growled with frustration.

If I knew I wouldn't be asking.

She'd kidded herself about his feelings for her so often that she refused to second-guess him.

I'm at ur tent. Where r u?

He was here. Poppy's gaze sought out her tent. She could barely see the green nylon between all the bigger more elaborate tents, but she could see the top of Mum and Jonathan's tipi, and yes, there was his mum's car, sunlight sparking off its silver paintwork. She texted him back:

I'm on my way.

She ran, grabbed her bag from the edge of the bluff

and was about to negotiate the steep slope down to the festival ground when she remembered the envelope Bob had asked her to post through the farmhouse door.

'Bugger!'

She blew the hair away from her eyes and walked in the opposite direction, away from Michael. She hadn't gone too far before she broke into a run.

The heat from the sun combined with tiredness, and by the time she reached the cobbled yard at the front of the house she felt hot and sick. Bright lights flashed before her eyes, the world tipped, and only a strong arm wrapped around her waist stopped her from toppling over.

CHAPTER THIRTY-THREE

On her way from where? Michael glanced at his watch and ran a hand through his hair. Her texts had been unusually monosyllabic. Understandable – he'd hurt her. She was his best friend, and instead of being honest with her he'd walked away. Twice. She had every fucking right to be mad at him.

He thought about texting her again, but that risked coming over as pushy and he didn't want that. He didn't want to do or say anything that would lead to them blowing up at each other again. He just wanted to see her, talk to her. Convince her, and maybe himself, that everything would be OK. Nervousness buzzed in his veins. It made him twitchy to do something – anything to pass the time until she got there.

He scanned the festival ground that was quickly returning to nothing more than a crescent-shaped field on the shore of Lake Scariswater. Cars were driving slowly over bumps and bouncing down into muddy dips, wrecking their suspension. And the only evidence that the wicker man had been there was the large black burnt spot at the centre. Most of the tents and caravans had gone; only a few of the food vans remained. Between two other larger trailers, he spotted the small white burger van.

Shit. Was that where she was?

He spotted Meg and Jonathan carrying what looked like a heavy box between them. He jogged over to them and took over from Meg.

'Michael, what are you doing here? We're just packing up,' she said, rubbing her hands together and stretching her fingers.

Michael soon knew why. The box weighed a tonne. 'What've you got in here? Rocks?' he asked.

'Yes, actually.'

He exchanged a glance with Jonathan, who grinned and shrugged.

'So, err, where's Poppy?'

'She had a few things to do. I thought she'd be back by now,' Meg replied.

Michael and Jonathan made their way to the boot of the Saab and dumped the box on the ground.

Jonathan opened the boot and frowned. 'It's never going to fit in.'

'I can take them for you,' Michael volunteered. 'Or you could put that in Poppy's seat and I'll drive her home.'

Meg and Jonathan looked at each other and grinned.

CHAPTER THIRTY-FOUR

'Are you all right?' Pete asked.

Poppy blinked away the flashing lights. 'Sorry,' she gasped. 'Got a bit hot.'

Pete smiled. 'Think maybe you've had too much excitement over the last couple of days.'

She smiled. 'Yeah. I don't want *that* much excitement ever again.'

'You and me both, love. What are you doing up here?'

'Bob asked me to give you this.' She grabbed the envelope from out of the bag.

The farmer snorted. 'Not something else to bring on the baby? The last batch of herbal tea weren't too successful.' He opened the envelope and Poppy saw a flash of purple bank notes. Money? Maybe it was what the festival owed for the ground rent, but why would they send that as cash?

Pete smiled and shook his head. 'Bob's a good bloke.' He handed the envelope back to Poppy.

'But...?'

'Tell Bob thanks, but we'll be OK.'

She nodded. Bob was doing his usual fairy godmother trick – he'd said he was worried about having to move the festival next year and the impact it would have on the farm. Obviously Pete knew a handout when he saw it.

'Sure?'

Pete nodded and so she stuffed the envelope back in the bag.

'Thanks for everything, Pete. I don't know what I'd have done if you hadn't been there when I found... Anyway, I should get going. My mum'll send out a search party if I'm not back soon.'

'I'll drive you down. Don't like the thought of you climbing down the bluff if you're not feeling too good.'

'Oh – umm—' Driving would take longer than walking, and if she didn't head back to the festival ground soon there was a very real possibility that either she would chicken out of talking to Michael or her head would explode with nerves. '—I'll be fine—'

'—Nonsense! Don't take this the wrong way, but you're as white as one of my sheep.'

Poppy laughed. 'Oh, thanks.'

Pete nodded in the direction of the house. 'Come on, I'll just grab my keys.'

To say no would be rude. She had no choice, damn it! 'OK. Thanks.' She felt her phone vibrate in her pocket. Another text from Michael, no doubt.

The front door to the farmhouse wasn't locked. Pete pushed it open and urged her in.

'Sally? Sally, we've got company,' he shouted up the stairs. 'She's supposed to taking a nap but she won't like it if she finds out we had a visitor and I didn't wake her. *Sally!*' He sighed. 'Why don't you go into the living room and sit down. I'll get you a drink. What would you like?'

Oh no, a drink too? 'Just water would be great,' Poppy said, trying not to sound too irked.

She headed in the direction that Pete had pointed, grabbed her mobile out of her pocket and opened the text.

WHERE R U?

Someone was getting shouty with the capitals. She was about to reply when she realised that the thick walls of the farmhouse had killed her signal. Great! She shoved the phone back in her pocket and sighed.

The hallway led into a living room dominated by a fireplace almost big enough to stand up in. On one of the whitewashed stone walls was there were the obligatory family photographs. Some were black and white, some more recent. Poppy forced herself to focus on the pictures rather than the queasy nervous feeling in the pit of her stomach. Pete and Sally smiling on their wedding day. Pete and Sally sitting on the bonnet of an enormous tractor – him dressed in his usual checked shirt, Sally in the pink female farmer equivalent, a scarf around her neck. And one photograph of a guy with a long stubbled face that was strangely handsome in a Sean Connery, ancient actor kind of way.

'That's my dad,' Pete said, nodding to the

photograph. 'He took over from his dad, and he handed it down to me.'

Poppy remembered Bob growling something about Pete's dad being an old bastard. A handsome old bastard though. She looked back at Pete, who she guessed looked more like his mum. He had the same ruddy farmer's complexion as his dad, and maybe the same hair colour, but the similarity stopped there.

Pete smiled and handed her a glass of water.

'Thanks.' Poppy took a sip. She spotted a walking stick leaned up against the fireplace. The handle was worn with use. 'Does your dad live with you?'

Pete shook his head. 'Died last year. He was out with the dogs rounding up the sheep. Heart attack, they said.'

'I'm sorry.'

He shrugged and almost managed a smile. 'It's how he'd have wanted to go – out on the farm. This land was in his blood.'

Poppy glanced at the door. There was still no sign of Sally. OK, this was too much. She needed to get out of there. 'Listen, I'd better get going. My mum'll freak if I don't get back to help her take down the tents.'

'But Sally's just coming.'

A scream itched to get out of her throat and her head felt like it was going to implode.

Pete's big hand squeezed her shoulder. 'You've gone awful pale again, you should sit down.'

At that moment, Sally walked in. Poppy smiled with relief until she saw the look on the woman's face.

'What's going on?' she asked, frowning.

Pete spun around, knocking Poppy's arm and sending water sloshing over her hand.

'Lass isn't feeling too good,' he said, defensively.

Sally stared at Poppy, her expression going from one of disgust to despair, then her gaze slid over to Pete and for a moment she looked totally lost. Pete rushed over to her and pulled his wife into a hug while Poppy stood awkwardly watching.

What the heck was that all about? She couldn't possibly think that she and Pete were...*ewww!*

'Sally's hormones are all over the place, aren't they, love?' Pete said. 'Sooner this baby comes the better.'

'Yeah, I'm sorry,' Sally whispered. 'For a second there I though you were—'

'—You should stay and look after Sally,' Poppy said, cutting off Sally before she could say something that would embarrass them all. 'I'll be fine walking.'

Pete nodded.

'And don't worry, I'll get that envelope back to Bob. Good luck with the baby, Sally, I hope it all goes OK.'

'Thanks,' Sally muttered.

'I'll see myself out.' Poppy had to stop herself from breaking into a run. She marched down the hallway, let herself out and pulled the door closed behind her. She sighed with relief, set off across the cobbles and pulled the phone out of her pocket. Damn it! Still no signal.

Michael would think that she was keeping him waiting just to be awkward. At this rate they'd end up having a domestic to rival Pete and Sally's. Poppy glanced back at the door to the farmhouse. Wow, had Sally really thought that she and Pete were up to something? He didn't look the type to go chasing after younger women. Unlike his dad, who'd looked exactly the type.

Poppy's legs stopped moving.

No! It couldn't be.

With all that had happened, she'd forgotten that Maya had been looking for her dad. She'd assumed he was someone at the festival, but what was it Kane had said about this place being in her blood? It was just what Pete had said about his dad. The question was, did Kane kill her before she got a chance to meet him?

For a second, Poppy thought about going back to the house – Pete had a right to know if Maya was his half-sister – but talk about an awkward conversation. *Hey, Pete, is it possible your old man might have had an affair?* Nahh. She'd talk to Bob first, and see what he thought. Right now she had to get back to Michael.

CHAPTER THIRTY-FIVE

'Excuse me?'

Michael looked up from willing his phone to ring. It was the detective who'd interviewed Poppy yesterday. Underneath his grey suit jacket, his shirt was creased and there was what looked like a coffee stain dribbled down his pale blue tie. He looked bloody rough and not at all happy.

'Is Poppy around?' he asked Meg.

She stuffed the bag she was holding into the back of the Saab and rested her hands on her hips. 'Do you need her for something?'

The detective rubbed his fingers over his lip and his eyes scanned the dismantled festival ground. 'Any idea where she's gone?'

'She wanted to say goodbye to a couple of people. I actually thought she'd be back by now.' Meg folded her arms over her chest, just the way Poppy did when she felt uncomfortable. 'What is it?'

Jonathan, who'd been taking down Poppy's tent, came to stand next to Meg and slid an arm around her shoulder.

'What's going on?'

'Sergeant Grant wants to see Poppy.'

Michael felt his chest tightening. There was

something about the way the detective wasn't looking directly at them that made him nervous.

'Has she got her phone with her?' DS Grant asked, pulling a radio off his belt.

'She texted a while ago to say that she was on her way,' Michael replied. 'I'm sure she won't be long.'

'Would you mind giving her a call?'

'What's going on? Why do you need her?' Michael asked.

'Please, just give her a call,' the policeman said, before holding his radio up to his mouth and turning away from them.

Meg squeezed Michael's arm. 'Try her again.'

He hit the speed dial.

'Hi, this is Poppy, leave a message.'

'It's going through to voicemail,' he said, waiting for the beep. 'Poppy, it's me. Can you call me as soon as you get this? I'm not mucking about. The police are here and I think they need to talk to you.' He cut the call and sighed.

At the same time, DS Grant looked up from his radio and raised his eyebrows. 'Any joy?'

Michael shook his head.

He put the radio back to his mouth. 'She's not here and nobody knows where she is. Yeah, ask the guys to keep an eye out.'

'What's going on? What's the panic?' Meg asked. Her voice had gone up in pitch and if the detective didn't spill some information soon, Michael suspected that before very long there would be shouting.

DS Grant bit his lip, as if unsure what lies to tell first. He slid the radio back onto his belt and inhaled deeply. 'A witness has come forward. Says he was with Kane the night Beth died. Says there's no way Kane could have killed her.'

If Kane didn't kill Beth, then who the hell did?

Michael called Poppy again. It went straight through to the answering service.

'Shit!' he cursed. Either she was somewhere with no signal, or she didn't want to be disturbed or... His gaze settled on the few remaining food vans on the other side of the festival ground.

He cut the call.

Meg raised her eyebrows at him in a question.

He shook his head and looked out across the field to the food vans. 'She's not answering. I have an idea where she might be, though.'

CHAPTER THIRTY-SIX

Poppy ran, slowing to check her phone signal every few paces. Only when she reached the bluff did enough bars appear to make a call.

'About time,' she muttered. She tapped in the first few digits of Michael's number when a voicemail message pinged up on the screen. She tapped *OK* and held the phone to her ear.

'Poppy, it's Michael. Can you call me as soon as you get this? I'm not mucking about. The police are here and I think they need to talk to you.' He sounded more tense than pissed off. Scared, almost.

What the heck did the police want with her again? She'd told them everything she knew in minute detail, signed her name to a dozen forms and statements. They might be interested in her new theory about Maya's father, but she wasn't sure it would make much of a difference to their case. It wasn't as if Kane would be going to court.

She had returned to the call screen when something moving caught her eye. It was the Druid card she'd left there earlier. The wind had blown it quite a distance from the edge of the bluff and it had caught in a mound of grass that was longer and greener than all the grass around it.

Something about the shape of the mound drew her. It was long and narrow, like a coffin. Like...a grave?

She didn't want to go any closer, but her feet moved towards the patch of bright green grass. It was as though someone had a hand on her shoulder, pushing her forward. By the time she reached the edge of the mound her legs were shaking. She had to kneel down before she collapsed.

Her hand cupped over her mouth as she stared at the earth.

Maya?

All the times she'd been here and she'd never seen it. But if this was where Kane buried her it would make sense of why he had come up here to kill himself. Kane might have murdered Maya, but he was in love with her in his own crazy way. Maybe he'd wanted to be close to her.

And Beth...had Maya drawn her here? It was *always* up here... Beth, Kane...her dream...

The implications made her head spin. The gas she was sucking into her lungs didn't seem to contain any oxygen. She felt like she was drowning, like she was going to throw up.

'Poppy?' a voice asked.

Poppy looked up to see Pete standing in the shadow of the trees. 'What's wrong?' He lurched to her side and crouched down beside her.

'Pete, look,' she gasped, nodding towards the mound.

'Look at what?'

'The grass. It's been disturbed. I didn't understand why Kane came up here...but that's why. I think she's here.'

Pete hugged an arm around her and squeezed her. 'What makes you say that?'

'I need to get down there, find the police.' She ran a hand over her dripping nose and pushed herself to her feet.

'No!' Pete grabbed her arm. 'You're in no fit state to go down there by yourself. Come on back to the house. I've got that detective's card on the fridge. We'll give him a call.'

He was right. Silly to go down there only to have to come back again.

Pete led her back along the worn pathway, through the strip of trees and across the cobbled yard to the farmhouse.

He pushed open the door and gave her a reassuring smile. 'Go on into the living room and I'll find that number.'

Poppy nodded and made her way back down the gloomy hallway to the room she'd been desperate to escape from not ten minutes ago.

Michael was going to kill her. She pulled out her phone. Of course there was no signal, but there was a text message that must have reached her phone before she'd gone into the house. She opened it and read.

u need 2 call me rt now! Kane didn't kill Beth. Need 2 know ur safe!!!

What?

Poppy's gaze flicked up to the gallery of family photographs on the whitewashed stonewall, to the picture of Pete's dad. But her eyes were drawn away from the black and white photograph to another – the one of Pete and Sally sitting on what looked like a sparkly new tractor. Sally in her farming gear, wearing a pink scarf over her patterned pink shirt. A pink scarf that looked a lot like the one Beth was found wearing. The one that had strangled her.

The air flew out of Poppy's lungs. Every muscle in her body tensed. She'd got it wrong. So wrong. Kane had told her, and she hadn't heard him.

She saw Kane again, the terror in his eyes. And he'd said that this land was in Maya's blood! He meant that it was hers, that she belonged here because...her father owned it so she had a claim on it. What if she had tried to claim it?

'Shit!'

Poppy heard footsteps approaching. She shoved the phone in her pocket and turned to face Pete.

He smiled uneasily. 'I've given the police a call. They're on their way.'

He was lying. There were no police coming. No one knew where she was – except for Bob! If the police were looking for her then Bob would tell them where she'd gone.

'Poppy, are you OK?'

She forced herself to smile at Beth's killer. 'I just feel a bit sick. Do you mind if I go outside?'

'Of course not.'

'Thanks.' Controlling each step, she walked past Pete, down the hallway, towards the door. If she could just get outside she stood a chance. She could run...call for help.

She reached up to turn the handle but could feel Pete behind her. He wasn't going to let her out there by herself. He wasn't going to let her lead the police to Maya's body. He wasn't going to let her live.

Unable to control the panic any longer, she wrenched open the door and darted into the sunlight.

A hand clamped onto her wrist and yanked her back.

Pete stared into her eyes and slowly he nodded, as if he'd seen the truth reflected there. 'You should have left well alone.'

CHAPTER THIRTY-SEVEN

While Meg and Jonathan went to check with Bob and Mo, Michael began walking towards the white trailer van. His pace quickened to a jog. And then a run.

Dealer Boy was bent over, attaching the trailer to an old clapped-out Ford Escort. Michael grabbed his shoulder and pulled him upright. Tariq's eyes widened and his hand closed into a fist.

'Have you seen Poppy?' Michael asked quickly. As much as he'd love nothing more than to get into it with this guy, fighting now would waste time.

Tariq frowned. 'Why d'you wanna know?'

'*Have you seen her?*'

Tariq yanked his shoulder out of Michael's grip. 'Yeah. She was here, about an hour ago.'

Michael swallowed against his dry throat. Of course she'd say goodbye to the guy, it made perfect sense, but he couldn't help feeling...*what...jealous?*

'Nothing happened,' Tariq said, breaking into his thoughts. 'It's not me she's interested in.'

Poppy had told him about what had happened between them? Michael nodded, but it didn't stop his muscles from tensing. 'Do you know where she went?'

'What's the problem, what's going on?'

'The guy who they thought murdered those girls?

Turned out he had an alibi. She said she was on her way twenty-five minutes ago.' Michael spun around. 'So where is she?'

There were a couple of kids playing with water balloons at the edge of the wood. There were adults too – chatting and mucking about. Not one of them was Poppy. He pulled out his phone and hit speed dial. As he expected – Poppy's phone rang out. He sighed and tried to hold back the profanities until the answering service kicked in.

There was a click and then a rustling noise. But there was no pre-recorded greeting. She'd actually answered. He started with a few choice words but then stopped and listened.

'I'll help you look for her, yeah?' Tariq said.

Michael put out a hand to shut him up. 'Poppy? Poppy, are you there? Can you hear me?'

CHAPTER THIRTY-EIGHT

'How did you work it out?' Pete asked. He had a tight hold on her arm and was dragging her across the cobbled farmyard. She stumbled but Pete hauled her to her feet and continued pulling her along. Her pocket was vibrating. Someone was calling her. She slipped her hand inside and dragged her finger across the screen, hoping it would answer the call.

'I don't know what you mean, Pete! Please don't hurt me!'

She tried to speak loud enough that whoever had called could hear. But what was the point? She wasn't even sure it had connected, and the further they moved away from the yard, the more likely it was that her phone would lose signal.

'Pete! Please! Can we go back to the *farmhouse* and talk? Whatever you think I've done, you've got the wrong end of the stick.'

'I liked you,' he said, angrily. 'Seemed like a nice girl. Not like a lot of them down there.'

He was talking about her in the past tense – that didn't bode well.

She tried to yank her arm out of his grip, but he just pulled her against his chest and part pushed, part carried her past the outbuildings, past a set of kennels where three sheepdogs wagged their tails excitedly.

'Let me go!' she shouted. He'd grabbed a shotgun from the house before dragging her out here. Even if he did let her go, she didn't stand a chance.

'I didn't know she was my sister. I'm not a bad person, Poppy. It was her. She threw herself at me. She didn't tell me she was my sister. Then she wanted money. Said that she'd tell if I didn't pay up. Said she'd get a lawyer and take the farm away from me. Might look rich, but we're in trouble with the bank. I couldn't afford to pay them and her.'

With one arm, he carried Poppy down a steep mud track.

She kicked her heels against his shins, but he didn't even seem to notice.

Ahead, down the steep mud track that was scarred with tractor tracks, Scariswater was coming into view. Not the shore she knew, but another, more secluded one. Trees hung over the grey waters like broken umbrellas, shielding the bay from view and waves sloshed against the shingle like they were trying to climb ashore; like they were coming to get her.

'She hurt me too, Pete! Maya – she's been messing with me. *I wanted her dead too!*'

He stopped and his grip on her loosened. She fought her way free of him, stumbled and fell hard onto the mud slope. Pain shot through her shoulder but she didn't have time to feel it. She scrabbled backwards until her feet got traction and she was able to push herself up.

Pete was staring at her. He didn't know whether to believe her or not. She was going to have to come up with a damn good story, and fast.

'Why do you think I was looking for her? She messed with my dad,' Poppy gabbled, saying the first thing that came into her head. 'She split up my mum and dad, Pete. I hate her. I was going to kill her myself if I found her. Look, I won't tell anyone. You can trust me. I won't tell them that you killed her.' She edged slowly backwards. But the lake was back there, waiting patiently like it had waited all year. Her gaze flashed around.

Woods. Lose him in the woods!

'Wasn't me,' Pete said quietly.

Her feet stopped moving. 'What?'

'It was Sally. She lost her temper. She does that – gets all het up. Stabbed her. Then that other girl came looking for her.'

The Other Girl. *Beth.*

'She knew, see. She knew that bitch was my sister. It were only a matter of time before she told someone. Then they'd work it out. They'd come looking and they'd take Sally away from me. And the baby. Baby needs a mother.'

'You only did what needed to be done, Pete. You did the right thing. You're a good man.'

He nodded, but there was a faraway look in his eye, like he wasn't really listening. She wanted to run. But her legs were shaking and he was so much taller than her – he'd catch her easily.

Slowly, he turned his gaze on her. 'I thought it would be hard – killing someone. But it's no different from slaughtering sheep. They struggle too. They all do. Then they go calm, like they know it's their time. She were like that. She knew.'

Poppy swallowed the bile that burnt the back of her throat.

He was going to kill her. Just like he'd killed Beth.

Would she struggle or would she be calm? Would he leave her floating face down in the lake or would he bury her in some forgotten corner of the farm?

Suddenly the very act of breathing seemed important. The sensation of the breeze on her skin. The sight of light dancing through leaves. She wanted to see it all and feel it all. It was all so beautiful and yet she'd ignored it all until they were special last things.

Mum and Dad would be gutted. Even Jonathan. Gods, she wished she could talk to them, tell them all the things she'd never said. And *Michael.* She never got to talk to Michael, sort things out. It wasn't fair! Wasn't fair that it should end like this.

Her heart and her head were so full of never-going-to-happens that she didn't notice that Pete was moving towards her, his big weather-worn farmer's hand reaching for her.

She grabbed the phone out of her pocket. The screen lit up. Someone was on the line. Someone was listening!

'At the farm!' she shouted. 'Pete. It's Pete!'

Pete grabbed the phone from her hand and stared at the screen.

From nowhere a surge of energy rushed through her body and she ran.

CHAPTER THIRTY-NINE

Michael ran. Instinctively, he headed for the lake. Nothing made any sense. Poppy's voice was muffled. All he knew was that she was in trouble.

But where?

'Where is she?' Tariq shouted.

Michael stopped, squeezed his eyes shut and tried to make out what she was saying through the crackles and rustles.

A scream. Fuck! Someone had her and they were hurting her. He spun around, searching the horizon.

'Pete, no!' she was shouting.

Pete? Who the hell was Pete?

To their right, the bluff rose steeply. A few scrubby plants clung to the hill that only sheep would be stupid enough to climb.

'Michael!' a gruff, out-of-breath voice called to him. He spun around. Bob was clutching his chest gasping for breath. 'She went to the farm.'

That was it. Pete was the farmer!

'Shit! Tell the police!' Michael threw himself up the steep rise of gravel and scrub. It wasn't so much running as climbing. His foot skidded out from under him and he slid back. A hand grabbed his shirt. It tore, but it gave him just enough time to find his balance again.

Tariq nodded at him and they were both on the move again.

Right then the clouds parted and the sun beamed its spotlight on them. Great! Now they were climbing under a heat lamp.

Sweat dribbled down his back and his lungs were on fire, but he couldn't stop, not even for a moment. A lot could happen in a moment. A moment was all it had taken for Poppy to hit her head on the side of the yacht. In a moment, filthy lake water had flushed the air from her lungs.

He charged forward, overtaking Tariq. He wouldn't let her die. Not again.

CHAPTER FORTY

Her breath was too loud. *Too loud!* She tried to hold it, but she couldn't. Her lungs kept on noisily sucking in air like it was some sort of bloody necessity. All around her birds were singing – tweeting their little heads of like today was just another day.

Somewhere, just beyond the broad trunk of the tree she'd flattened herself against, a twig snapped.

Close. So close. He was circling her like he knew she was there. Playing with her like a cat pawing a sparrow before it rips its tiny head off.

Sunlight shimmered through the tree canopy, tiny spotlights appearing and disappearing like the dance of the water sprites on the lake. Probably some of their distant cousins, come to finish her off.

'*Please, someone? Help me!*' she whispered under her breath. But why? No one was listening. Not now that Pete had the phone. Had it been Mum on the line? Or Michael? Maybe whoever it was had realised that she was in trouble and had sent help. Knowing her luck it was a sodding cold caller from the phone company.

For the first time in a long time, she squeezed her eyes shut and prayed. She wasn't sure to whom or to what, but faced with the prospect of dying again she was willing to give anything a go.

Help me!

A bird screeched an alarm call, shattering the serenity of the woods. It was a blackbird, Druid Dhubh...the Druid of the forest. She saw the image on the card she had left on the bluff. For a second she, and the whole woods, held their breath.

Something flashed between the trees. Her eyes tried to find the movement. There.

A shadow passed between the trees disturbing three woodpigeons. They were flushed into the air with a clatter of wings and snapping twigs.

Heavy footsteps pounded away from her. She dared a glance and saw Pete running between rustling banks of saplings. He'd seen the shadow too. He must have thought it was her.

She pushed away from the tree trunk and headed down the steep bank towards the lake. If she could make it to the lake she could probably shout for help. Maybe even swim to safety. Surely someone would see her?

The breeze switched directions, blowing her hair into her face. Somewhere in the distance she heard voices. Shouting. Those voices, they sounded familiar... like...oh God, *Michael!*

CHAPTER FORTY-ONE

Sally screamed. She held her stomach and panted like she was going to drop the sprog any minute.

Michael threw up his hands and tried to keep his voice calm. 'I just wanna know where Poppy is!' He glanced at Tariq, but Dealer Boy looked just as much at a loss.

Work boots clunked against the cobbles behind them. Out of the corner of his eye he saw Pete marching towards them holding a shotgun.

Not good. And shit, where was Poppy? If he'd touched her...

The farmer glanced at his wife and then flew at them. Before he could do anything to defend himself, a heavy fist struck the side of Michael's head. Sickening pain turned the world to darkness. He didn't even know he'd fallen until his knees crunched onto the rough stone cobbles.

'What are you doing to my wife?' Pete shouted.

'Nothing! Nothing at all!' Tariq said. 'We were looking for Poppy, that's all.'

Their voices were distorted. There was a ringing noise in Michael's ears, like feedback from a bad speaker. A hand grabbed his arm and hauled him to his feet, but his vision was messed up like he'd just got off a spinning fairground ride. Pain throbbed through his skull, but he had to get it together – the bastard had Poppy.

'Where's Poppy?' he spat, trying to focus on Pete.

The farmer shook his head. 'Don't know. Not seen her.'

'You're lying!' This time, it was his turn to throw a punch. His fist connected with the side of Pete's face. Pain ricocheted all the way up Michael's arm. That didn't stop him from doing it again. '*Where. Is. She?*' The shotgun clattered to the cobbles. He saw Tariq make a dart for it, but too late. Tariq slid to a stop as Sally raised the gun to her shoulder.

'Get away from him!' Sally stared through the shotgun's sight, one eye squinted. 'Get away from him!' she screamed.

Michael stumbled back.

'What do we do?' she asked her husband. 'They know, Pete. What are we going to do?'

Michael wiped away the blood that was muddying his sight and glanced around. Where the hell were the police?

At the corner of the farmhouse, a flash of auburn hair caught his eye. Then Poppy's head popped around the grey stone wall. His knees buckled with relief. He glanced to the side, but Psychopathic Pete seemed too preoccupied with his equally psychopathic wife to notice. Tariq had seen her though; his eyes were wide with panic.

Michael caught Poppy's eye and shook his head. *Stay there! For God's sake stay there! Better still – run. Get help.* But that wasn't Poppy's style and he knew it.

'You! Get over there,' Sally shouted.

The crazy woman was talking to him. Slowly, he edged further away from Pete. The barrel of the gun followed his movement.

'Turn around,' she said, squinting through the sight.

'No! Sally, don't!' Pete gasped.

'I can't go to prison! The baby...they'll take the baby away from me!'

Michael stopped breathing. His heart pounded in his throat. If he turned around that was it. She would kill him. His gaze connected hopelessly with Poppy's.

'No!' she mouthed.

'I said, turn around!' Sally shouted.

'You think you can get away with this?' Tariq yelled. 'I called the cops. They're on their way. Can't you hear that, bitch? That's a siren, yeah? They're gonna lock you up and throw away the key!'

'Turn around!'

'Nooooo!' Poppy burst around the side of the farmhouse, running at Sally and screaming like a banshee. Tariq raced to head her off. Sally swung around ready to fire. And for a second, Michael thought Poppy was dead. His heart froze. He ran at Sally. But as he grabbed her shoulder a shot rang out.

He screamed, but it was too late. Poppy and Tariq fell to the ground like leaves blown from a tree. He got his arms around Sally's shoulders and tried to grab the barrel of the gun.

'Police! Stop! Put the gun down!' a voice called over a loudhailer.

Suddenly, Pete was moving. Michael made another grab for the gun. He and Sally stumbled backwards. Another shot cracked the air and Pete fell.

The farmer lay face down on the ground. Blood ran down the cement between the cobbles until trickling red lines formed a grid. It was like a perverse computer screensaver. For a second there was nothing but the sound of gurgled breathing. Then silence.

Sally stopped struggling. She let go of the gun, dropped to her knees and wailing like an injured animal, she crawled the short distance to where Pete lay.

Poppy! Michael spun around. He realised he was holding the gun and froze, afraid to drop it, afraid that if he moved a finger another shot would be fired and another life gone.

Out of nowhere, what felt like hundreds of shadows appeared from behind outbuildings and walls. The gun was snatched from his hands. Michael's face hit the cobbles as he was shoved to the ground. His arms were yanked behind his back and metal clasped around his wrists. His heart hammered in his throat.

'Poppy! *Poppy!*' he shouted.

He was dragged to his feet and through the mayhem, his eyes sought her out.

She was kneeling, squeezing Tariq's arm. Blood was pouring from beneath her fingers. Tariq was nodding and talking to a police officer. The officer relieved Poppy from blood-stemming duties and she scrambled to her feet.

'This way, son,' a big guy said, yanking Michael towards a police car.

'Wait, I just need to...'

Poppy darted over to him and threw her arms around his neck. He wanted to hold her, but all he could do was press his head into her hair. It was OK. She was shaking and scared, but she was safe. 'It'll be OK,' he whispered, before the police pulled them apart.

EPILOGUE

The light from the streetlamps was just enough to see by to get the key into the lock. This wasn't going to be the problem. Getting the door open without waking the whole street was going to be the problem. He pushed it an inch – so far, so good – and tried another. That's when the door's hinges began to screech.

Thunder on the stairs, and a low growl, forced him in through the door before Dawkins could give the game away.

'It's me!' he whispered to the ghostly white dog, whose tail was wagging so fast that it seemed to blur in the middle. Dawkins jumped up. Paws landed squarely on Michael's chest, forcing him back against the door. It slammed into the frame.

He winced and pushed the dog down. At the top of the stairs, Meg appeared, rubbing her eyes.

'Really smooth, Michael!' she stage whispered, making a face at him.

He shrugged hopelessly.

Meg smiled. 'Have fun tonight,' she said, before heading back to bed. 'Or this morning...or whatever time it is.'

He waited a second and then climbed the stairs with Dawkins stuck to his side like a guard dog. His legs complained at being made to work when they should be in bed. It had been a gruelling afternoon, talking to Julia. Apologising for what had happened. Apologising for not loving her. But he felt better now that they'd talked and officially broken it off. At least it was one thing off his conscience.

He crept through the grey and black shadows, along the landing to Poppy's room. These days, she slept with the bedside light on, but Meg had compromised by throwing a sparkly blue scarf over the lampshade that made the room look like it was cast in moonlight. From the door, he could see her, wound up in the bedclothes like she'd tossed and turned for hours. One bare leg was hooked around the quilt, long and pale. And her face was half turned into the pillow with her hair spread out about her like rusty sunbeams. He crossed over to her and kneeled beside the bed. It seemed a shame to wake her. There were no lines across her forehead; no fear lurked in the creases around her eyes.

He was about to shake her when he noticed that clutched in her hand was what looked like nothing more than a shiny black pebble. He slid it out of her fingers and held it up to the bedside lamp.

He didn't get it. He wasn't into the whole Pagan thing. To him, it was just a stone. But to her, this thing was keeping her safe and that was good enough for him.

* * *

'Poppy, wake up.'

'What?'

She forced open her eyes. The blue light from the bedside light illuminated Michael's face, making him look drowned and dead. She bolted upright.

'What's wrong?' she gasped.

'Nothing.'

Dawkins jumped on the bed and panted in her face. She pushed him aside. 'What is it? Why are you here?'

'Come on, we're going out.'

'What do you mean? What time is it?'

'It's three a.m. and if you don't move we'll be late.'

Before she could object, Michael grabbed the quilt and dragged it off her.

'Hey!' she shouted, while simultaneously yanking her nightie down over her bum. 'What do you think you're doing?'

She caught his gaze drifting up her legs. He grinned and her heart stuttered like it had forgotten how to beat.

'It's a surprise. Get dressed.' He walked out of the room, taking her duvet with him.

Feeling like she was stuck in a dream, Poppy forced herself out of bed, found her jeans where she'd deposited them on the floor and grabbed a clean sweatshirt out of a drawer. She threw on the clothes and some trainers, and stumbled downstairs.

Michael was standing by the front door.

'I should tell Mum.'

'No need, she knows.'

'What? Don't tell me you sneaked into her bedroom too? And how the hell did you get in?'

Michael dangled a key in front of her face.

This was seriously weird. She made Dawkins sit on the sofa in the pitch-black lounge, and then followed Michael out onto the street. 'Where are we going?'

'You'll see,' Michael replied, getting into the driver's seat of his mum's car. She sighed and went to the other side. As she opened the door, she saw the curtains of Mum's and Jonathan's bedroom window twitching. Whatever was coming, they were in on it – buggers! She stuck out her tongue before ducking into the car.

Michael drove through deserted streets, down into Bowness and then onto the road that followed the shape of Lake Windermere. He didn't look at her, not even when he had to look past her before making a left turn. He was trying desperately not to smile, but she could tell he wanted to.

'You're really not going to tell me where we're going?'

'I'm *really not going to tell you*, so you might as well shut up about it.'

'We're going to sit in silence for...how long? An hour? Two?'

'Nice try.'

'Are we going to a strip club?'

'*What?*'

'Or a casino? No, I know: the twenty-four-hour Tesco? I'm trying to think of places that are open.'

'I didn't say that we were going somewhere that was open. I've got a sledgehammer in the boot.'

'Great! A night of crime – just what every girl dreams of.'

She regretted the words as soon as they were out of her mouth. Over the last few weeks, the two of them had spent hours in separate police interview rooms, answering questions about everything that had happened that weekend – Michael more than her. Although the police had been more than a bit suspicious when she'd told them where they could find Maya's body – on the bluff, under that patch of bright green grass. Apparently a couple of dreams and a Tarot card didn't make for good court evidence.

Tariq caught a bit of flak too. The police eventually figured out his role at the festival and he was hauled in again. But he'd sent Michael a text the other day, saying that the police didn't have enough to charge him and had sent him home with a slapped wrist.

'Would some music help you not talk?' Michael asked, with a smile.

She laughed. 'You're a real charmer, you know that?'

He leaned down and switched on the stereo. A line

of violins filled the car. The Verve album he'd made her download. The drums kicked in, reverberating through the seats.

'You never said whether you liked this,' he said over the music.

'It's OK,' she said, suppressing a smile.

The road swung around millionaires' row, as the locals liked to call it: all 1980s ten-bedroom palaces with no character and nothing to boast except a lakeside view. Then on to Newby Bridge, across the deserted train line, and up the other side of the lake. Well, that ruled out a whole lot of nowhere.

She glanced over at Michael, who thankfully had his eyes on the road – he wasn't the best driver in the world, even if he liked to think he was a test driver for Top Gear. He'd been great though – since the festival. Spent all day every day with her, when they weren't at the police station or talking to solicitors. They'd watched every crap DVD the library had, and when they'd run out of films, they'd moved on to audio books, tucked up in a quilt on the sofa. He'd been careful to choose nothing with bloodshed – nothing that could remind them of that day.

He'd even agreed to a bit of romance, which she knew really *wasn't* his thing. They'd sat cuddled before the fire, Poppy sitting between his legs and his face buried in her hair while Darcy pissed off Elizabeth and some Latino guy pulled a cheerleader, all without complaint. He held her hand, hugged her – he was never far from her. It was almost as if he was scared that something bad would happen if they weren't touching. But none of it had moved him to kiss her.

Michael leaned down again and flicked forward to the second track. The guitar picked up the first notes of *Sonnet*, the melancholic love song she'd listened to over and over again, and she couldn't help wondering whether they'd ever get past this strange limbo they found themselves in.

Lights twinkled on the opposite shore of the lake. Bowness came into view, blocked only by the trees on the intervening Belle Island, a place that strangely held no fear for her any more, even though it had been close to there that she'd nearly drowned.

Eventually, Michael pulled the car off the road, onto the grass, and stopped.

'This is where we're going?' she asked, raising her eyebrows.

He cut the engine. 'Yeah. This is it. Are you getting out, or what?'

Poppy opened the door and got out. The drop in temperature after the artificial heat of the car made her shiver. Michael had already popped the boot and was getting stuff out. He handed her a coat. *Her* coat, in fact. And a thermos flask.

'This has been planned,' she said.

He just returned her smile, slid on his own fleece,

the one normally reserved for hiking up mountains, grabbed a picnic blanket and nodded towards the lake.

'What is this?' she asked, following him. 'You fancied a three a.m. picnic?'

He glanced at his watch, then up at the sky and began unfolding the blanket.

'Y'know how everyone thinks *I've* lost it? It's drawn attention away from you! They haven't noticed that you've cracked. You definitely need more counselling.'

He ignored her, but the smile had turned to a grin. He sat down on the blanket and rubbed his hands together. 'You going to keep that hot chocolate all to yourself?'

She collapsed down beside him and handed him the flask.

'You really don't know why we're here, do you?' he asked.

Oh no! Was this something she was supposed to remember? Some weird anniversary of theirs? 'Of course I do. I'm just faking surprise so as not to upset you.'

Michael did a double take then laughed. 'Nahh. You haven't got a clue.' He poured out a steaming cup of hot chocolate, handed it to her, and started pouring out his own. At the same time, he glanced up at the sky and nearly poured it all down himself.

She giggled. 'What are we doing here?'

He licked the spilt chocolate from his hand and took a sip. Again, his eyes flashed up to the sky.

'You are soooo annoy—' Just then, she saw something. A faint flash of light. She dumped the cup of cocoa on the grass and pushed herself to her feet.

Above them the skies were dark. The moon had nearly set but there were stars and planets and...*meteors!* There was another – just a faint whisper across the sky. And then another, clear and bright and beautiful. She gasped.

Arms wrapped around her waist and he rested his chin on her head. 'I didn't want you to miss it,' he whispered, as if making too much noise might frighten them away. 'It seemed important to Beth that you saw it.'

With everything that had happened, she'd forgotten about the Perseid meteor shower and the dream she'd had about her and Beth watching for meteors from the bluff. But Michael had remembered.

She got hold of his arm and squeezed tightly. She felt breathless with panic. She didn't want to lose him, and yet at all around her lives were being extinguished – quicker than the light from a falling star.

Beth.

Maya.

Kane.

And Pete.

All gone.

'In preparation, I've been reading about meteors,' Michael said. 'So I could astound you with my brilliance.'

She sniffed back a tear. 'Oh yeah?'

'Did you know that meteorites consist primarily of iron and that when one of them hits the earth's atmosphere they reach temperatures of almost one thousand six hundred and fifty degrees Celsius?'

'You sound like a Wikipedia entry.'

'That's probably because that's where I got most of this from. I bet you didn't know that in some parts of Europe, it was said that everyone had their own star, and when a person died, their star would fall to the earth.'

'There's a bit of a rush on tonight. What do you think? Coach crash? War, maybe?'

Michael turned her to face him. His wide eyes were sad, and just for a moment she saw the young boy she'd grown up with. The one who cried when his favourite Action Man lost a leg or they came across a dead rabbit on the side of the road.

He swallowed and his bottom lip trembled. 'I keep wondering if there was something – if I'd done things differently—'

'Don't! You didn't kill him. The police have said so. And you wouldn't have been there if it wasn't for me. I'm so sorry, Michael.'

Hot tears spilled over her cheeks. He shook his head

and brushed them away but there were tears in his eyes too. Then, as the sky exploded with flashes of light so bright that it looked like the entire heavens were crashing down around them, Michael leaned down and kissed her.

She'd waited so long for this kiss that tasted of tears that she had no intention of letting it slip away. She locked her hands around Michael's neck, and just for a second, as her heart sang like it was free for the very first time, she saw Beth smiling, the silver of falling stars reflected in her eyes.

ACKNOWLEDGEMENTS

It's only when your first book is accepted for publication that you realise how many people contribute to its production so please forgive the long list of names to follow...

My first thank you must go to the Society of Children's Book Writers and Illustrators, and particularly to the organisers of Undiscovered Voices who really are in the business of making dreams come true!

Heartfelt thanks to my lovely agent, Jenny Savill, without whose careful eye and sound instincts this manuscript would never have made it to publication, and to Megan Larkin, Rebecca Frazer, Rosalind Turner and all the team at Orchard, for believing in *Dead Jealous* enough to give it a home, and for shepherding the book (and me) through the publication process. Thank you!

I owe a huge debt of gratitude to Scooby pals and critique partners, particularly to Ellen Renner, without whom this story would have never been entered into Undiscovered Voices, and to Liz, Sarah, Teri, the whole gang from the Birmingham critique group and the crazy land of Twitter who have walked this road with me, and given me the best gift of all: their friendship.

And finally, thanks to my mum, Denise Jones, for her endless support and dog sitting services!

Read on for an exclusive extract
from the next Poppy Sinclair thriller...

DEAD SILENT

'Are you sure you're holding the map the right way up?'

Poppy tried glaring at Michael. Instead, a guilty smile inched across her face as she kicked at the pile of slush that had collected in the gutter.

Snowflakes the size of cotton wool balls drifted out of the night sky with haphazard elegance. Clumps of them caught in Michael's dark hair and for a moment she could imagine that there was just the two of them, in some magical snow globe.

Michael stared at her, his face deadly serious and his gaze so steady that she knew the game was up. 'Poppy, have you – by any chance – been taking us in the wrong direction?' Before she could answer, Michael rolled his eyes. 'You can't put off seeing your dad forever. In case you haven't noticed the cold white stuff, it's snowing and I'd rather not spend the night out here.'

'But don't you think it's pretty?'

Michael turned his face to the heavens as a smile tugged at his lips. He shook his head. 'You're unbelievable. Where are we?'

'Not in Kansas any more.'

He grinned and leaned closer to her. 'Where are we?'

'Somewhere in Cambridge?' Poppy said, shrugging

and taking a step back.

Again, Michael advanced on her. '*Where* are we?' He made a grab for the map. Poppy just managed to dodge him and set off running down the cobbled street. Her foot hit a patch of ice. She skittered to a stop as the weight of her backpack combined with gravity to tug her towards the ground. A hand grabbed her arm just in time to stop her from toppling over and, before she could object, the map was snatched from her grasp.

Michael's smile was victorious and just a little bit cocky. Oh, how she'd love to wipe that smile off his face – and maybe she would...*tonight*.

There was no room for them to stay at Dad's and so he'd arranged for her and Michael to stay in guest rooms at the college where he worked. Student rooms. Where there would be no parental supervision. And that presented them with certain...*possibilities*. A shiver of nervous energy tingled up her spine.

Michael looked at her strangely. 'What is it?'

'Nothing.'

He smiled and brushed away a flake of snow that landed on her upturned cheek. 'Please tell me you know where we are.'

Time to put him out of his misery. 'That's King's College,' she said, nodding down the alleyway.

Michael's eyes widened. 'Really?' Her transgression was instantly forgotten. He stared open-mouthed like she'd just told him they'd found Atlantis. She grinned, grabbed his jacket and pulled him down the street, past a church with a squat golden-brick tower that looked like it had been squeezed in between other buildings, and a pub where people had spilled out onto the pavement, smoking and stamping their feet against compacted snow. The road opened onto a wider street, lined with shops on one side and King's College on the other.

Poppy and Michael stopped moving.

Carefully placed streetlamps lit the stone façade. The college looked more like a film set than an actual building, let alone a place where teenagers drank, partied and occasionally picked up a book. Everywhere, the bone-coloured stone was adorned with archways, chimneys and intricately carved turrets that seemed to have been chiselled out of the billowing snow clouds.

She'd seen the pictures in the prospectus – Michael had kept it open on his desk for the last two months so it had been hard to miss – but the photographs hadn't done the college justice. And for the first time she felt a small pang of jealousy that Michael might be living here in just over nine months' time.

She glanced up at him. His lips were parted, and his eyes clouded with dreams of his future. She was happy for him – she really was. Going to Cambridge had been his ambition since he was ten years old. But a nagging, selfish voice couldn't help complaining that after all the time it had taken for them to admit to each other that they were more than *just good friends*, he was going to leave. And come here. Without her!

'It's certainly impressive,' she forced herself to say.

Michael nodded. 'It's only a building but...' He shrugged.

'There was an article in the *New Scientist* that said that listening to Bach can actually make you smarter – something to do with the structure and the intricacy of the patterns. I wonder if it's the same with architecture. Because I'm pretty sure that just looking at that college could make you smarter.'

'What about kissing smart girls? Does that make you smarter?' Despite his smile, his brow creased and she wondered whether he too could hear the clock ticking down on their relationship.

'I don't know. I've never tried it.'

'Nahh. Me neither.'

Poppy whacked the back of her hand against his stomach.

'Oof!' Michael groaned, doubling over like she'd lamped him. 'Right, that's it!' He looked up and grinned from beneath the sodden fringe that flopped over his eyes.

Poppy set off, dodging between the groups of students huddled together, holding each other up after a night in the pub, their college scarves wrapped around faces and hoods weighed down with snow. She could hear Michael's feet pounding the cobbles behind her, and a disgruntled someone shouting, 'Hey! Watch where you're going!'

She kept running, despite the way her feet were sliding off cobbles, and took the road she thought would lead to Trinity College. With every step, the straps of her backpack cut deeper into her shoulders and the freezing night air stabbed her lungs with icy little daggers. She wished she had left her Mac at home, and a couple of the books weighing her down. She was almost relieved when a hand grabbed her arm and yanked her to a stop. She giggled as her legs wobbled dangerously.

Michael's cheeks were blotched red and he puffed out clouds of steam like a racehorse that had just won the Grand National. He grinned, and before she knew what was happening, he'd pushed her up against a shop window, his lips were on hers, and his hands were seeking her body through the padded waterproof.

All the breath that was in her disappeared, creating a vacuum; a need stronger than she'd ever felt for anyone or anything. It made her head whirl and her heart dance. *Don't stop*, she wanted to tell him. *Don't ever stop*. But he did.

Michael broke the kiss and stepped back. His eyes were wide and just for a second, she thought she saw that same need in him, and like a black hole it sucked her closer to him.

He looked away, took a deep breath and brushed his

sopping hair out of his eyes. 'Come on,' he said, with an almost shy smile. 'It's this way, isn't it?'

She took his warm hand and they walked up the winding street in silence as if neither one of them knew what to say about what had just happened.

When they'd first started going out the kissing had been a bit awkward. They'd been so careful with each other, as if after years of being best friends they were frightened of breaking this new thing that they had. But four months later that fear had melted away. And now after five months it had been replaced with something dangerous and even more scary: need.

The snow was falling more heavily now, whirling around them so fast that it was hard to see beyond the dance of the snowflakes. They tingled against Poppy's cheeks and cooled her kiss-bruised lips but she felt dizzy, like she was falling with them; tossed around on waves of wanting that seemed to creep up on her and then drown her. Would tonight stop her from feeling so overwhelmed by all of this? If they just *did it* would she feel less out of control?

'It'll be OK,' Michael said, softly. And for a second she thought he was talking about tonight. Oh God, did he know? Had he guessed why she'd really wanted to come with him?

'Terms here are really short. And then when you go to Manchester next year we can see each other at weekends.'

Oh. He was still thinking about that. 'Yeah,' she agreed, although she doubted it would be that simple.

He squeezed her hand. 'Hey, I think this is it.'

Ahead of them was a strange building of red brick and golden stone. Between two turret-like towers was an arched oak door and above that a statue of a king who had gained a few extra pounds where the snow had clung to his waistline. The scene reminded Poppy of something from a book: the gateway to another kingdom, another world. A world she knew nothing of.

Dad's world.

She sighed. She'd almost forgotten that she was about to see Dad.

Tension knotted in her spine. Her feet stopped moving. Michael stopped too. He'd just turned to her when a smaller door to the right of the main entrance opened and that Other World spat out three of its creatures.

The first was a dark-haired guy dressed in a tuxedo and bow tie that was partly undone, like someone had tugged on it, but not quite managed to unknot it. He tripped out of the door, turned and held his hand out for the next: a girl with ice-blonde hair and a red dress that, although floor-length, was slit almost to her waist and left very little to the imagination.

The last guy had on a dinner jacket similar to his compatriot, but this guy had finished the look with a black gangster hat and two bottles of wine that swung from his hands like he was about to juggle with them. Instead, he took a swig from one and handed it to the girl.

She put the bottle to her lips, threw back her head and drank. She shuddered.

'Was this from the dining room? Tastes like cat piss!'

The guy laughed as she turned the bottle upside down. The yellowy white wine poured out onto the ground and where it met a patch of white snow it did indeed look like something, or someone, had taken a leak.

As the last drops drained, the girl's gaze connected with Poppy's. She threw the empty bottle back to the gangster and walked slowly and unsteadily towards Poppy and Michael.

'Well, what do we have here? Tourists?'

Poppy and Michael exchanged a wary glance.

'I'm here for an interview,' Michael piped up.

Snowflakes sparkled in the girl's long, straight blonde hair, making it appear almost as white as her bloodless skin. She had the face of a doll; wide blue eyes, sweetheart lips framed by flawless porcelain.

The girl stopped in front of them and those large blue eyes examined Poppy's face like someone would a painting. Her expression remained fixed: inquisitive, almost perplexed. Then her gaze slid over to Michael.

She was almost as tall as him and seeing this beautiful and unworldly creature toe-to-toe with him made Poppy slightly nauseous.

The girl reached up a hand and caressed his cheek.

'The face of a poet,' she murmured, as if lost in a dream.

Michael swallowed, but said nothing.

Suddenly she whirled around. 'Snow!' she squealed excitedly, as if noticing the weather for the first time.

'What are you doing?' one of the guys called to her, as the girl ran to the roped-off triangle of ground that Poppy imagined had once been grass before becoming a snowdrift. She hopped over the chain-link barrier and, without hesitation, flung herself backwards into the snow. Not worrying what she might be showing to the world, she began flapping her arms and legs, carving out the wings and gown of a snow angel. But her skin and hair was so pale that she seemed to disappear into the white, leaving only the red dress a bloodstain against the snow.

The guy with the gangster hat laughed, but the other swore under his breath and bolted over to her.

'What the fuck do you think you're doing?'

'I'm going to be an angel!' she said, grinning and crunching snow between her fingers like it was warm sand and not frozen water.

The guy grabbed her arm and yanked her to her feet.

'Where's Danny? I want my Danny,' she said.

The guy brushed the snow from her skin and dress, hastily took off his dinner jacket and put it around her bare shoulders. 'He's meeting us at the club. He had something to do.'

She smiled contentedly. 'Oh Danny boy-o-boy-o-boy.'

As the two guys helped her over the chain fence and back onto the icy pavement, the girl smiled in Poppy's and Michael's direction.

'Goodnight, sweet poet,' she said, blowing Michael a kiss before being dragged, stumbling, down the road.

'This place is seriously weird. Are you sure you want to come here?' Poppy said, watching them go.

Michael didn't reply. His eyes were fixed on the students who stumbled down the road like characters from one of the old movies they used to watch when they were kids.

For a second he seemed so very far away, like a little bit of him had gone with them.

Michael swallowed and suddenly turned to her. 'We should get inside and find your dad.'

'Yeah,' she agreed, and forced her lips into a smile.

As they headed for the open door, Poppy heard the girl's voice singing: *I'm lovin' angels instead.* Michael turned to look in their direction, and Poppy couldn't help wondering if, in his head, *Poet Michael* was waxing lyrical about the angel in the red dress.